I'm With Anxious

SUZANNE BROWN

I'M WITH ANXIOUS is a work of fiction. Names, characters, places, and feelings are all in the author's wild and unruly imagination. Any resemblance to actual events, locations, situations, or persons, living or dead, is entirely coincidental.

ISBN: 978-1-7321706-6-7

www.sbrownbooks.com

To my amazing family!
There's no one else I'd want laughing, crying, and
freaking out with me on our adventures around the world.

Table of Contents

CHAPTER 1

It's 8 AM, and all is not well

I have to admit that so far this day totally sucks.

I'm locked out of school, freezing my tush off. The first bell just rang. And I'm pretty sure I just killed my boyfriend.

Well, I guess he's my ex-boyfriend now.

Crap.

CHAPTER 2

Earlier that morning before my day went down the crapper

The first thing I do every day is draw on my wall calendar. I know, wall calendars are so old school, but I like the visual. I have a smiley face on every day of the past eighteen months (and four days) to celebrate the new, happy, positive, anxiety-free me. And I started the hearts six months ago when Dillon and I went on our first date.

Dillon. Happy sigh.

He's six-feet of eye candy. Ocean-blue eyes. Wavy, brown hair. Captain of the soccer team. Sweet. Thoughtful. And the reason I'm going to be nominated for prom queen today!

I know! I can hardly believe it! Sophomores aren't even invited to the prom, but Dillon is a junior, and they're making an exception because we're like the most loved couple in school. (Even Mama and Daddy love us together. Which totally amazes me because Daddy doesn't ever think anyone is good enough for his little girl).

I walk into my closet. I promised to meet Dillon and my besties this morning before they announce the nominations and I have to wear my favorite sweater. It's light blue, like happy clouds on a sunny day, and it's spun of the softest cashmere, making me feel like I'm wrapped in a Daddy hug.

And I can't find it.

Eighteen months ago, this would have been a really big deal. I would have freaked out, had a major panic-attack, and probably wouldn't have made it to school. I know it sounds a little extreme for a missing piece of clothing, but that's how I used to roll. I used to freak out about every little thing. And I mean. Every. Little. Thing.

God, I was so pathetic. I know everyone gets anxiety, but I made it an Olympic sport. I didn't just worry about how to cheat the dress code, or if I over plucked my eyebrows. No. I mutated everything into catastrophic, life-altering, world-ending disasters. KA-BOOM!

Like when I overheard my daddy tell my mama that his company was downsizing. I didn't just worry that Daddy would lose his job. I worried that we'd have no money so we'd starve to death in the middle of winter, and our carcasses would be frozen to the couch until the mailman found us in the spring thawing and stinking up the joint. (I still have protein bars and matches hidden under the couch... just in case.) I worried that my twelve-year-old brother, Berg, would get drafted into a war, lose a leg, get a really cool prosthesis, and then I would run it over with the car and crush it to smithereens. I worried that my Mama would get cancer and need my blood to live, but my fear of needles would make me run away from home, and she would die. You get the point. My imagination worried things into a senseless oblivion.

It was near the end of eighth-grade when my school counselor smiled sadly and told my parents I had Generalized Anxiety Disorder.

"Oh my God, I have Oh my GAD!" I joked. No one laughed, but I didn't care. I was just happy to finally know what the heck was wrong with me. I hated worrying. I hated my anxiety. I hated feeling so depressed and angry that on some days all I could do was crawl into bed, turn off all the lights, and hope I disappeared.

I hated myself for allowing those feelings to win. But most of all, I hated myself.

So... POOF! I changed. Overnight! Just like in a fairy tale!

Well, that's not exactly how it happened. Nothing is ever that easy. Especially when you're a teenager... and a girl... and a freak. Triple whammy sundae. And not a tasty one.

I did change. That's not a lie. But it took a long time. I didn't want anyone to know that I had Oh my GAD, so Mama and Daddy did lots of voodoo, hippie crap like deep breathing and guided mindfulness with me until I finally found something that clicked. I call it Breathe and Bury. I think about happy things while I breathe in, and I exhale out all the crap. I taught myself to bury my emotions so well that no one has seen me yell, or cry, or freak out since I started high school last year. Not my family. Not my besties. And definitely not Dillon.

My anxiety is now just a thing buried in my past. It takes a ton of work to be happy every day, but it's so worth the effort. Negative nellies don't get the perfect life. You never see the pissed-off girl dressed in combat boots nominated as homecoming queen. Or the vegan chick crying over the mistreatment of cows elected president of her class.

Nope. It just doesn't happen.

No one wants to share pain, or see anger, or feel sad. We avoid these emotions like a flesh-eating disease. (Yikes! She's sad. I don't want to catch it. RUN!) Everyone wants to hang out with someone who's happy and living the dream life. That way we can totally ignore our own crappy, little existence, and pretend we're living the dream life, too.

I wrap my fuzzy robe tight around me, making certain all my parts are covered before I open my bedroom door. I'm very private about my privates, if you know what I mean.

"Mama!" I holler down the hall. "Have you seen my blue sweater?"

There's no answer.

I pad down the hall and into her bedroom. No mama. I continue into her bathroom and find my little brother making faces at the mirror.

I close my robe tighter around me. Berg is only twelve, and I'm sure he's stumbled upon a few internet sites that he shouldn't have, but his sister should definitely not be the first girl he sees naked.

"Hey, Berg."

He doesn't look my way but swivels his head back and forth. "Does my hair look okay?"

His short, brown hair is spiked up into a mohawk in front and neatly pasted to his head in back. Usually his hair looks like that picture of Albert Einstein, so I'd have to say this is an improvement.

"Looks good to me."

His mouth turns up into this embarrassed smile where only one of his dimples show. And that makes me grin. I love when he's happy.

"You're wearing your Barcelona jersey." I arch my eyebrows. "Special day?"

He shrugs and tries to act all cool. "Not really," he says, but his dimple deepens so I know he's totally bluffing.

"Liar," I tease. I know that he only wears his favorite soccer jersey on special occasions. I lean against the bathroom sink. "So…who's the lucky girl?"

"No one," he grumbles, his smile widening.

He's a terrible liar.

"Awww, come on," I beg. "You can tell me."

He presses his lips together.

"Is it Emily?"

He crosses his arms and frowns at me. I'm not deterred. I'm his big sister. It's my job.

"Is it Samantha? Morgan? Alexa? Maddie? Carrie?"

A huge smile wide enough to ignite both his dimples erupts onto his face.

"Carrie?" I repeat.

He tries to frown, but utterly fails, and giggles and nods instead.

I clap my hands together and squeal. "Are you going to ask her out?" I pause. "Do kids your age do that?"

He nods. "Brady's asking Morgan to walk up to Treats after school, so I thought I'd ask Carrie if she wanted to go." He opens his hazel eyes wide. "Will you and Dillon please meet us there?" He tries to hide his enthusiasm and looks down at the counter and rubs his finger along it. "You know, just in case… you know… I need more money, or something."

I smile. I know what he needs. He needs his big sis, and that makes my heart feel all fuzzy and good.

I smile. "No problemo! Dillon and I will meet you there after school." I'll do anything for my little brother.

"Thanks." He nods his head toward the closet. "Um, well… Mama said I could use some of Daddy's cologne."

I suppress a smile. My little brother wants to wear cologne. Too cute. I steer him toward the closet, but he wiggles out from under my arm.

"I can do it. Daddy showed me how."

"Okay."

I watch him walk into our parents' closet, ready to spritz his way to manhood, and I suddenly feel that time has passed me by. I'm five-nine, and he's a whole foot shorter than me, but suddenly he seems all grown up. Asking out a girl. Wearing cologne. Where did my baby brother go?

"Love you, Little B," I say.

He peeks around the door and grins. "Love you, too, Big L."

I suddenly want to hug him. But I only have ten minutes until we leave for school and I'm not dressed, so I'll just have to be nostalgic and ponder the passage of time later.

I rush out of the bathroom and into the hall. "Mama?" I call out. "Mama?"

"I'm in the kitchen!"

I dash down the hall and meet her at the bottom of the stairs.

"Looking for this?" she asks, her eyes crinkling. She's wearing my sweater on her head like a turban.

"Yes!" I throw my arms around her. "You're the absolute best mom ever!"

"Ha! Remember that the next time I ask you to scoop the dog poo," she laughs, and hands me the sweater.

My mom is tons shorter than me, a little wider, and always wears her light-brown hair up in a messy knot. Sometimes I wish she took more care with her hair and clothes like other moms, but I hope she never changes her smile. Because when she smiles... Wow! Her bright blue eyes wrinkle at the edges. Her teeth try to break free from her lips. And I feel like sunshine has warmed my entire body. And I love that.

"Thanks, Mama. You're the best!" I yell over my shoulder, and race back up the stairs. I run into my bedroom and close the door behind me. I'm feeling a bit rushed and this is going to be a day that changes everything, so I take a second and focus on my soft blue walls. The color helps calm my emotions. Inhale. Usually I picture happiness as a cute little smiley face fluttering into my body. Today I just picture Dillon, and it works.

I slip into my dark, skinny jeans and pull on my favorite, blue sweater. I check my phone. Four minutes until we have to leave. Perfect. Because I desperately need one more thing. My lucky earrings.

I walk over to my desk and sit down. The desk is heavy and clunky and made of some kind of dark wood, but I love it. My great-grandfather built it for my great-grandmother years and years ago. I never knew either of them, but every time I sit down I can feel how much he must have adored her. He even cut a huge heart out of swirled glass and set it on top of the desk.

My great-grandmother loved keeping up with her friends all over the world, and her favorite postcards are still under that beautiful glass heart. There are ones from exotic places like Morocco and Bangkok, a few from South America, and tons from Europe. But my absolute favorite is of the Eiffel Tower in Paris, France. I love the angle. The photographer was standing under it at night time when it was all lit up in golden lights. Where others saw boring structural supports, the photographer saw something else, and made it look beautiful.

My mama and my daddy promise to take me to see it someday if I keep my positive, anxiety-free attitude. And stay out of detention. I have to admit it's a smart move on their part. Attitude I can do. Detention? Well, that depends on whether that moron vice-principal keeps measuring the length of my skirt. Ugh. I can't help it if I'm tall… and like to wear short skirts.

I slide open the top drawer of my desk and pull out my lucky earrings. They're small white circles with dark blue, lotus flowers painted on them. They're quite simple compared to what I normally wear, but Daddy brought them back from Morocco right after I was diagnosed with Oh my GAD. The lady selling them gave Daddy some mumbo jumbo about how lotus flowers help awaken the light within the wearer blah blah blah find her true self. I don't believe any of it, and I'm pretty sure Daddy didn't either, but they're really pretty and my real name is Lotus, so I wear them when I don't want to worry. Just in case they do help.

I close the drawer and inhale a deep breath. It's time. Today's the day my life will change forever!

CHAPTER 3

Some crappy time before 8 AM

I think I'm losing my mind. Why else would I be laughing when I just saw my boyfriend playing tongue hockey with someone else?

Dillon is supposed to be holding my hand as we accept the prom queen and king nomination, not starring in a private screening of Let's Freak Out My Girlfriend on the auditorium stage. And lucky me I walked right into the opening scene.

"Lottie!" Dillon's eyebrows shoot up. "What are you doing here?"

I guess I'm laughing maniacally. I do that sometimes when I feel my anxiety rear its ugly head. And seeing my boyfriend's lips going to town on another boy has taken me somewhere WAY beyond anxious. It's really only a matter of time before pimply guys in white jackets come to take me away. And it's way too early in the season to wear white.

"Do you think she saw us?" the boy toy whispers.

I squelch my hysterics and slowly turn around. I'm thinking I exit the stage, go back out the door, and pretend I was never here.

"Lottie, wait. Please."

I start walking. I pretend I didn't hear Dillon. I think my ears might be clogged. I may be getting allergies. It is spring. There surely must be flowers growing under the crusty snow somewhere out there.

Dillon grabs my arm. "Lottie, we need to talk."

I make the mistake of turning around and looking into his bright, blue eyes. Those same eyes that lit up only moments before when he kissed someone else. That wasn't me.

But we're all alone now. That boy is gone. Now it's just me and him on this stage in the auditorium. And I wish this were just a play. Starring beautiful me, and my sweet, perfect boyfriend.

My boyfriend. Who taught me the right way to eat cheese puffs. (Never lick your fingers until the end!). Who brought me five boxes of popsicles when I had strep because he didn't know which flavor I would like best. Who drew cartoon heart people on my palms during algebra.

The pain hits me hard in the gut and my stomach churns, turning this morning's happy blueberry pancakes sour. I recognize that old, anxiety pressure building, like when you eat something bad and it doesn't hit you right away but you know you're sure going to be paying for it later.

I need to breathe and bury. I can't let the old Lottie out. I've worked too hard to keep her locked away. I struggle to think of happy things. Ice cream sundaes topped with lots of cherries… which, of course, Dillon and his boy toy will be feeding to each other.

STOP!

My brain is disgusted with my imagination, and that awful anxiety pressure expands into my chest. I feel as if I'm trapped underwater, and if I dare to breathe watery tears will smother my lungs. So I squeeze my hands into tight fists, and imagine I'm a mighty dam holding back a raging river. I haven't allowed myself to feel this way in over eighteen months, and I refuse to let a little kissy face ruin the new me I've worked so hard to be.

"I have to…" Dillon starts, and then pauses. He closes his eyes and sighs. A bead of sweat trickles down from his soft, brown hair, and as he wipes it away, his fingers ruffle his right eyebrow. The tiny hairs stand up and make him look like a little boy just waking up from his nap.

I'm about to reach up, smooth out that eyebrow, and kiss it all better when his blue eyes pop open and shoot me a look of pure determination.

Uh oh. I can guess where this is going. Nowheregoodville. Population me.

I grab both his hands and walk backwards, trying to tug him with me across the stage. "We should go," I beg. His fingers are so warm on mine that they make my stomach hurt.

He pulls me to a stop. "First, I have to tell you something."

I shake my head. "Nope. You don't have to tell me anything. In fact, let's not talk all the way over to the commons so we can save our breath and get there faster. Ok?" I paste on what I hope looks like an encouraging smile.

Dillon's face falls. "You saw me kiss him, didn't you?" he whispers.

The pain punches me hard in the gut. POW! Just like in the cartoons.

"I was going to tell you," he murmurs. "I just…" His shoulders slump. "I'm so sorry, Lottie."

My heart beats faster. All my muscles contract, and my pancakes are trying really hard to launch themselves out of my stomach. I swallow. My heart races. I know what's happening. I'm starting to panic. I'm starting to freak. And I can't go back down that road again. I've worked too hard.

I close my eyes and inhale a deep breath. I can do this. Sunshine. I inhale again. Daisies. Inhale. I sure wish I had my vape right now.

I exhale and open my eyes. "We better go now," I murmur.

"Lottie," he says softly, rubbing his thumb gently over mine. "I don't think you understand."

He's actually very wrong. I do understand. I just don't want to.

"Lottie, I think…"

I know what he's about to do, and I can't let him.

"I know you're sorry," I interrupt. "No need to say it again. I said I forgive you, and now it's all over and behind us, and we don't have to talk about it ever again."

I hate this play. I want this to be over. I tug his hands and try to pull him off the stage with me, but he doesn't budge. He just stares at our entwined hands, and then very slowly, one by one, unwinds every one of his fingers away from mine.

He gazes back up at me, eyes wide with hope. "I think I may love him," he whispers.

And those words plunge my mind into blackness.

"What?" I croak. "You said you love me." I feel everything inside me boiling up, snatching the oxygen from my lungs.

"Lottie, I do love you."

I feel my lungs inflate again, until he adds.

"But not as my girlfriend anymore."

And that doesn't just make my heart stop. It crushes it. Into a million, shattered, un-fixable pieces.

Snot floods my nose. Cramps gouge my stomach. My lungs shrivel in on themselves like deflated balloons as wretched sobs vomit from my body. I can't stop them. I can't control them. All I can do is thrash in agony as they burn their way up from my heart and spurt out.

"NO!" I scream. I slap his perfect cheek. "You can't do this to me!" I slam my fists into his chest. "I was going to be prom queen! Prom queen! How can I be prom queen if my king is a flaming queen?!"

I'm spitting out the bitter words, hating the taste of them in my mouth, but I'm out of control. I can't stop even if I wanted to.

"Do you know what people are going to say? DO YOU?!" I stab him in the chest, hoping it will hurt him as much as he's hurting me. "That I wasn't good enough. That I made you this way." My eyes narrow into slits and I feel the anger sear my throat as my voice turns raspy. "But it's not me. It's you. Something is wrong with YOU. You're the weirdo. You're the one that's not good enough. You're the freak."

I slam my hand over my mouth. What the crap? I sound like a feverish shrew who rips apart still-beating hearts with her bare hands. Oh my god. I need to apologize. I need to make this better!

But as I watch his face crumple and the tears he shouldn't be feeling roll down his cheeks, I know I screwed up. It's too late. The disgusting words are out there. Hanging between us like a poisonous gas. And the worst part is that I allowed them to escape.

Again.

I scream inside my head. I squeeze my eyes shut and scream so loud that I see black and red swirls of anger. I feel like I'm in a horror movie and I can't find my way out. I keep screaming and see flashes of white, all exploding inside my brain, killing any happiness I may have left. It's all I can see. All I can feel. Pain. I take a deep, gurgling breath and can't help thinking that it sounds like my last.

Inhale, dammit!!

Breathe!

STOP SCREAMING!

BREATHE!
GET OUT OF HERE!
OPEN YOUR EYES!
I slam my eyes open.

And see Dillon. Staring at me. His eyes wide with fear and horror. And I know he heard me.

My heart plummets. I wasn't just screaming in my head. Dillon heard me freak out! After eighteen months of hiding, he knows the lunatic I was before I came to high school. The monster who can't control her emotions. Or what she feels. Or what she says.

Or who she is.

And I hate that girl. I hate her with all my heart and soul!

I can't stand this. I can't stand the way he's looking at me. I have to get out of here. I lunge toward the nearby stairs, and I only see a fraction of the fear in Dillon's eyes when he realizes I'm coming towards him, and he tries to get out of the way of the freak express. I don't even have time to tell him that I won't hurt him before he stumbles too close to the edge, teeters for a second, and then tumbles backwards down the steps, landing with a crack on the tile floor ten feet below.

Someone screams, and I realize it must be me.

Because Dillon's not moving.

I stop screaming. I blink. I blink again.

Dillon's eyes are closed. His neck is crooked. His legs are sprawled awkwardly open, split at the seam. I walk slowly down the stairs and check his pulse. He's alive. I should call for help. I should get help.

But then they'll know.

I pull out my phone. I press*67 so no one will find me, and I call 911. I tell her I want to be anonymous. I tell her to send an ambulance to the high school auditorium. I tell her to hurry. The operator wants me to stay. To tell her who I am.

But I can't. Because I don't even know anymore.

And right then, something inside me slips.

I hang up, and without looking back I run out the exit door and yank it closed with both hands. Only when I hear the lock click me out do I finally exhale, and I just stand there, outside the school, deep in a shadow the sunrise hasn't found yet.

CHAPTER 4

And now I'm in deep

I'm hoping for a miracle. Or an anomaly. Like the moon slipping out of orbit and causing tsunamis and blizzards that are so catastrophic no one knows I just killed my boyfriend and disappeared.

I know I should go back and make sure Dillon's okay, but I don't want to face my mess. I don't want to freak out again. I don't want anyone to know what lurks inside of me.

I try the door. I'm locked out. I can't go back, even if I wanted.

I guess I could knock, or pound on the door until someone hears me. Either would be better than going around to the front door and running straight into that moron vice-principal just so he can give me another detention.

Or send me to jail. For murder.

I hear sirens. Good. They're coming for Dillon.

I wipe my face on my not-so-favorite-anymore sweater, leaving smears of black mascara that look like ominous storm clouds against the blue. I burp up a giggle. I must look awful. Probably even worse than that time Dillon and I walked home in the rain.

Dillon.

CRAP.

I can't go back. My life will be over. Everyone will hate me. And if anyone sees me like this, they'll never elect me prom queen.

Especially after they find out what I did to the king.

I shake my head. I need to get out of here.

I unzip my boots and carefully stash them in my backpack. The grass looks dry, but it's April in the mountains and I know better. Melted snow, or dew, or some kind of wet crap is lurking under last year's dead grass. I babysat too many kids to buy these boots, and I don't need anything else to ruin my day. Besides, I don't mind wrecking my socks. I borrowed them from Dillon, and I'm fairly certain he won't want them back now.

I heave my backpack onto both shoulders, tighten the straps, and sprint across the football field. I half expect someone to see me and demand that I come back. Like my first-period, AP English teacher. And I really want someone to beg me to come back. Like Dillon.

I zigzag through a small opening in the fence and decide not to look both ways as I dash across the street and into the safety of the neighborhood. The houses are spaced farther apart in this section of town. Acres of weedy meadows and towering pines separate neighbor from neighbor. There are no well-manicured lawns and elk-resistant fences like in my neighborhood, and I find it peaceful here.

I veer off the street and snake through the trees until I find the trail leading to Conifer Lake. Deer and elk created this shortcut, and high school kids looking for a place to escape help maintain it.

I run faster. My legs are on fire and my back aches from where my backpack is slam-dancing against it. But none of that matters. I'll take anything over the awful pressure building again in my chest. It feels like a giant hand is squeezing my body so tight that soon my head will pop off. I can't let that happen. I kind of like my head. So, I run even harder, focusing on physical pain, instead of the emotional one that's shredding my heart apart.

When I start gasping for air, I know I need to think of happy things.

Daisies. Yes, they're happy. And sunshine. And puppies!

I inhale a deep breath and imagine a meadow, overflowing with perky daisies, their faces warmed by the bright sunshine.

I exhale, and my pace slows a little.

I inhale and picture wrinkly puppies, stumbling over each other as they cross the meadow, tumbling into my arms to smother me with gentle kisses.

Kisses.

Dillon is a great kisser. Was a great kisser. Or maybe is. Crap I don't know! I'm desperately hoping I didn't kill him. I'm not that barbaric.

Either way, he was a great kisser, because it appears he loves someone else, and since I almost killed him, he likely won't be to open to kissing me anymore.

My legs screech to a stop. Oh great. I roll my own eyes. That did it. I'm glued to the ground as my brain sucks up all my energy and runs away with my imagination.

Why was Dillon playing tongue hockey with that boy? Is he a better kisser than me? Are his lips softer? Does he exfoliate? Boys aren't supposed to kiss boys. Boys are supposed to kiss beautiful girls like me, so it's really not my fault I reacted the way I did.

I sigh. That's not true. It's ALL my fault. It's always my fault. Because of who I try not to be. I hang my head. This is bad. Way worse than the last time.

I stand there alone in a meadow of crushed weeds, and I long to cry. I want to sob and scream and snot all over myself, but I don't know if I remember how. I stand there for a really long time. I don't know how long. Maybe too long. Maybe not. Time is tricky like that. Sometimes it won't leave even when you ask nicely, and other times it doesn't even give you a hug goodbye before it's gone.

I think I'm losing my mind.

Soft, white kittens. Inhale. Gooey, chocolate-chip cookies. Inhale. Ice cream sundaes topped with lots of cherries…

Which, of course, Dillon and his boy will feed each other while they nuzzle their sweet soft kitten.

"STOP IT!" I hear someone scream, and I guess it's me.

My brain is disgusted with my imagination, and I'm disgusted with myself. My legs are wobbly, my feet bruised, and so far this skipping school day sucks. I'm sure I could think of at least one other thing I'd rather be doing than standing on top of a hill yelling at myself.

Below me Conifer Lake glistens in the morning sun and the lake house shadows the shoreline. I love the lake house. I love the floor-to-ceiling windows. I love the view. I love that brides and grooms pledge their lives to each other while gazing out over the sparkling lake and soaring mountains. It's silly since I'm only a sophomore, but I actually thought about what it would be like when Dillon and I were married there. I imagined it would be late summer. The setting sun would unfurl reddish-orange streaks across the sky and the warm air would ruffle Dillon's hair.

Oh my god! Are you serious? STOP IT!

I inhale and focus on emptying my mind. When all thoughts of him are gone, I limp down the hill to the back of the lake house. The grass here is even more soaked, and water seeps through my socks like tears, almost as if every blade is crying for me.

Which is fine by me. Tears are overrated and they're crap on a good makeup job.

I plop down on the deck. The aspen trees along the shoreline are still bare and chalky white. Over the next month, the branches will adorn themselves with bright green leaves to help soak up the longer days of sunshine, but right now they look like dead sticks on the outside, while life thrives on the inside. Like me.

I pull out my vape, load it with oil, inhale a drag, and then very slowly blow it out. The smoke twirls and dances until it disappears. A beautiful wisp snuffed out too soon.

Crap. This philosophical stuff has got to stop. I'm thinking way too much. I want to feel nothing.

I empty my mind and take another drag. I've vaped for almost two years now. My eighth-grade counselor suggested it when she diagnosed me with Oh my GAD. She thought it may help. And I guess it did.

Until today.

CRAP!

I inhale another drag, and without bothering to take off Dillon's socks, I plunk my feet into the lake. Since my hometown is 8,000 feet above sea level, the lake is sometimes still frozen on April 3, but today it's mostly melted and stupidly cold. As my feet grow numb, I order my emotions to follow.

Your mind is a blank wall. A black wall. That's good. Forget everything that happened. Just forget. It never happened.

I think about the happy times I've had here at the lake. Playing Frisbee with Berg. Inhale. Running the trails with Mama. Inhale. Skipping rocks with Daddy. Inhale. Paddle boarding. Ice skating with Dillon when he first told me he loved me.

"NO! STOP IT! STOP IT! STOP IT!" I scream, kicking the water over and over until I'm as soaked as Dillon's socks.

Great. Now the freak is crazy, cold, and wet.

The lake is deserted this early in the morning so my freak out only disturbs a gaggle of geese. They all bolt out of the lake squawking and squealing their disapproval at my lovely scene. One goose that didn't follow the gaggle swims a little closer to me. I imagine it's curious, like people gawking at a car wreck, and I wonder what I look like through beady goose eyes. Probably like a typical, blond-haired, teenager who can't wait to turn sixteen in two weeks and drive her besties around in her new yellow Jeep, laughing and having the time of her life. The perfect life.

But that's not really me.

I'm not perfect. And I'm not exciting. I'm a nobody. Duller than dirt, really. In fact, I think they named dirt after my real hair color. I secretly get highlights every month and tell everyone I'm a natural blond. And I binge eat cheesy puffs. And my stomach is too fat. And I wear blue contacts to make my dirty brown eyes sparkle. I'm dull. And I'm nobody.

And I hate it. I wish my inside would change to match my outside.

I eye the duck. "You think I'm crazy."

It eyes me back. I'm pretty sure it nods.

"Maybe I am." I shrug. "I am talking to you." I pull my frozen feet out of the water and wiggle my toes trying to regain some feeling. I sigh. "I didn't mean to hurt Dillon. I really didn't. It was an accident. He has to know that, right?"

The goose doesn't respond. Smart goose. Never interrupt a teenage girl when she's overthinking.

"But he looked so scared." I stop. My eyes widen. "Oh my god! He was afraid of me! Of what I did." My voice drops to a whisper. "Of who I am." I close my eyes and hang my head. "Of course, he was. And he'll tell everyone, and they'll all know I have Oh my GAD."

"Would that be so bad?"

I snap up my head. "What did you say?"

The goose just looks at me.

I squint my eyes. "Are you talking to me? Like my fairy goose mother or something?"

I hear laughter behind me. And it's not goose laughter. Or at least I don't think it is. I whip my head around and come face to face with my eighth-grade counselor. And I mean face to face. Her bright red lips are inches from my forehead, curled up in a big, crooked grin.

"Hiya, Lottie," she says.

Someone's found me. Crap.

CHAPTER 5

Ms. Foofaraw is crazier than me

Ms. Foofaraw found me.

Yep, my eighth-grade counselor's name is Ms. Foofaraw, and it totally fits her. She has bright red ringlets of hair that stick out from her head like fireworks. She's short, curvy, and always wears faded mom jeans and an outrageous t-shirt. Today she's wearing a too-tight, lime-green-zebra-print that reads, "Dear Karma, I have a list of jerks you missed."

I should be worried she's going to bust me for skipping school, but her shirt has me all discombobulated. She has to be over thirty. That seems way too old to be wearing such a tight shirt. Then again… what do I know? I almost killed my boyfriend today, and I'm sure that's frowned upon in some circles.

She motions to the deck. "This seat taken?"

I shake my head.

She slips off her lime green hiking boots (who makes them in that color? Ugh!), and plops her big bottom down with a plunk.

"So, are you going to offer me a toke, or what?"

I cough. My middle-school counselor wants to vape with me? You've got to be kidding me. This has to be a trick. Or… maybe not. Maybe she just needs a smoke. She was the one who whispered to my parents that it may help me.

I decide to take the safe route. She is an adult after all, and I'm probably already in enough deep doo-doo.

"Um… well… as you know," I stumble. "It's just flavored oil. I'm not smoking weed or anything. And this is for medical purposes so I'm not supposed to share." Which is a total lie because I do share. But not with adults.

Ms. Foofaraw bounces up and down on her knees and laughs and laughs. "Hoo wee! I love that answer. Medical purposes." She snatches my vape out of my hand, holds it over the water, and grins. "Are you sure you need it?"

I raise one eyebrow.

She raises one of hers.

"Um," I stumble. "You were actually the one who recommended I start vaping."

She looks thoughtfully at the vape. "I did?" She shrugs. "Then I should be the one to tell you to quit." And before I can stop her, she turns her palm over and drops my vape into the lake.

"No!" I plunge my hand into the water, but it's too late. I can't reach it. I watch my vape disappear into the murky water.

I turn and glare at her. "Why did you do that?"

She grins. "Because you no longer need it."

I shake my head "Um, yeah I do! You have no idea what happened today."

"Ah, but I do," she says quietly.

She knows? But how? Is Dillon awake? Did he tell everyone what I did? Does the entire town know?

My eyes widen. "You know?"

She shakes her ringlets, and I lean away to avoid a whipping.

"What is done is done," she says. "And you no longer need the vape."

"But Ms. Foofaraw! You don't understand how much it helps me." I know I sound super whiny but I couldn't care less. This whack job just tossed the one thing I could count on into the lake.

She tilts her head. "It helps you what?"

"What?"

She sighs. "The vape. How does it help you?"

I know she's the one who diagnosed my Oh my GAD, but I'm still embarrassed to say it out loud. "You know, with my anxiety. My emotions." I pause and then mumble, "My Generalized Anxiety Disorder."

She waves her hand. "I know all that. But you do not need it. You need your emotions."

I snort. "Um, no I don't. They're horrible. They're out of control. They suck and I hate them. And I hate who I am when I feel them. They're my curse."

She grins ever so slightly. "You think they are a curse?"

I raise both eyebrows. "Uh, yeah. The crappiest curse ever in the history of curses."

"Why not a gift?"

My mouth drops open. Ms. Foofaraw has obviously lost her mind. A gift would imply something happy and fun and exciting to open. Like a soft sweater on Christmas morning. Anger and sadness and pain would be a gift you give to someone you hate.

She tilts her head. "You do not see your emotions as a gift? Yes, they are strong, but to feel so strongly means you are living life to its fullest." She grins like she just announced that I won a year supply of cheesy puffs. "And that is a beautiful gift."

I shake my head. "Nope. Totally disagree."

She frowns. "Really?"

"Yep."

"And that is really how you feel?"

"Not feel," I correct her. "I know."

"You sure?"

"Yes! Totally."

"And nothing will make you change your mind."

I laugh. "I will never change my mind. I hate my emotions. I hate feeling them. I hate who I am with them."

"You are sure?"

"Yes!" I yell, and then frown at my own outburst. "See," I whisper. "This is why I need to bury my feelings."

She purses her lips and closes the distance between us to stare into my eyes. She's way too close for my comfort, but I don't budge. Maybe this is some voodoo counseling stuff that will make me feel better so I play along. Her eyes are a muted green, and her black pupils look like a swirling galaxy of teeny white stars. They're really beautiful for such a weirdo. So green. With all the black and white stars spinning and twirling. Around and around. It's so mesmerizing.

"Then it must be," she whispers.

I shake my head. That was weird. I lean back and regain my personal space.

Ms. Foofaraw slips on her boots. "Okie dokie. Whether you return to school or not today, that choice is yours. Either way our time here is up." She stands and winks at me. "I will be seeing you again very soon, Lottie."

And with that nifty promise hanging over my head, I watch her saunter around the lake house and out of sight.

Okay. That was beyond weird. Her swirling galaxy eyes? And what was up with her tossing my vape in the lake? Doesn't she know those things cost money?

"Lottie?"

Seriously! Can't a girl skip school in peace?

"Is that you, sweet girl?"

And with that I know it's my mama.

"Hi," I say without turning around, and that feels so lame after the day I've had. I want to run over and bury my face in her chest. I want to be three again so she can pick me up and swing me around until we both collapse with laughter and dizziness. I want her to make this all go away.

She sits down close to me and wraps her arm around my waist. She's wearing capris and a baseball cap and must have been running because she feels a little sweaty and she smells like her baby powder deodorant. But I don't care. I snuggle into her. I need my mama.

"You okay?" she asks.

I snort. "I thought a goose was talking to me, so probably not." I frown. "How did you find me?"

"Your school called."

I suck in a breath. I'm totally dead meat.

"What did they say?" I barely whisper. This is it. This is the cherry to top off my wonderful day. This is the end of my life.

Mama shrugs. "That you didn't show up for first period so they were wondering if you were sick."

Sick? Most definitely. I'm beyond sick. I'm a freak.

She tucks my hair behind my ear. "I tried your cell, but you didn't answer. I was worried so I tracked you here." She's trying to keep any feeling out of her voice, but her forehead is swollen with wrinkles and her eyes are red and puffy.

Oh my god. What kind of girl makes her own mother cry? Exhaustion slaps me in the face and I sag into her. I'm too emotionally exhausted to even say I'm sorry.

She wraps her other arm around me and kisses my forehead. "Want to talk about it?"

I shake my head. "I just want to go home."

I feel her inhale like she's going to say something, but she doesn't. She must have known this day would come. The return of the freak with GAD. It's been a while, but we've been through this before and she knows just what to do. And for that I'm so grateful.

She doesn't say anything about my soaked socks. She doesn't say anything about my limp on the way to the car. She doesn't say anything until she helps me into my bed. I think she knows I've slipped, but instead of scolding me, she just lies down next to me and wraps me in a strong hug.

"It's going to be okay, my sweet girl. I love you, and it's going to be okay."

I picture a catfish taking a huge drag off my vape, and I allow the comforting darkness of sleep to wash over me.

CHAPTER 6

Back to reality

When I finally wake up, it's dark outside. I must have slept all day. I yawn, and bury myself deeper under my feather comforter, clutching my stuffed zebra so tight that my fingers start cramping.

Slowly, the sweet amnesia of sleep fades away and memories crowd into bed with me. Seeing Dillon kiss that boy. Freaking out. Probably killing him.

Crap.

Or… could it all have been just a dream?

A light illuminates the hallway and spills into my room. I hear voices coming up the stairs.

"I have to!" Berg yells.

Berg never yells.

"Not right now," Mama says.

"But she promised!" Berg cries, and suddenly he's in my room.

He pauses for a second when he sees I'm in bed, but anger quickly overtakes the confusion on his face.

"You promised me!" he yells. "You promised you'd be there, and you weren't! You promised that you and Dillon would meet me at Treats, and you never showed up. I needed you!" His voice cracks. "I needed you," he whimpers, "and you never showed up."

What? God, no. I hurt Berg, too?

Tears stream down his baby face, and now he doesn't look grown-up at all. He looks hurt and angry, and I long to hug him.

"I needed you," he repeats softly. "I needed you, and you weren't there for me, and now she hates me." He narrows his eyes, swipes his tears, and crumples his dimples into thick lines as anger consumes his face. "And I hate you!" he screams, and storms out of the room.

I feel like I've been punched in the stomach. Berg has never yelled at me before. Never.

Oh god. What did I do?

Mama pauses in the doorway. I wait for her to say something to make me feel better like she always does, but instead she just sighs.

"Lotus," she starts.

And I immediately panic. She only uses my full name when I'm in trouble.

"Dillon is…" Her voice cracks.

Oh god, no. Please don't say Dillon is dead. Please don't say Dillon is dead. No. No. No. I think I'm going to puke.

"Dillon was hurt today."

"Oh thank god!"

She takes a step into my room, a look of confusion on her face. "What did you say?"

Crap! Double crap!

"I meant, oh thank god he wasn't hurt bad. I mean, he wasn't, was he?"

My mama's eyes narrow. "From the little I've heard, he's hurt pretty bad."

Crap. Crap. Crap. My heart is racing. I hope she can't see the sweat pouring down my face.

"Um, how bad? Like will he be healed in time for prom?"

What? Why did I ask that? I could care less about that now. I just want to know how bad I really hurt him.

How bad I really am.

Mama shakes her head. "Really, Lotus. I know you think you've had a bad day, so you've shut everyone else out, but sometimes I wish you would think about someone other than yourself." And without another word, she leaves.

I'm stunned. I think I had a bad day?

I think?!

I KNOW I've had a bad day! No one else in the entire world has EVER had a day as bad as mine! First of all, Dillon dumps me for a boy! A BOY! Then I completely freak out after 18 MONTHS AND FOUR DAYS of excruciatingly hard work trying NOT to ever freak out again! And THEN my brother YELLS AT ME, AND MY OWN MOTHER TELLS ME I'M SELFISH!!

YES, I'VE HAD A BAD DAY!

I sniffle. I expect tears, but something else boils up instead. Something red, and hot, and torrid.

It's anger. Again.

And it grows, like the heat from a fire when you keep your hand there too long. At first you can stand the warmth, but then it gets hotter, and hotter, and hotter, until you either shriek out in pain as it engulfs you or wrench your hand away to escape it.

And I can't escape it.

I HATE Mama for being mad at me! And I HATE Berg for yelling at me! And I DOUBLE HATE Dillon for not loving me! I HATE THEM ALL! HATE! HATE! HATE!

My heart races. Swirls of red and black and white cloud my vision, and I grab the closest thing I can find and channel all my rage into hurling it across the room.

Time slows as I watch my cell phone fly across the room and crash onto my desk. The shattering of glass is like a soft purr to my anger, and I smirk at my destructiveness.

Until I realize what I just did.

I broke the glass heart my great-grandfather lovingly crafted for my great-grandmother. I broke it. Into hundreds of shattered and un-fixable pieces.

Just like me. Shattered. And un-fixable.

I'm awful.

I hate letting my feelings overpower me, because when they do, I hurt people. I mean, what kind of person calls the sweetest boy on earth a flaming queen? And who doesn't keep a promise to her brother because she's so caught up in her own problems?

I'll tell you who.

Me.

The freak.

I hate myself for breaking that precious heart. I hate myself for getting angry. I hate every single atom in my being that makes me the freak with Oh my GAD. I hate the sour taste in my mouth. And the churning in my stomach. And the pounding in my head.

I hate who I am.

I will bury these awful emotions so incredibly deep that they will disappear forever, and I won't ever have to be me again. The freak will be gone. Forever. I will inhale happiness and bury every last bit of pain and anger and sadness… even if it kills me.

I gaze out the window into the night. The stars are blinking and iridescent in the blackness, but all I can think about is how their light is tainted and sad because I know they are the remains of lives burned out millions of years ago. I inhale the deepest breath I've ever taken in my entire life, and I hold it. I will always remember today and how it felt to be in such pain. And that will remind me to never, ever feel it again.

I curl up into a little ball, close my eyes, and wish myself far, far away from today.

CHAPTER 7

Now this is much better

I groan. I don't feel so good. In fact, I feel like that time I ate four cream-filled donuts in five minutes, and then promptly threw up.

"Are you ready?" someone asks from the other room.

Ugh. Berg must be watching TV. And it's so loud! I almost yell at him to turn it down, but then I remember he's super angry at me, so I don't. I feel around for my pillow to help drown out the sound.

"Aicha, what are you doing? Mum will be home soon, and you know I'm not supposed to be wearing this yet."

Mum? What the heck is Berg watching? And where is my dang pillow?

Someone pinches my arm.

"Ouch!" I cry out.

I try to open my eyes, but they're so heavy I can't. I reach up, pry them open with my fingers, and immediately wish I hadn't. A hazy wheel of vibrant colors spins around and around in front of me. I can't focus on any one color, or any one thing. It's like I'm inside a whirling, rainbow tornado. My stomach lurches so I quickly snap my eyes closed. I am not going to throw up. I am not going to throw up.

Inhale. Exhale. Inhale happy. Exhale icky.

It takes me a few more seconds, but I finally get my stomach to settle down and I open my eyes. This time the bedroom is in focus.

But it's not my bedroom.

I'm sitting on some kind of fat beanbag next to an opulent bed drowning in orange and purple pillows and covered with a pink, wispy veil. The walls are painted a bright teal blue. The ceiling is covered in ornate metallic tiles, and red and purple bejeweled lanterns hang under arched doorways in every corner. There's only one explanation. I've obviously stumbled into the magical lair of a rainbow unicorn.

I notice a woman standing in the corner frowning at me. She looks dressed for some kind of party. Maybe prom? Is it time for prom already? How long have I been sleeping?

I look closer. She's older than me, and her dress looks too fancy for prom, so maybe she's going to a ball? Her dress could be a ball gown. It's long and flowing and looks like green velvet. The sleeves and skirt are embellished with swirls of golden lace, and fat pearl buttons define a perfect line from her neck to her toes.

"Well, what do you think?" she asks, twirling around, her long dark hair rippling out behind her.

I think she looks like a princess going to a ball.

"Isn't it the most stunning kaftan you've ever seen?" she asks.

She glances back at me, and when she smiles wide, I gasp. A huge dimple creases her cheek and makes her look a little like my brother, Berg.

I shake my head. "You're not my brother."

I clamp my hand over my mouth. And that was not my voice!

The woman sighs, puts her hands on her hips and pouts. "Aicha, quit playing. You begged me to try it on, and then you talk nonsense. Do you like it or not?"

I don't know who Aicha is or why she's talking nonsense, but the woman seems to want an answer from me and I do like her dress, so I nod.

She claps her hands and grins. "I knew you would! Oh, this is going to be so wonderful!" She bounces over and throws her arms around me in a hug. I don't want to be rude, so I hug her back. She smells of roses and mint, and that makes me smile.

She straightens up and arches one perfectly sculpted black eyebrow. "Now I better take this off and put it away before Mum comes home." And before I can ask her who the heck she is and where the heck I am, she bustles through one of the arched doorways and disappears.

Maybe she's my fairy godmother. I loved reading fairytales when I was a little girl. Bad things would happen and then a fairy godmother would always appear to save the day. I definitely had a bad day today. Surely, I earned a fairy godmother visit?

But, where am I? And why is she calling me Aicha? Every nerve in my body tells me to flee. To run away from this unfamiliar place and go back home. But something in my heart tells me to stay, because for some strange reason I feel like I belong here.

So, I stay.

On my pouf.

Yes! This isn't a beanbag. It's a pouf. Pouf. That's a fun word.

"Pouf." I repeat it three times fast. "Pouf! Pouf! Pouf!" I giggle and feel happy. Which is completely opposite of how I felt when I fell asleep.

That's it! I'm asleep and I'm dreaming. About fairy godmothers and poufs.

Awesome! I'd much rather be here than at home with all the deep doo doo happening there. I smile, close my eyes, and snuggle into my pouf. This is my dream, where I can be happy again, and I'm going to enjoy every delicious second.

"What are you saying about a dream?"

I open my eyes to see my fairy godmother standing a few feet away. She must have slipped back into the room while I had my eyes closed. She's traded her fancy, ball gown for a white, blousy top and a pale-gray, gauzy skirt that reached her knees. Very chic.

"So what are you saying about a dream?" she asks again.

My cheeks feel hot. I'm so embarrassed. She must think I'm an idiot talking to myself and… wait a minute. This is my dream. It doesn't matter what I say. I'm in control. I'm the star here. I don't have to be embarrassed!

I grin at her. "I like this dream."

She laughs. "I know! It's finally here. My dream wedding."

Wedding? My fairy godmother is getting married? I clap my hands together. This dream is awesome!

Fairy G walks over to three low tables on the other side of the room. The tables are surrounded by plump pillows covered in the same purple and gold tapestry print as the bed. She plops down on a pillow and motions for me to join her.

"Come on then, let's have tea."

I shrug. "Okay."

My tan, gauzy skirt tickles my legs as I walk across the room. I glance down and notice that my blouse is blue. I grin. Of course, I'm wearing my favorite color in my dream.

Since the tables are only about a foot off the floor, I feel like I'm in a remake of some Arabian movie as I tuck my skirt around my legs and sit down on a pillow next to my Fairy G.

"I can't believe my wedding is finally here," she sighs. She picks up a silver pot with squatty legs and a long, tapered spout and pours tea into a red, frosted glass rimmed in gold. "I know we're ten years apart and you're only fifteen, but I'm so happy that after all these months of preparations and all the waiting, that you're going to be standing right beside me during it all." She smiles and hands me the glass.

I take it from her, and inhale the steam. It smells of herbs and warmth and mint. I don't know if I can burn my tongue in a dream but I hate when I do that so I very carefully take a sip. It's hot, but quite delicious. Sweet and minty like a peppermint candy, and I love it.

"I wouldn't miss my fairy godmother's wedding," I gush, and take another long sip.

Fairy G looks puzzled. "Fairy godmother? Why are you calling me 'fairy godmother?'"

"Cause that's who you are."

"Who I am?"

I nod. "Yes, aren't you my fairy godmother?"

Fairy G tilts her head back and laughs. "Oh, Aicha, you have such a wonderful imagination. You know I'm not your fairy godmother, silly. I'm just your sister."

"My what?" I sputter, and almost drop my glass. My hands start to sweat, and I start to panic. I don't have a sister. I have a brother, Berg. And he's awesome.

Fairy G (although I guess I can't call her that anymore because she's no longer my fairy godmother and is now my sister -whaaat?) is staring at me, mouth open, clearly thinking that I'm a lunatic. I worry she might be right.

Wait a minute…

This is a dream! This woman is not my dream fairy godmother, she's my dream sister. And Berg is still my brother. He will still be there when I wake up. My heart rate slows, and I lounge back into my pillow.

"You looked so gorgeous in your kaftan that I thought you looked like a fairy godmother," I explain, congratulating myself on my clever cover-up. Kaftan. That's what her dress is called. How did I know that?

My sister gives me a funny look, but a voice in the hall distracts her from asking me more about it.

"Girls?"

"We're in our bedroom, Mum!" my sister calls out.

I guess our Mum is here. I take another sip of tea. My dream sister is model-gorgeous. I can't wait to see what my dream mum looks like. Don't get me wrong. I love my real mama, but she could use some tune-ups in the beauty department.

My dream mum saunters through the arched doorway, and I'm not disappointed. My real mama is pretty in an average, this-is-my-mom way. My dream mum is an exquisite beauty. Her dark eyes are almost navy, and lined with black kohl; her glistening, black hair is styled in a chic bob, with not a gray hair in sight; and a silver embroidered belt cinches her rose-colored kaftan tight around her tiny waist.

Wow.

My dream mum pursues her glossy red lips into a charming frown. "My lovely daughters, I thought you would be ready." Her words drip like honey, sweet and thick, coating me in relaxing warmth. She waves a red manicured hand. "No mind, we shall just be late."

Late? Really?! My mama would never allow us to be late. Mostly because she knows I hate to be late and might freak out. Being late makes me super anxious. I'm usually the first person anywhere I go.

But this is a dream. I can do anything, and be anything, so I think I'm going to be a person who will just be late.

I exhale a freeing breath. I like this.

My dream mum gracefully seats herself on a pillow between us. She smiles at my dream sister. "Malika, please pour me some tea."

Malika. My dream sister's name is very pretty, just like her.

I hold out my glass and grin. "Malika, may I please have some more, too?"

My dream sister stares at me for a split second before she starts laughing. Then my dream mum joins her. I notice they both laugh the same way- with barely any sound, but with crinkles of happiness around their eyes.

"What?" I grin, wondering what I did that was so funny.

My dream mum pats my leg. "Oh, silly Aicha. I have not heard you call your sister by her name in so long. You always do make us laugh."

I smile. I like the sound of that. I want to make them laugh. Laughing makes people happy. And I love making people happy. It's a crap ton better than making people sad.

I want to sit here forever drinking delicious mint tea and making them happy, but Malika has other ideas.

"We must really get dressed," she says, and sets down her tea glass. "Mum's ready, but we're not."

She stands and walks over to a towering wardrobe painted pale pink with white scrolling. When she opens the doors, I see that it's crammed full of what look like long tunics in every color imaginable.

I stand up and cross the room to join her. The tunics are exquisite. I caress all the silken fabrics, marveling at the beautiful colors. Burnt orange. Pale yellow. Vivid red. Deep purple. It's like the most exquisite dress department at the mall is all in this one wardrobe.

Malika pulls out a lavender tunic and hands it to me.

"This is so beautiful!" I gush.

Malika leans close to my ear and snorts. "That's not what you said yesterday." She glances back at our Mum, but she's sipping her tea and not paying any attention to us. "I know you didn't want to wear this jilbab, but I know you'll look so beautiful in it," she whispers.

Jilbab. That's what these tunics are called. A jilbab. And this one is gorgeous! It's a soft lavender with dark purple piping lining the long sleeves. I'm about to ask why in the world I wouldn't want to wear this one when she pulls out another jilbab. That one is a soft, pale blue silk with a row of delicate, silver pearls cascading all the way from the neckline to the bottom hem. My jilbab is the ugly duckling compared to what she's holding.

I drop mine on the floor. "I'll wear that one," I say, and reach for it. When Malika doesn't let it go, I try to pull it from her fingers.

"Aicha, what are you doing?" she cries, holding tighter to the blue jilbab.

I tug harder, but she won't let go. This is my dream. I should get to wear what I want. Blue is my favorite color. Why won't she give it to me? I feel my muscles tense and my heart race. I'm getting angry and this is supposed to be a happy dream.

I swallow my anger and stick out my bottom lip. "But I love the blue one, and I think you should let me wear it because it will look much better on me than on you."

"Aicha!"

Mum's thundering voice startles me so much that I drop my hold on the jilbab. Malika squashes it protectively to her chest.

Mum frowns. "What is wrong with you? This is your sister's wedding. This is not about you."

"But blue is my favorite color, and I want to wear it."

"This is not about what you want!" Mum screeches in a voice more nails on a chalkboard than sweet honey.

I drop my eyes. I didn't want to make anyone angry. I want this to be a happy dream.

Mum takes a deep breath, smoothes her skirt, and stands. "This is Malika's wedding. I don't want to remind you again. Do you understand me?"

I nod, hoping it will make the happy Mum return.

She replaces her frown with a forced smile. "That's better. Please get dressed. I'll meet you at the front door." She blows us both a kiss, and then waltzes out the door as if her impression of a pissed-off monster didn't just happen.

Malika is still clutching the blue jilbab to her chest, her long eyelashes glistening with tears. "I'm so sorry," she whispers. "I didn't mean to get you into trouble." She shoves the blue jilbab into my hands. "Here, you wear it. Please."

I should take it. I mean, this is my dream and I should get to do whatever I want. But instead, I just sigh and let her keep it. "Obviously, this dream is not totally under my control," I mumble.

She must hear me because a look of confusion crosses her face. "I don't know what you are saying about a dream, but please wear it, Aicha." More tears form in the corners of her big eyes as she whimpers. "I don't want anyone to be angry. I want everyone to be happy. I want this day to be perfect."

I totally get ya, sister.

I pick the lavender jilbab up off the floor and paste on a smile. "I really want to wear this one, and you should wear the blue one."

"Are you sure?"

I nod. "Positive." I lean closer and arch my eyebrow. "And I'm pretty sure that will make Mum happy, and I really think we should keep her happy."

Laugh wrinkles form near Malika's dark eyes, and she nods in agreement.

After I watch Malika put on her jilbab, I put mine on in the same way. It covers everything from my neck to my ankles like a long shirt. It kind of reminds me of my grandmother's fancy nightgown with the buttons down the front, except it's more fitted and a million times more beautiful.

Malika squeals when she sees me. "Aicha, you look gorgeous! We must take a picture." She grabs her cell phone off the table, presses her cheek against mine, and quickly snaps a few selfies, coaching me when to smile and pout, just like my besties do with me.

"Ok, let's make sure we have a good one." She scrolls through the pictures. "Ooo! I love this one!" she squeals and shows me.

Malika looks gorgeous in the picture. She has glossy, dark-brown hair, chocolaty brown eyes, and dewy smooth skin. She's the most beautiful Moroccan woman I have ever seen.

And I look just like her.

I sink down onto the pouf. "I'm Moroccan," I marvel.

Malika giggles. "Of course, you are." She raises her eyebrows. "Were you hoping your fairy godmother had turned you into a happy, blonde bombshell?"

My heart sinks and I close my eyes. That's exactly what I was trying to be in real life. When everything went wrong.

CHAPTER 8

Home, Not Sweet, Home

My stomach cramps up and my head spins. I feel like my body is rocketing around a rickety, old, roller coaster after I ate a greasy, corny dog covered in cotton candy. Ugh. This feels like the start of a panic attack, but how can that happen if I'm dreaming?

"Malika, I'm not feeling so good," I mumble. "What exactly was in that tea?"

A large, warm hand covers my forehead.

"Lottie?"

"Daddy?!" I slowly peek open one eye because I so don't want to blow chunks on the most amazing man in the world.

I'm back in my own bed in my own bedroom, and he's sitting beside me. He's still wearing his scrubs so he must have just come home. His eyebrows are drawn, and his blue eyes look tired. All I can think is that I wish I had his eyes and his crazy long eyelashes. I got boring, brown ones.

"I'm here, Lottie." He presses his stubbly cheek against mine. It feels cool, like a refreshing breeze on a steamy day. "I think you have a fever." He leans away and peers into my eyes. "And what's this tea you're mumbling about?"

I snort. He thinks I'm on something. My daddy is an internal medicine doctor and has seen too many patients strung out on whatever new fad drug is going around.

I try to laugh, but I have so little energy that I can only manage a tiny snuffle. "The tea wasn't real. It was in this dream I was having. At first I thought it was my fairy godmother but then she turned out to be my sister. And I was so beautiful, and so happy, and I didn't hurt anyone. Not at all like…" I stop.

Crap. I'm back in my real life. Which means I'm either in a boatload of doo-doo, or I'm going to jail. Either way sucks.

"Not at all like, what?" my daddy asks.

I shake my head.

He doesn't push for an answer, and we just sit in silence staring at each other, waiting for the other to speak. Finally, he sighs.

"Mama said you skipped school today. And I think I know why."

Then I think I'm going to be sick.

"It's because of what happened to Dillon, right?"

Yep. I'm definitely going to blow chunks. I close my eyes.

He gently rubs his thumb over my hand, maybe hoping it will distract me from the fact that he's about to tell me something I really, REALLY don't want to hear. Surprisingly, it does settle my stomach a little.

"I was in the ER when they brought him in," he murmurs.

I keep my eyes closed. I wish I could close off my ears, too.

"He was unconscious by that point, but the paramedics told me he was awake on the ride over and kept saying Lottie over and over again. I think he was worried about you. That you wouldn't know where he was." He squeezes my hand. "This was a big day, I know. You two were supposed to meet for the prom announcements this morning, right?"

I don't say anything. I'm so afraid to open my mouth. I don't know what will come out.

"I'm sorry," he continues, "but he's in really bad shape. I won't elaborate unless you want to know more, but just know that he's in a medically-induced coma and we're doing all we can." He leans over and embraces me in a hug. He smells like breath mints and bandages and coffee.

Crazy emotions billow up from my deep, dark depths and I want to puke them all up and tell my dad exactly what happened and how I freaked out and hurt Dillon, and how I am so ashamed and furious at myself.

But I don't. I can't. He's so proud of me, of all that he thinks I am, and I can't let him know that the real me, the freak me, is back.

So, I swallow all my emotional puke, bury it back inside me, and release his hand. "I love you, Daddy," I murmur as I close my eyes, and wish myself far, far away.

CHAPTER 9

A white kitten and a colorful souk

"Aicha, are you okay?"

What?

"You look really pale. Are you going to be sick?"

My stomach heaves, but my heart soars when I open my eyes and see Malika's sweet eyes looking at me with such concern. I'm back in my dream! This is so much better than all the pain I was just trying to bury. I must have fallen asleep again. My dad did say I had a fever. I hope I don't wake up any time soon. I love myself here! My hair is the color of shiny, dark plums. My skin is like a smooth caramel. I'm gorgeous, my sister loves me, and there's going to be a wedding which can only mean happy, happy fun!

"I'm okay," I reassure Malika and lift myself off the pouf.

She frowns. "Are you sure?"

I nod. "Really, I'm fine. And don't we need to get going?"

Her eyes widen. "We do. But if you aren't..."

I interrupt her. "I'm fine. Really!" I link my arm through hers. "Lead the way beautiful, bride-to-be."

We walk out of our bedroom and into an indoor courtyard. Blue-and-white, diamond-shaped tiles cover the floor. A fountain bubbles in the center and green palms in silver urns sprout from every corner.

Mum is sitting on a plump, gold-and-rust striped couch. She sees us, and her red lips break into a smile.

"You both look so very beautiful."

Malika grins. "Thanks, Mum." Her phone buzzes. She glances down at it and frowns. "My friends are wondering where I am."

Mum rises. "You run along and meet them. Aicha and I will meet you there."

Malika glances at me with concern. "That okay with you?"

I nod. "Of course," I answer, although I'm still not sure where we're meeting her.

"Okay, great!" Malika hugs me and then Mum, and then hurries out of the courtyard typing into her phone.

Mum looks at me. Her big eyes look a bit watery. "I'm so very sorry for before, Aicha. I never should have lost my temper like that. Will you please forgive me?"

Um no. This is my dream, and I want to yell at her for yelling at me and calling me selfish and making me feel like something is wrong with me.

But I don't.

Because I understand her regret and remorse. I was so angry with Dillon that I punched him and yelled hurtful things and physically harmed him, but I never meant to hurt him. Never.

But I'm not thinking about all that right now. I'm in this happy dream where I can make everything else disappear.

I smile at Mum. "Of course, I forgive you. It was my fault anyway." I gesture to where Malika disappeared. "And we better go. I can't let my sister face her friends alone. I know how my besties would be if I was late."

"Besties?" Mum arches her perfectly waxed eyebrow and chortles. "I love you, Aicha. You do make me laugh."

I don't know Mum well enough to tell her that I love her, but it feels good to have her like me again, so I allow her to give me a quick hug before following her out of the courtyard. We stop in the foyer where a row of shoes is neatly lined up by the front door. Mum slips on a pair of black, pointy-toed, open-backed slippers that are embellished with gold leaves, and I put on a simple pair of flip-flops.

I follow Mum out the front door and into what appears to be a thin alleyway barely big enough for me and my three besties to walk hand-in-hand. White-washed, concrete walls rise three stories tall on either side of the narrow street, punctuated by a few brightly colored doors and windows. The door to my dream house is painted bright green, outlined with multi-colored mosaic tiles, and surrounded by green plants in simple ceramic pots.

Mum closes the door and turns to me. Her eyes are shining with excitement.

"I have something to pick up on the way to the hammam, so I will meet you there." She pecks me on each cheek and then hurries down the narrow street.

She has just turned the corner and disappeared out of sight when I realize I have absolutely no idea where, or even what, a hammam is. I hurry to catch up with her and almost trip over a thin, tabby cat. It meows loudly at me, probably scolding me for not watching where I'm walking.

"Sorry, kitty," I apologize, and lean over to give it a scratch.

The tabby immediately arches up to meet my fingers and begins to purr loudly.

"That feels good, huh?" I smile.

The tabby meows again and glances over at one of the pots by the front door. I follow its gaze just in time to see four, teeny kittens tumble out from behind the pot. The tabby meows again and the kittens slip and slide across the cobblestones in a race to reach us. A soft gray kitten arrives first, and the tabby mama gives it a quick lick. Two, black-and-white kittens bound up next, and are also rewarded with their mama's tongue. But when the last kitten approaches- a pure white cutie with brown eyes and a black spot on its forehead, the tabby mama arches her back and hisses loudly until the kitten skitters away and disappears around the corner.

My eyes widen. I glare at the tabby. "Why did you do that?" I rush after the white kitten, but when I turn the corner I'm assaulted by chaos. I've left the quiet, residential streets for the bustling souk- the marketplace.

The souk is noisy and colorful and jam-packed. Every stall along the cobblestone street is stuffed with people and stalls selling everything imaginable. Black, plastic barrels overflow with herbs and spices. Raw chicken parts line glass cases. Silk jilbabs in happy colors like peach, cream, teal, amber, and coral shimmer in the sun. Pointy-toed shoes like Mum's are stacked in blocks of gold, red, purple, and pink, all nestled on top of one another so snugly that there must be thousands of shoes in one little stall.

I'm in heaven! The souk is like the mall at home, only way cooler! I know I need to find this hammam place to meet Malika and Mum, but I'm sure I can look around for a few minutes. I mean, this is my dream.

A lady passes me wearing a lavender jilbab similar to the one I'm wearing. Her head is covered with a brilliant pink scarf which really sets off her darkly-lined eyes and vivid pink lips. I'm definitely going to try that back in my real life. I bet my brown eyes would pop if I wore a headscarf.

I pass the stall selling spices. A man who looks to be about Mum's age stands proudly in front of the barrels. He's wearing a long white tunic and a red fez on his head. He glares at me when I lean down to smell his barrel of orange cumin, so I move on to the next stall selling jilbabs. I squat down to admire the detailing on the hem of a blue jilbab, and suddenly the most gorgeous sandals on earth walk up beside me.

"Are those the summer Jimmy Choos?" I gush without even looking up.

"Why, yes they are," the voice above me answers.

I drool over the black-and-white, hounds-tooth pattern and the silky-thin tassels for a few seconds before I stand up and come face to face with what I swear is me, twenty years from now. This woman is bottle-blonde, blue-eyed, big-chested (well, that's probably not likely), a little wrinkly, and a lot smiley.

I smile back. "They're so beautiful! How did you get them? I didn't think they were coming out for another month."

She grins wider. "I know a buyer who was able to get them for me right before I left Nashville for this vacation."

I sigh. "You are so lucky. I totally want them for my sixteenth birthday, and I've been asking my parents for them for like months but seeing them now in person I want them even more. They really are as fabulous in real life as they look online."

"Well, shock ran."

I tilt my head. "Shock ran? Is that like a Nashville thing?"

Her eyebrows knit together. "I'm sorry. Am I saying it wrong?" She laughs nervously. "I'm trying to say thank you in Arabic."

I smile. "Oh, you mean shukran."

What? How did I know that?

"Aicha?"

Uh oh. It's Malika. Her face is tight, lips pursed, hands balled into fists at her side. Uh oh is right. She's pissed.

"Are you speaking English?" she hisses under her breath.

"What?" I thought she was going to yell at me for being late. I raise an eyebrow. "Um, yeah. What else would I be speaking?"

She looks at me like an olive tree just sprouted out of my head. "Arabic. Like we are now."

My eyes widen. "We're speaking Arabic?"

She nods.

I turn to the woman. "Am I speaking Arabic to you?"

She shakes her head. "No. You're speaking English. And it's quite good as a matter of fact." I'm about to tell Malika she's hearing things when the woman adds. "But it sounded like you were speaking Arabic to that young woman."

What?! My eyeballs feel like they're going to pop out of my head. When in the world did I learn Arabic?

Oh wait.

Of course, I can speak Arabic. This is a dream. I can do anything in a dream. I can speak Arabic. I can see the new Jimmy Choos up close. And I can be a Moroccan girl.

It's a dream. Anything is possible.

I grin at the woman. "Well, my sister and I are off to the hammam. Have a nice vacation!"

She waves goodbye, and I watch those beautiful sandals walk away. "Good-bye Jimmy Choos. Thanks for visiting me in this dream. I hope to see you on my birthday." I turn to Malika. "Allrighty sister-of-mine, off to the hammam we go." I hold out my arm and wait for her to latch onto it so we can go skipping through the souk laughing and giggling in my beautiful dream.

Malika eyes narrow. "I can't believe you were talking to an American," she hisses.

I raise my eyebrow. "Why?"

"What if Mum had seen you?"

"Um, hopefully she would have loved the Jimmy Choos, too?"

Malika shakes her head. "Quit trying to be funny. This is not funny." Her eyes sag as her frown deepens. "You know Mum is extra sensitive because he's not here for the wedding." She sighs. "Aicha, sometimes I wonder if you care about anyone but yourself."

What?

What is it with this selfish theme? This is my dream, and I want this dream to be happy; not this shame-on-you crapola my psyche is trying to get away with.

"I do care," I snap back. My heart starts racing as I feel my anger rising. I inhale a happy thought of that cute, white kitten. "I let you wear the blue jilbab, didn't I? I forgave Mum for yelling at me. And besides, why would Mum care if I talk to an American?"

Tears drip slowly from Malika's eyes, and my stomach instantly hurts because I know I somehow caused them, even if this is just a dream. Her eyes turn darker than black, and I don't understand why, until suddenly I know what she's going to say and it plunges my stomach into darkness.

"They hated him," she whispers, almost so softly that I can't hear her over the clamor of the souk. "They hated him so much that we'll probably never get to see our Papa again."

CHAPTER 10

More than I can handle

Tears are streaming down Malika's face, and I hate watching it. And seeing all this sadness. I don't want to feel it. I try to turn and run, but the crowd is suddenly too thick, suffocating me against her pain.

"You were too young, but I remember," she whimpers. "They hated Papa. Not because he was bad, but because he was Muslim. He wore a headscarf. He prayed to Allah. And they thought he was just like those horrid men who killed everyone in America."

I don't want to hear this. I try to step back, but I can't move.

"They never saw Papa for who he really was," she says. "He was our sweet father, and Mum's loving husband, and he was an amazing chemist working on a cure for leukemia." Her eyes light up. "He was going to cure cancer. I just know he was!" She shakes her head. "But they never cared about any of that. He went over to share his research, and they thought he was a terrorist and they took him away from us. We don't know why. We don't know where." A sob escapes and her voice cracks as she whispers, "We don't even know if he's still alive." She buries her face in her hands, shoulders shaking, quietly sobbing.

Sadness bubbles up inside of me. I can't help it. All I can think about is if my Daddy was killed and he wasn't there to sing his wacky, off-key, happy birthday song to me. Or to give me my special, fist-bump kiss goodnight. Or to tell me to stop growing up so I can always be his little girl.

I can't even imagine.

And I don't want to.

I swallow those awful emotions. I shove them deep down, refusing to feel them. I'm not doing this in my happy dream. I inhale a vision of that sweet, little, white kitty again.

But Malika is not finished playing with my emotions. "I remember how Mum cried and cried, and tried to understand and forgive, but then she just completely fell apart." She wipes her eyes and stares past me. "And then we almost lost her, too."

Losing my mama… Nope! I'm not even going there.

I watch Malika wipe her tears and remember how streaked with black my favorite blue sweater got after my freak-out crying fit in the shadow of the school.

She grabs my hands, and stares at me with big, round, puppy dog eyes. "Aicha, I can't bear to see her like that again. Especially for my wedding. I just want everyone to be happy so please no more talking to Americans."

I nod. Crap, I'll agree to anything if we can just get past all this icky emotion. Malika looks so relieved, but I have a funny thought. If I can't talk to Americans, does that mean no more talking to myself? Because I'm American.

Or am I Moroccan?

What are we in a dream? Are we our real selves with all our hopes and dreams? Or do we become the person we dream we are, and forget about who we once were? Am I nobody in my dream? Merely a figment of my own imagination?

Malika saves me from over-analyzing by hugging me. I slowly put my arms around her and find myself really hugging her back. I focus on the happiness growing in my belly and bury any residual sadness deep, deep down.

Malika pulls away first. Her eyes look brighter and her face is flushed. Hugs definitely have a special healing power. I need to remember that.

"Okay." She inhales a deep breath. "Now we are beyond late. My friends are covering for us, but no one can deceive Auntie for that long." She links her arm through mine. "Promise you'll stick with me at the hammam?"

I nod. "Like glue."

Malika grins, looking like her happy self again. "Oh, Aicha, I'm so lucky you're my sister."

I smile at that, and find myself sort of wishing it were true.

We push our way through the souk crowd until Malika stops in front of a bright green, wooden door.

"Auntie and Mum think I went to the bathroom," she confides. "Please don't tell them I went looking for you. I don't want them to be mad. I just want us all to have fun."

I feel really guilty. She left her special hammam party to find me, and I was shopping. Maybe Mama was right. Maybe I am selfish?

I put my hand on her shoulder to stop her. "Hey, Malika."

She turns around. "Yes?"

"Thanks for coming to get me."

She smiles. "Of course. You're my sister. I'd do anything for you."

Wow. Just like I said I'd do anything for Berg. But I didn't. Because I let myself get in the way.

Malika inhales a deep breath. "You're going to stay with me?"

"Of course. You're my sister."

She grins, opens the door, and we walk together into the hammam.

Oh crap. I don't know what I expected to see, but a dozen women, topless and hanging out in their underwear in a huge bath hall was not even close.

"They're here!" someone shrieks, and boobs of all shapes and sizes bounce over to greet us.

Oh my. This is slowly turning into a nightmare.

We're standing in a long, thin room under an arched ceiling. The floor, walls, and ceiling are an earthy-green marble peppered with bright-green mosaic tiles. And that's all I have time to take in before the attack of the boobs descends upon me.

"Aicha, you look so lovely!" says saggy boobs.

"Aren't you so proud of your sister?" says small boobs.

"Where have you been?" says oh-my-god-look-away boobs.

I'm bombarded by woman of all ages... and all of their boobs. I'm not exactly prude. I mean, I have seen Mama in her underwear and bra. But I don't even know these people! And they're all hugging me to their boobs!

Wait. Actually, I do know them. That one is Mum's best friend. And that one is my cousin. And that's Malika's best friend. And that's Auntie.

I shake my head. Dreams are so bizarre.

I catch sight of Mum. She didn't bounce over to greet us. Thank god! She's sitting crossed legged in the middle of the floor, with her chic hair all wet and slicked back, and somehow without her red lips, she looks very sad.

Or maybe she looks that way because now I know what she's been through.

I quickly avert my eyes because I don't want to feel her pain.

Malika sheds her clothes and hangs them on a hook. "Remember your promise," she whispers before the gaggle of woman drag her away.

I groan. Why did I promise her? I don't want to be here times infinity. I don't want these women to see my boobs. What if they stare? Or point? Or…oh my god… talk about how perky I am?

Crap. And now I'm worrying again.

I'm seriously thinking of sneaking back out the door when Malika calls my name.

"Aicha, come on!" She motions to me and then pats the mat next to her. Mum is sitting on her other side.

Aicha! That's right. I'm Aicha, and I'm in a dream. There's nothing to worry about. The only person that will see my boobs is myself because I'm the only real person here. These people are all in my imagination.

I strip down to my panties, and even though I keep reminding myself this is a dream, I still feel exposed so I fold my arms tightly over my chest.

Auntie appears in front of me. "Finally, you are ready," she scolds and links her arm in mine, exposing my boobs to everyone. As my cheeks heat up, I remind myself that this is only a dream. Auntie drags me to the center of the room and pushes me to sit on the mat next to Malika. I'm wondering if the drain that runs down the center of the hall is deep enough to swallow me up and whisk me out of this dream when Malika leans closer.

"I'm happy you didn't leave," she whispers.

I raise my eyebrows. "Now why in the world would you think I was going to leave?"

She snorts. "Your hand on the doorknob."

I bite my lower lip, but she only laughs.

"Don't feel bad," she giggles. "I was thinking about joining you."

I can't help but giggle with her. I like seeing her so happy. And I like to think it's because I'm here. With her. For her.

And that can't be selfish. Maybe my mama was wrong.

Auntie hands me a bar of black soap. "Here is the sabon bildi. You need the olive oil to soften your scaly skin."

Um. Gee, thanks, Auntie. Just call me lizard girl.

While Malika, Mum, and I lather up with the soap, the women surround us and start singing. The tune is rhythmic and joyous, and a few of Malika's friends even start dancing.

I set the soap down on the mat next to me and close my eyes. I inhale and let the music and the steam lull me into a deep relaxation. Too bad I didn't have a hammam handy when I ran into Dillon in the auditorium. I would have…

"Yow!" I shriek. Something is scratching the skin off my back! "Ow!"

My eyes fly open. Malika looks mortified. Mum is frowning at me. And, of course, the singing has stopped and everyone is staring at me like I just announced that I'm part of the I-hate-spa-day club. Auntie is behind me, giving me a funny look, her hand inside a black glove that's poised above my back.

"What's wrong?" Malika asks, concern in her eyes.

Suddenly, I know that the black glove of pain is actually a loofa used to exfoliate dead skin and make my skin super soft.

How do I know that? Is this for real?

Man, this dream is taking such a weird turn.

Everyone is still staring at me so I fumble for an explanation. "Nothing's wrong. It's a… it was a song." What am I saying?!

Inhale. Remember this is a dream. You can do anything.

I give Malika what I hope is a grin. "It's a new song I wrote for you."

She claps her hands together. "Really?" she squeals. "Will you sing it again?"

Ok. Oh geez. Here goes nothing.

I sing softly to the tune of Row Your Boat. "Wow, wow, wow, wow, and wow. This is Malika's day." Malika is smiling so I take that as a good sign and keep going. "And now you all sing with me, 'Wow, we're all bathing in the hammam, for her wedding day.'"

No one joins me. No one smiles. In fact, no one moves. This may only be a dream, but I am definitely feeling like a humongous idiot. My stomach starts to knot up. My cheeks get really hot. And then Mum saves me.

"Bathing," she sings softly. "Bathing in the hammam." Her voice is deep and rich, and really soulful, like an old-time jazz singer. "Bathing in the hamman, for her wedding day."

Malika squeezes my hand. "I love it," she cries.

And this prompts everyone to start singing my dorky, ridiculous, made-up song. Everyone sings at different times and in different chords, but somehow that transforms it into something rich with life and love and happiness. And surprisingly, it sounds beautiful.

This does not, however, distract Auntie from her task of skinning me alive. She rubs my body with that scratchy glove, and after a minute, I must lose all nerve endings because it feels less like barbaric needles and more like fine sandpaper. I close my eyes and listen to the singing until, finally, Auntie sets down the glove (Hooray! Hooray!) and rinses me with a pitcher of water. This I love. The warm water rushing over my body feels like every molecule of my skin is getting a cozy, warm hug. Malika is rinsed with warm milk, not water, to purify her for the wedding, and I wonder if it feels the same. Or if she feels like she's in a big bowl of cereal.

Once I'm all rinsed, Auntie massages argan oil into my pink skin. It smells like a mixture of olive oil and lemons. I'm limp as spaghetti when Auntie finishes, but my skin feels softer than anything I've ever felt and smells so fresh. Maybe I should see if there's a hammam near my house when I wake up.

Mum smiles. "I am so happy that this day is here. You both look so beautiful. I just wish…" Her words trail off.

"I know, Mum," Malika murmurs, and pulls Mum into a hug.

I watch huge tears drip from Mum's closed eyes and I know they aren't happy ones. Her lips are pressed together trying to hold in the pain she must be feeling because her husband isn't here to share what should be a perfect wedding celebration.

Malika whispers something in Mum's ear that must make her happy because Mum's face relaxes a little and the tears slow. Then Mum opens her eyes, sees me, and tries to smile.

"I love you," she mouths.

And for some weirdo reason that hurts. Like really hurts.

And it shouldn't. Mum's just being sweet, but it makes me miss my mama. My real mama who does love me. For real. Even when I'm selfish. Even when I freak out.

NO! I don't want to feel my heart ache! I don't want to share this pain of missing someone with Mum. I want to wake up! I want to see my mama!

The steamy heat. The loud laughter. Mum's face. The emotions. They all overwhelm me, and, suddenly, I don't feel very good.

Auntie announces that mint tea and cookies are in the next room, and I don't want either. I want a huge bag of cheesy puffs, my stuffed zebra, and my mama. It's time for this dream to end. I want to go home.

I close my eyes, and wish myself far, far away.

CHAPTER 11

Home. Can you hear me?

I feel so sick. Like I'm on a rickety, old, roller coaster that won't stop doing loop-de-loops that are slamming me into the metal seat.

Ugh! I need out of this dream.

I keep my eyes closed, inhale a deep breath, and think of happy things. Like cookies and mint tea and boobies. Wait. I need to think of happy things in my real life. Like Berg jumping on my bed with me. And Mama dancing with Daddy on the deck at sunset.

My nausea starts to fade. I inhale another deep breath and open my eyes.

It worked! I'm back in my bedroom!

There are my soft blue walls. Hi walls! And my great-grandmother's desk. Hi desk! And there's Mama, Berg, and Daddy! My heart soars. I'm so happy to see them standing next to my bed that I start babbling away.

"Oh my god, I just had the weirdest dream. I was this girl who lived in Morocco. And I was really beautiful with this long, glossy, dark hair. And I had a sister named Malika, and a mom, who we called Mum, and she was so incredibly gorgeous, but she wasn't happy because her husband had been thrown in prison and could be dead, and all I could think about was how sad I would feel if something happened to all of you, and how horrible it would be."

I stop to take a breath and tears threaten to leak out of my eyes. I blink them back. I am not allowed to be sad anymore. I will not be sad. I refuse to be.

I exhale a huge breath and paste on a smile. "But that's all behind me now. I'm back. In my real room. With all of you. And I'm my beautiful, blond self, again, right?"

No one answers me. They just stare at me, zombie faces full of sadness.

"What?" I reach up and touch my face. "Why are you all looking at me like that? Do I have something on me? Do I have a big zit? What?"

Berg shakes his head.

"No zit? Then what?"

He doesn't answer.

My eyebrows knit together. "Are you still mad at me? Is that why you're giving me the silent treatment?"

Berg just stares at me. No expression. No smiley dimples. Nothing. Oh- kay.

I wave my hand in front of his face. "Berg? Hellooo? Anyone home?"

My heart picks up, and I feel a little sweaty. Is this my punishment? Is that what I get for losing control of my emotions?

"I love you, Little B," I whisper, hoping that will snap him out of it. It always works. Berg never stays mad at me when I call him that.

I wait to hear, "I love you, Big L," but he doesn't say anything as big, fat tears drip from his green eyes.

Ok, now I'm starting to freak out.

I turn to my Daddy. "What's wrong with him?"

He doesn't answer me either.

"Daddy?" I whimper.

He doesn't answer. He just walks over to the window, turns his back to me, and hunches over, shoulders shaking.

What the crap is going on here?! Why is no one answering me? And why are they so sad? It's making me sad. And I don't want to be sad! I want to be happy!

I turn to my Mama. She'll know how to fix this. She'll know just what to do to make this all better.

"Mama," I moan. "I need you."

She walks closer and sits down on the bed next to me. Her eyes are red and puffy, and her lips are squeezed into a thin line. She reaches out her hand, and I close my eyes, yearning for her soothing touch.

But it never comes.

CHAPTER 12

How did I get back here?

Instead of my Mama's soothing touch, I feel my stomach squeeze and twist and turn so violently that my head starts spinning.

I open my eyes.

%%%$$** Crap!

I'm not in my room anymore. I'm still in bed but I'm staring at wispy pink veiling and drowning in orange and purple pillows.

Double crap on a kebab. I'm back in the bedroom I share with Malika.

In my dream.

In Morocco.

Away from my family.

But how? I was home! I thought I woke up from this dream and was back in my real life. With my real family.

I feel that familiar tightness building in my chest. It starts as a cute, baby elephant sitting on me and mutates into a fatty-fatty-two-by-four glomming bananas by the truckload. My heart starts to race. My temples throb. I know anger and sadness are in the ring throwing punches to see who can escape first.

And. I. Hate. It.

I grit my teeth. I will not let myself feel this way. I inhale a deep breath of happiness. I think of popping open a fresh bag of cheesy puffs. I exhale my anger. I inhale the sun shining on my face. I exhale the sadness.

The elephant on my chest barfs up the bananas, and my heart rate slows.

It's okay. I'm going to be okay. I'm just still dreaming. Being back in my bedroom was just part of my dream. That's why no one could hear me. That's why no one was talking to me. Yep. This is all one big, weird, totally-crappy dream.

Except... my heart is whispering that it might be something else.

Mum peeks into the room. She's back to her beautiful self. Glossy-black bob. Red lips. Darkly-lined eyes. And she's wearing a floor-length, vivid-teal kaftan with elegant gold swirls. She looks stylish, and thankfully, totally in control of her emotions again.

"Oh good, you're up," she says, her voice failing to surround me with warmth like my Mama's. She glides over and sits on the bed next to me. She kisses my cheek. Her lips are warm, but not particularly comforting. She's not my real mom. My mama. The one who painted a daisy on my cheek on the first day of sixth grade to cover the humongous scab I got from jumping my bike over a log pile the day before.

"Are you feeling better?" she asks.

Um no. I'm feeling like crap, but I don't want her to know. I quickly paste on a smile and lie. "Yes, much better. Thanks."

Mum strokes my cheek. "Malika will be so pleased. We had to start the henna celebration without you, but you still have time to participate."

She shows me the intricate swirls of orange-red ink forming vines and flowers surrounding a sun on the top of her right hand and the moon on her left.

"What do you think?" she asks.

I glance up at her face. She's gazing thoughtfully at her henna, and I'm almost afraid to answer because for some reason I know the sun and moon symbolize an everlasting love between two people. She still loves her husband deeply, and that makes me so sad.

No. No sadness.

I am so over this dream.

I force a grin. "It's beautiful."

Her face opens into a smile. "Thank you. I think so, too." She stands and straightens her kaftan. "Shall we join the party then?"

As I climb out of bed, I notice I'm dressed in a pale pink kaftan with tiny, dark green embroidered flowers blooming at the hem. Since the last thing I remember was being half-naked at the hammam, I probably don't want to know how I got dressed. Or who dressed me. Yikes.

Mum picks up a thick, gold necklace from the dresser. "Turn around, darling, and I'll fasten this for you."

I lift my hair and she lays the heavy chain around my neck. It feels cool on my skin.

"Lucky girl," she murmurs, tucking a piece of hair behind my ear. She smiles. "Just out of bed, and as lovely as a blooming flower."

I know this is only a dream, but my heart warms like a ray of sunshine. Who doesn't like to be told she's beautiful? Maybe this dream will be good again. That would be nice.

I follow Mum across the indoor courtyard and up an ornate, iron staircase leading to the rooftop. Sounds of music and laughter grow louder with each step, and when I follow her through a doorway I see the henna party is in full swing on the roof.

I feel like I've stepped into a fairy tale. An ethereal, white tent billows overhead. Plush, red rugs cover the rooftop. Delicate, paper lanterns seem to float overhead. A DJ is pumping out rhythmic music, surrounded by men dressed in cream robes and dark sandals, dancing with their hands in the air. Malika and her girlfriends are clustered at the far end of the roof. She's perched on a red velvet couch, and her friends are lounging around her on plump red poufs and purple pillows.

Malika spots us and waves. She's wearing the dark-green velvet dress she had on when I first met her in this dream, and she looks absolutely stunning. A lacy, golden veil waterfalls down from the tiara that's perched atop her sable hair. Delicate, gold chains cloak her neck. Her eyes are darkly-lined, and her lips are a deep maroon. She looks like the exquisite princess in this fairy-tale dream.

"Oh, Aicha," she cries when we walk up. "I'm so sorry we couldn't wait for you. Are you feeling better?"

I really don't know what I'm feeling, but I want to be happy and enjoy this dream so I squeeze her hands tightly and paste on a huge grin. "Yes! And ready to party!"

She laughs, and I feel relieved.

"And she's ready for her henna," Mum adds.

Malika claps her hands, and that huge Berg-like dimple creases her right cheek when she smiles. She tugs me down next to her on the couch.

"Take Youssef's spot. He won't mind because he's over there dancing with his friends." She glances over at the group of men and a different kind of smile forms on her lips. It's easy and natural like I've seen on my mama when she looks at my daddy. A blush swells across Malika's cheeks, but then she brings her attention back to me and shows me her arms.

"What do you think?" She traces the henna designs that flow from her wrists all the way up to her elbows. "I chose flower buds since I'm starting a new life with Youssef. Vines and leaves for longevity and devotion in our marriage. The sun and moon for eternal love. And…," she pauses and giggles, "paisleys. For luck… and you know," she lowers her voice, "fertility."

I bust out laughing. I don't know why that's so funny. It's probably not. But I can't help it. Malika looks shocked for a second and then starts laughing with me. The sadness and anger I felt before is officially buried. I'm so happy right now I might burst.

"Okay, silly girls, settle down." Mum says, but there's a sparkle in her eyes. She gestures to a squat, plump, old woman standing beside her. "Aicha, this is Karima. She will do your henna. I must go see to the cookies."

Mum walks away and Karima shuffles closer. She's wearing a basic white jilbab trimmed in silver. Her skin looks as wrinkled as a walnut, and her white headscarf is wrapped so tightly around her head that her eyeballs look like they're about to pop out. Especially when she thrusts her face inches away from mine, and stares right into my eyes.

She's so close I have no choice but to stare right back. Her eyes look cloudy, and I wonder if that's why she's totally invading my personal bubble, but as I look closer, something about her eyes is familiar. They're muted green, but her black pupils are what really stand out. They look like swirling galaxies of teeny, tiny, white stars, all spinning and twirling. Around and around. It's so mesmerizing...

"Do you remember me?" she whispers, and my eyes about bug out of my head.

Oh my god! Her eyes. I know those eyes. They're Ms. Foofaraw's eyes from the lake!

I press my back deeper into the couch, but she just leans closer and grins.

"Ah, so you do remember?" Her eyes widen. "I know who you are, too," she whispers.

My heart thumps. She knows? But how is that possible? How could she know that I'm a girl who worries too much? Who can't control her emotions? Who hurt Dillon. How could she know that I don't belong here because I'm not good enough to be Malika's sister?

I'm not good enough for anyone.

My heart thumps faster. My palms start sweating. I feel the familiar freak out coming on…

Oh, for crap's sake, stupid brain. Get a hold of yourself! This is a just a dream. None of this is real. My freaking imagination is just running away again.

I close my eyes and inhale a deep breath. "This is just a dream."

"You must stop believing that, Lotus, or you will never find the way."

My eyes fly open. Did she just call me Lotus?!

The old lady tilts her head, and frowns. She brings her nose so close to mine that it almost touches. "This. Is. Not. A. Dream," she whispers.

I shake my head. She's wrong. I know this is a dream. I know I'm dreaming.

She shrugs. "Okey dokie. Suit yourself." She stands back up. "Guess we'll continue on then." She hums what sounds like the tune to "Happy Birthday" as she reaches down beside the couch and pulls out a large, black album. She drops it into my lap. "This one," she says, tapping a picture on the open page. "I will give you this one."

My breath catches. Her gnarled finger is pointing to a lotus flower. And it's not just a drawing like the other designs on the page. Nope. This is a photo of my lucky, lotus-flower earrings. The ones Daddy brought me from Morocco. The ones I wear when I need strength.

When I don't want to worry. The ones some Moroccan lady told him would awaken the light within.

The ones I wore when I almost killed Dillon.

She fixes her galaxy eyes on me. "A lotus flower roots itself in the mud yet blooms above the darkness and murk anyway. This is you, no?" she says in a thick voice.

I'm not quite sure what she means by all that, but I'm definitely darkness and murk when my anxiety comes to the party. Or did she mean that I'm stuck in my dream world, away from my real family, and she thinks I may never go back to them? That I may never wake up?

I snort. Or maybe I'm just a lunatic having a weird dream and overthinking all of this in my head?

This is just a dream. And she's just a nice artist who wants to draw a lotus flower for my dream sister's henna party.

Malika turns back to face me. "Which one did you choose?"

Before I can answer, the old woman points to the lotus flower. And now it's just a drawing. Of course.

I want to roll my eyes at this dream.

"I love it!" Malika cries. "The lotus symbolizes the awakening of your soul. That will be so beautiful." She grins. "And be sure to get lots of vines and leaves like mine!"

I nod, because really what else am I going to do. Malika turns back to her friends and Karima pulls out what looks like a bag of icing I would use to decorate cupcakes. When she grabs my hand, her fingers are surprisingly warm and comforting, and I find myself settling back into the couch. Dark-green ink spills from the bag and tickles my hand as she paints. Her warm fingers, the sensation of the henna, and Malika and her friends chatting lull me into such relaxation that I almost forget about my worries, until Youssef walks over.

He kneels in front of Malika and gently takes her hands in his. A cheek-to-cheek grin overtakes his face. "I hope the most beautiful girl I've ever known is enjoying herself tonight?" he murmurs.

Malika nods. "Oh Youssef, this has been so wonderful."

He exhales a happy breath. "And this is only the beginning of our beautiful life together. I promise to try my best to make you this happy every day."

Youssef and Malika are gazing at each other like Mama and Daddy always did. With a mixture of respect and awe, and I'll do absolutely anything to make you happy. They don't even realize that the rest of us are here because they're in love. Real love.

And then suddenly it hits me.

Dillon and I were never in love. He never looked at me like Youssef is looking at Malika. But he did look at that boy like that. That boy he was kissing.

Zings of raw emotion shoot through me. My body throbs with pain. It feels like someone punched me in the gut and their fist went all the way through. Why didn't he love me? Boys should love girls. Just like Mama and Daddy. And Malika and Youssef. Was it my fault? What did I do that made him gay? Am I really that awful?

I might be. Because I have no idea who I am anymore. I still feel the same on my inside. I want people to like me. I want to be happy. And as much as I adore jilbabs and mint tea, I would kill for the new Jimmy Choo sandals and a bag of cheese puffs right now.

So who am I? Am I the happy girl? Or the Oh my GAD girl who lashes out at her boyfriend and almost kills him? Am I American or Muslim?

Am I dreaming or not?

"What about calling Omar?" Malika says with a giggle.

I was so deep in thought that I didn't notice Youssef has left and all the girls are giggling about someone named Omar.

"Call him?" her friend shrieks. "I could never do that!"

And that gives me a crazy idea.

I'm going to call my house. Maybe if I hear Mama's voice I can get out of this wacky dream. Maybe that will help me wake up and go back to my real life.

"Um, excuse me," I say softly, trying not to startle the old woman who seems to be in a trance. "Are you...?"

"Yes, I am finished," she answers. She closes her eyes and nods. "Go call her. You need to know."

My eyebrows pop up. What did she just say? How did she know I was going to call my Mama? Did I say it out loud?

She grins at me with crooked teeth. "Just go."

Oh- kay. First, my lucky earrings and now this. This woman is like a mind-reader or something. Although, anything is possible in a dream, right? Because I'm creating all these people. In a dream.

Or at least that's what I'm going to keep telling myself.

"I added a butterfly to help with your transformation," she says and traces the closed wings of the butterfly on my hand. She nods. "I am hopeful they will open soon."

I yank my hand away. She's starting to really freak me out now.

I lean over to the girl sitting on a pouf closest to me. "May I please borrow your phone?" I whisper. "It's a surprise for Malika."

My lie rewards me with a huge grin, and I feel a little guilty. When Malika looks the other way, I take the girl's phone, hide it under my sleeve, and excuse myself.

I hold my breath as I escape downstairs. I need privacy. I don't know why since this is my dream and all, but for some reason I don't want anyone to hear what I'm about to do. I slip out the front door, yank it closed with both hands, and only then do I exhale, standing outside the door, deep in shadows.

I dial Mama's cell. This has to work.

Someone picks up and my breath hitches with excitement, only to hear a voice telling me I need to dial the international code.

Oh right, I'm in Morocco and she's in Colorado. I guess that makes sense.

EXCEPT THAT THIS IS A DREAM!

I shake my head, and dial again, this time adding the "1" in front of the number for the crazy annoying phone company in my dream. A deep tone buzzes twice, and then someone answers.

"Hello?"

My heart leaps for joy. "MAMA?" I yell. "It's me!"

I'm greeted with silence.

"Mama?"

Maybe I don't have a good signal between these concrete walls. I'm quickly learning that anything is possible in dreams. I glance at the phone. Three bars. That should be enough but I walk a few steps down the cobblestone street anyway in case I get a better signal. Now that I have Mama, I don't want to lose her.

"Mama? Can you hear me?"

"I'm sorry," she answers. "I'm afraid you have the wrong number."

And then she hangs up on me.

My heart constricts so tight I can't breathe. My palms sweat and my stomach roils. No. Don't hang up on me, Mama. I have to talk to you.

I pinch myself. WAKE UP!

Nothing happens.

I try to inhale. It's jagged, but I get it down. Okay. It's going to be okay. You heard Mama's voice. That was her voice. Now close your eyes. Think of her voice. Think of her. She's wearing your favorite sweater on her head like a turban. Think of Berg spiking his hair in that mini-mohawk. Of Daddy dousing you with flour the other night when you helped him make fried chicken. I pinch myself really hard again. WAKE UP!

I inhale, open my eyes... and my heart plummets. I'm still surrounded by what feels like a prison of white walls. I inhale another deep breath. It's still okay. I'm still okay. This is going to work. I'm going to make this work.

I re-dial her number, hear those strange tones again, and beg Mama to pick up. "Pick up. Please. Pick up. Pick up."

"Hello?"

"Mama, it's me!" I scream. I don't want her to hang up again so I rush into my explanation. "I'm in Morocco. But I'm in a dream. So, I guess I'm dreaming that I'm calling you. But I just saw all of you and no one would talk to me. And then I ended up back here. But I want this dream to end. I want to come home."

I hear Daddy's voice in the background. "Darling, who keeps calling?"

Mama's voice is muffled when she answers him, like she's holding the phone away. "I have no idea. I can't understand a word they're saying. I think they're speaking another language."

What? Why could I speak English to that American lady, but not to my own mama?

I focus really hard. English. Speak English!

"Please don't hang up!" I plea. "I need you to help me!"

"I'm sorry," Mama says politely, "but you need me to help you do what?"

My hearts soars. She understands me!

"Mama, it's me! It's me, Lottie!" I'm so choked with happiness that I almost can't speak.

"What did you say?" Mama whispers.

"It's me, Lottie," I laugh. "It's Lotus. Your daughter! I'm stuck here and I can't leave. I need your help! I need you!"

"Is this some sort of sick joke?" Mama growls. "WHAT HAVE YOU DONE WITH MY LOTUS?" she yells. "If you hurt her, I will hunt you down and I will…"

I don't hear the end of her threat because I hear myself say, "Mama, what's wrong? I'm right here."

Except…

Except I didn't say that. Those words didn't come out of my mouth. They came out of someone's mouth standing next to my Mama. Was that me? If I'm at home then why I am here? As Aicha?

"Mama?" I whimper, aching for her to help me make sense of all this. But all I get is bitter anger.

"Do not ever call here again," Mama growls. "I am not your Mama."

And then she hangs up on me.

I'm frozen. My heart has stopped. I keep holding the phone to my ear, desperately hoping Mama will come back on and apologize, and I'll wake up. But nothing happens. I slump against the wall and try to ignore all the emotions swirling inside of me like a terrible tornado.

This dream used to be fun and happy. What happened? I loved doing all this wedding stuff with Malika, and I really do love being her sister. She's so sweet and caring. But to have Mama tell me that she's not my Mama. That hurts. It really, really hurts. Like when you slam your hand in the car door and the pain won't stop throbbing.

And I don't want to hurt. Which is why I have always buried my pain.

I inhale a deep breath. This is just a dream. It has to be. A dream that's turning into a friggin' nightmare, but still, it's just a dream. Exhale. I will get out of here. Inhale. I will wake up soon. That's what happens in a dream. It all seems so realistic, but you always wake up and go back to real life.

A spot of white behind one of the pots catches my eye. I walk over, kneel down, and find the little white kitten from this morning. The one with the brown eyes like me. I reach down to pick it up but the minute my hand touches its body, I recoil. It's limp, and cold... and dead.

I crumple to the ground, one hand still on the kitten's listless body, neither of us moving.

This dream really is becoming a nightmare.

I pick up the dead kitten and cradle it close to my heart. "My mama rejected me, too," I whimper and kiss its tiny head. I notice the black spot on its forehead is in the shape of a butterfly just like my henna. A butterfly that should be alive and flitting around exploring the beauty of the world, not cold and lifeless.

Anger and despair try to wash over me. Sobs crawl up my throat like vomit. But I swallow them back and refuse to feel the pain. For the kitty, or for me, I don't know. Maybe for both of us. Either way I'm so done. With this dream. With feeling. With everything.

The front door slowly opens, and the old woman who did my henna shuffles out and kneels in front of me.

"What have you discovered?"

I raise an eyebrow.

She raises both her eyebrows. "Well, what?"

Seriously? Is she friggin' blind? I feel laughter bubble up in me. I giggle. "I found death."

She shakes her head. "I was not referring to your little friend."

I roll my eyes. "Of course, you weren't. You are just another part of this annoying dream that makes absolutely no sense and is driving me crazy." I don't care that I'm being a jerk. I'm so sick of everything that I'm finding it really hard to care anymore.

She reaches out and strokes my cheek with her wrinkled hand. "Whether it is a dream, or it is not," she murmurs in a voice that is somehow soothing and unnerving at the same time, "you must care enough to feel the pain so that you may choose to live."

I snort. "No thanks."

"And that is how you feel?"

"Nope." I stand up and hand her the stupid, dead kitten. "I don't feel anymore. Feeling is overrated. I am done with feeling."

She gently tucks the kitten into her jilbab. "Are you sure?"

"Yep."

"Even if it means never waking from what you think is a dream?"

I roll my eyes. "Whatever, lady. I'm done here. I'm done feeling. I'm done worrying. I'm done being angry." I bounce my chin in a way that I think looks cool but probably looks like a dorky, bobble-head. "Lottie is out."

She nods so slowly that I wonder if time is ceasing to exist. "Then that is the way it will be," she murmurs and shuffles down the street.

I close my eyes, imagining my Mama's comforting hands hugging me close, and wishing myself far, far away.

CHAPTER 13

Home, Painful, Home

I'm done with this dream. I need to wake up. I scream inside my head. WAKE UP! WAKE UP! WAKE UP!

This.

Is.

Going.

To.

Work.

I inhale a deep breath, open my eyes… and let out a whoop of joy. I did it! I'm back in my room!

My room. With my blue walls, and my cozy comforter, and my stuffed zebra, and my desk that my great-grandfather built. I exhale for so long that my legs feel like jelly and I have to sit down. I sink into the chair at my desk and my joy fades when I see all the shattered pieces of the glass heart and remember all the pain and sadness waiting for me here.

Does Berg still hate me because I wasn't there for him? He was so sad and heartbroken. And so angry… at me.

Tears form in my eyes.

Does Mama still think I'm selfish? I acted like such a jerk, and she was so disappointed.

A huge sob escapes my chest.

And Dillon. Is he okay? I know he must hate me. And by now everyone must know what I did. How I totally lost it and exploded and almost killed him. How I'm the freak with Oh my GAD. Everyone must hate me.

Pain rockets through me. I lay my head down on the shattered glass and explode into gut-wrenching sobs. The sharp pieces cut into my cheek, but I don't care. I deserve it. I deserve to be punished for who I am. This crazy monster who can't control her emotions. Who cries and screams and freaks out with feelings.

I wish I didn't have to feel anything ever again.

I wish I didn't have to be me anymore.

I lift my head from the desk. One of my great-grandmother's postcards is stuck to my cheek so I peel it off. The front is a photograph of baby elephant, with "Bangkok" written in black script above it. I flip it over and read the writing on the back.

Dear Lotus,
Until you choose to feel all that life offers you, you will never be home.
See you soon,
Venerable Bhik

The postcard falls from my fingers. My great-grandmother's name was Rita.

My lungs seize and my eyes drift shut as I wish myself far, far away.

CHAPTER 14

Crushed by my emotions

I can't breathe. That postcard. Where did it come from? Why was it on my desk? And what is a Venerable Bhik? And what does "I will never be home" mean?

I think of never seeing my loving Mama, my sweet Berg, and my fun Daddy ever again, and that makes my chest ache. Crushingly bad.

I think I'm going to puke.

No! I need to get control of myself. I need to shove my emotions so deep that I don't ever have to feel them again. I struggle to inhale a deep breath… and find that I can't.

Holy crap! My chest has never felt this heavy before. These emotions are crushing me! I need to get rid of them!

I hear voices. They're muffled, but they sound angry. No, not angry. They sound frantic. Panicked, almost. I hear words tumbling over words, every voice begging to be heard.

Oh crap. My heart seizes with fear. Did they finally find out what I did to Dillon? Are they coming to arrest me? I try to open my eyes, but they're glued shut. I try to raise my arm to wipe them off, but it's stuck to my side and I can't move it. What is happening?!

I feel hands clawing at my scalp.

Oh my god! Get away from me!

I ache to punch them away but I can't move either of my arms. It's like they're pinned to me. I open my mouth to scream and beg them to stop, but nothing comes out, and I taste dirt.

Dirt?

Oh my god! I'm swallowing dirt! I'M SWALLOWING DIRT! I can't find any air! I'm drowning. I'm dying…

"Breathe!" a man yells.

Hands are clawing at my mouth now.

"Breathe, boy! Breathe!"

I really don't want to eat any more dirt, but my chest feels like it's going to explode so I breathe… and finally get air. Sweet, sweet air! I inhale deeply, the smell of musk and earth and something else I can't place fills my senses, and the aching pressure on my chest eases.

"He's breathing!" the man says, but his voice is muffled, like I'm wearing headphones.

Hands claw at my chest, my arms, and my belly. Why are all these people touching me? Leave me alone! This is my body! I want to cry, but I can't get the words to my lips. I try again to stop them and this time one of my arms is free and I connect with something solid.

A warm hand grabs mine. "Stop fighting," a different man's voice orders. "You're almost out."

Hands grasp under my armpits and lift me into the air. I feel so light. I can breathe again! But I still can't open my eyes so I lift my other arm to wipe them and pain rockets through my body so fast that I see stars in the darkness behind my eyelids. I cry out.

"Boy, quit moving. It's broken."

Someone wipes my eyes.

"Try to open them," a man says.

I do as he says but it's so bright that I'm blinded. I want to close my eyes, but I don't. I'm afraid I may not be able to open them again. My eyes burn but I keep blinking them until I can make out shadows of men crowded around me. There's a loud ringing throbbing in my head, but the voices beside me are starting to drown it out.

"Let's get him out of here."

"Find him help."

"We found another one!"

Whoever is holding me under my armpits hands me off to another shadow. I feel like a limp puppet. My legs won't hold my weight and my arm feels like a million bees are eating it alive. The shadow grabs me around the waist and lifts me off the ground. I don't resist.

My eyes finally adjust and take in the man carrying me. He's wearing a knee-length tunic, trousers so baggy they look like a skirt, and a turban. His face and beard are cocoa-colored, but streaked with what looks like grey dust. He's quiet, but I hear wailing and angry yelling around us. I want to ask him where I am when four armed policemen sprint by, their huge machine guns poised and ready.

I watch them race past, and immediately know where I am. This is the souk, packed with stalls selling colorful fruits and vegetables, racks of raw meats, clothes, spices, and who knows what else. But I'm not in Morocco anymore.

How do I know this? Because I'm still dreaming? Then why does this all feel so real?

The policemen stop near the last stalls where cheery, red-and-white awnings are engulfed in flames. Billows of smoke hang in the air. And the three-story building next door looks like a giant took a huge bite out of it and then spit a tower of rubble beside it.

The rubble that could have been my burial site.

I'm in Afghanistan. In the middle of Kabul. And I've just been buried alive by a bomb.

The men who rescued me are still on top of that tower of rubble, scrabbling away at the rocks and dirt, desperately searching for any more survivors.

A man dashes out of the smoke, screaming and cradling a body in his arms. I have to turn away. My stomach roils and gurgles. I start seeing black spots. I hear another explosion and I close my eyes.

The man lowers me onto the ground. "Rest now, boy," he demands in a tight voice.

I know he's speaking Dari, the most widely spoken language in Kabul, because I speak it, too.

"We may need you to fight soon," he adds.

I don't like the sound of that, so I just keep my eyes closed and nod.

I'm totally lying, of course. No way am I fighting. I'll be lucky if I don't throw up and pass out in about five more seconds.

I feel a small hiss of air and know he's rushed away. Careful not to move my injured arm, I shift my seat to face away from the destruction and feel something between my legs. I almost giggle. So this is why everyone keeps calling me boy. I wrinkle my nose. Crap, what is that smell? Is that me? It smells worse than when that girl brought egg salad to school and left it in her locker for two weeks.

I open my eyes to find out what's stinking up the place… and immediately wish I hadn't. I'm surrounded by bodies. Scorched, dead

bodies. A woman and man still holding hands. A boy Berg's age…
with no legs. A small girl in a tattered dress. No head. Just a body.
And there are more. Dead. All of them dead. All around me. Dead.

I somehow crawl one-armed as far away as I can and start puking
my guts out into a mound of shiny, red apples. Sobs rip through me. I
can't even think to stop them.

I'm not in my room. I'm not even at a happy henna party in
Morocco anymore. I'm halfway around the world, surrounded by
bodies that used to be someone's mother, and someone's father, and
someone's brother. And they're all dead. Not pretend dead. Not video
game dead. No. They are all real-life, no-more-breathing ever dead.

All I can think about is that these rotting corpses could be my
Mama, or my Daddy, or my Berg. Wretched emotions flood my brain.
How could someone do this? Did they know their life was over? Did
they suffer terribly? Do their families know they're dead?

Will anyone miss them?

I cry out in anguish. For their lost lives. For being so far away from
those I love. For my grisly, broken arm, and for my throbbing,
chaotic, utterly confused brain.

What in the world is happening to me?

A horrid thought saturates my aching body. Is it possible that
Lottie in Colorado and Aicha in Morocco only exist in my dreams and
this wretched place is my real life? Am I that good at burying my
emotions that my body really lives here, while I live in happy dream
worlds in Colorado and Morocco?

I shiver with fear, desperately hoping that's not anywhere near the
truth.

A stooped woman shuffles towards me. She's wearing a light blue
burqa that completely covers every inch of her body, head, and face.
There is only a slit for her eyes. I can't tell if she's young or old, or
even a friend or an enemy. She could be the bomber for all I know.
But she kneels next to me and begins wrapping my limp, bloodied
arm with a rag, so I guess she means no harm. And honestly, at this
point I'm so confused that I'm beyond caring.

I start laughing. I must be delirious.

The woman stops wrapping my wound and leans in close, probably trying to decide if I've lost my mind. She stares into my eyes so I stare back into hers, and I don't believe what I find. Her eyes are green and her pupils are black with white specks that look like galaxies. Yep. I've seen this before. It's that old bat who looks like Ms. Foofaraw and who did my henna in Morocco. Why the heck is she here? Is she following me?

Or does she live here with me? And I just dreamed she was in Colorado and Morocco?

Oh my god. My mind is spinning. I wish I had my vape to melt away all this anxiety and pain. Or maybe that's what caused all this? Who knows what those oils actually contain!

Wait a minute.

My eyes narrow. "Why did you throw my vape in the lake?" I demand of the woman.

She just stares at me through the slits in her burqa.

"Ms. Foofaraw?" I whisper.

No response.

"Henna lady?" I know Mum introduced her but I can't recall her name.

Nothing.

I laugh. And not just a little snort. This is full out, I've-completely lost it guffawing.

The woman returns to bandaging my arm, not at all bothered by my complete breakdown. She tugs the bandage closed and the pain gets so bad that black stars dance in front of my eyes. My arm. It hurts. The pain. I'm scared. I hurt. I'm in pain. THE PAIN!

HOLY CRAP! I'm losing my mind! I'm in wretched pain, and I'm stuck here, and I WANT TO GO BACK TO MY REAL LIFE! Or my dream life? Or whatever the heck life I had that wasn't this!

My heart is racing like crazy. My chest feels so tight that I think it's going to explode. Oh my god. I know the signs. I'm about to completely lose it. And the last time that happened, I almost killed Dillon. My mind is spinning. Am I Lottie from Colorado, or am I Aicha from Morocco? Or am I really just a "boy" in Kabul?

I don't even know who I am anymore!

This has to be another dream. Nothing can be this dreadful. The pain. The anger. The terror. All these dead bodies. I seize so hard icicles of pain sear into me, and I can't stand feeling any of it.

Enough! I'm done with this dream and feeling so bad! I grit my teeth. I will put every ounce of my soul into ignoring this pain so I can wake up.

The woman cups my chin. "That is not what your soul wants." Her sour breath washes over me as she whispers, "Not all pain is unbearable."

I shake my head. "Wrong. Wrong! WRONG! ALL pain is unbearable, and miserable, and definitely not worth feeling. I hate pain." I narrow my eyes. "I hate everything about pain."

"What do you know of pain?" she asks.

That maniacal laughter bubbles out. "Way too much! My heart cracked with pain when I found Dillon kissing his new boyfriend. My heart ached with pain when I disappointed my mama and Berg. My heart sank with pain when I found the dead kitten. My heart roared with pain seeing all these dead bodies." I shake my head. "I am done with pain. I am done with feeling. I am done with all of it!"

"Are you sure?"

"YES! OH MY GOD, YES!" My head is pounding and my insides ache to explode. "I want to never feel anything ever again."

"You are absolutely sure?"

I feel a sense of calm wash over me. "More than anything in my life."

The woman slowly nods. "I see it is time." She stands up, reaches under her burka, pulls out a machine gun, and holds it out to me.

"Others caused you pain," she says matter-of-fact. "Now it is your choice. You can make others suffer for the pain you feel, or you can choose to feel the pain and then move on, back to your life and all the goodness it has to offer you. It is your choice."

I shake my head. "I don't choose either. I don't want to feel, and I don't want to hurt anyone."

"But you are hurting someone. You are hurting yourself."

I snort. "Only by feeling."

I've barely spoken the words when her eyes grow wide, and her body spasms and jerks and explodes blood all over me. I don't even have time to scream before a thousand splinters rocket through me and launch us both ten feet in the air. I feel light and pain-free for a brief second, and then crash to the ground, the old woman landing with a thud on top of me.

I know she's dead. And I'm pretty sure I'm not far behind her. Yet... I feel nothing. No sadness. No fear. No anger. No anxiety. Nothing. I only feel a hole. It's somewhere near my heart where I've been burying all my negative emotions. Where I've been hiding all my anger and sadness and pain. I feel them leaking out, one by one, staining my body with their revolting blackness.

This hole in me is real. And this pain can't be fixed by burying my emotions, or hiding in my bed, or even by killing someone else.

So, I do what I do best. I close my eyes, and wish myself far, far away.

CHAPTER 15

The glass is totally empty

A warm hand caresses my forehead. It doesn't feel like Mama's, or even Mum's, so I flinch away from it and open my eyes.

I'm sitting on a dirty, tiled floor, my back leaning against a metal-framed bed. A completely bald woman wearing a burnt-orange robe is kneeling next to me.

"Your suffering is almost over," she says, and offers me a small smile.

I don't smile back. Funny she would say suffering because I don't feel like I'm suffering. I don't feel any more pain. It's gone. Poof. Like magic. I think I should shout out my glee, but I don't feel any joy either. In fact, I don't feel anything. No pain. No happiness. Nothing. I just feel… empty.

Wait a minute. Am I dead?

I turn to the woman. I realize she's a monk.

"Is this heaven?" I ask her.

The monk's lips narrow as she shakes her head. "No, kid, this is hell."

CHAPTER 16

Things are looking up

Hell appears to be a tiny room with paint peeling off the walls and a single light bulb hanging precariously above me. There's a small window to my left, a closed door about ten steps across the room, and the female monk squatting next to me. I'm wearing a black, lacy bra and pink boy shorts that are so skimpy I can feel the cold tile floor on my bum. Both my wrists are tied to the bedpost behind me.

I feel like I should be upset that I was so bad that I ended up in hell, but again I feel nothing. Zip. Nada.

The monk touches my arm. "You won't be here much longer."

A key jiggles in the door.

"He's here," she hisses. She jumps up, races over to the open window, and climbs up on the sill. She glances back at me. "I'll be back. I promise," she whispers and then jumps out the window.

I want to say I feel confused and afraid, and realize I should feel both of those emotions, but I don't feel anything. I feel nothing.

Are my anxiety and pain gone forever? Maybe hell was the answer all along.

The door opens and dull light spills into the room. A hulking shadow fills the doorway and I guess I'm about to come face to face with the almighty devil, the King of Hell himself, but, surprisingly, I could care less. I feel nothing.

The devil shuts the door, locks it, and then flips on the one light bulb in the room. It casts an eerie shadow on the walls yet illuminates him like he's onstage. He's dressed in jeans and a black t-shirt, and his brown hair is cropped close to his head like a normal person. He honestly doesn't look anything like what I imagined as the devil. I don't see any horns. No tail. No fire. No brimstone. His brown eyes are bloodshot, but that's the closest he comes to resembling the ruler of the underworld.

I change my mind when he walks over and grabs my breast.

"I like having you tied up in here," he moans.

Something in my brain screams at me not to move. So, I don't.

He spits out a string of curse words; spewing ones I've never been allowed to hear. When he finishes his rant, he takes a step back and leans down until his face is even with mine. Beads of his sweat drip down his creased forehead and onto my bare legs. He's so close that I can see a girl with short hair reflected in his gloomy eyes. He doesn't look like a monster. He just looks sad and pathetic. But somehow my body must know differently because everything inside of me tenses when he caresses my face. I want to head butt him, but I don't dare move.

"My beautiful Thai flower," he croons, rubbing his rough finger over my lips. "As much as I want to be with you now, I need you to wait just a bit longer. I have something I need to finish." A disturbing smile creeps onto his lips. "And then I'll have lots of time just for you and me."

I wait for something inside of me to scream in fear, or to cry out in anger, or to utterly panic… but nothing happens. I still feel nothing. And deep down I know that's probably a good thing.

My devil straightens up, stomps across the room, and opens the door. He glances back at me. "I will be back very soon." His lips spread into that wacked-out grin as he growls. "And if you escape, I will hunt you down and kill you."

I stare at the door long after he's left and bolted the door behind him. I should be frigid with fear, but I feel nothing. No anger at him touching me inappropriately. No terror of what will happen when he returns. Nothing. I'm just an empty shell, devoid of all feelings.

Which means, I'm either really dead and in hell… or I'm still dreaming. I try to feel angry or even just slightly miffed, but I can't conjure up any feelings at all. My heart doesn't seem to want to do anything but beat.

I garner all my strength and channel it into my brain. WAKE UP! YOU'RE STUCK IN A DREAM I yell in my head. I pinch the back of my hand really hard. Nothing happens.

I close my eyes and imagine all the details of my real life bedroom. My calming blue walls. Great-grandmother's writing desk. Snuggling under my feather comforter. Curling up in Mama's hug. Hearing Berg's laughter when he beats Daddy at a video game.

I open my eyes… and the bald monk is kneeling in front of me.

"I'm still here," I drone. I sound like a zombie.

"Not if I can help it." She reaches behind me, fiddles around for a moment, and unties my hands. "You're free." She stands up and grins. "Let's go, kid."

I rub the red marks on my wrists. "But he said he'd kill me if I leave."

Although when one is already in hell, how does one get killed?

The monk gently grabs my hands and helps me stand. She holds my gaze with her small brown, make-up free eyes. "You know he will kill you if you stay."

I think she's probably right.

"You can stay here with him," she says, "or you can come with me. The choice is entirely up to you, kid."

Being killed in hell can't be that fun. And if I'm not in hell, I'd rather not spend any more quality time with that guy.

"Okay. I'll go with you." My voice sounds so weird, like I'm a robot programmed to bore people to death.

She nods. "Let's get outta here then." She walks over to the window, pulls up her robes, and climbs up onto the windowsill. She grins at me. "See you on the other side," she says and jumps out the window.

A memory floats by like an apparition. I know why I was chained to the bed. He bought me. From my family in Burma. My mom sold me to him so they could afford to buy food for my baby brothers… so that maybe they would survive.

I should definitely feel some hatred, and lots of pain. But I don't. Huh.

I walk over to the window and look out. The neon lights of the surrounding buildings illuminate the night enough that I can see it's about a three-foot drop to the flat roof where the monk is waiting. She waves to me, and mouths, "Hurry."

Well, I'm either dead, or I'm dreaming that I'm this Burmese girl, who is really good at keeping all her feelings buried. I'm not feeling any pain so I guess either is okay with me. And going with this monk is probably better than waiting around for that devil man. So, I climb onto the windowsill, jump into the muggy night and tumble onto the roof.

The monk gives me a thumbs up then presses her fingers to her lips and takes off across the rooftop. I follow her, although I'm not sure why we have to be quiet with all the honking horns and city noise assaulting us from the street below.

The monk stops at the end of the building, and points to the rooftop of the next building. There's two-foot gap of empty air between the two buildings. She grins at me, leaps easily across the gap, and holds out her hand.

I glance down. I don't know how many stories up we are, but I'm pretty sure I'd be a flat splat if I fell. I wait for my limbs to seize with fear, but again, I feel nothing. I shrug. Okay then. I take her hand and jump over. No splat today.

She gives me a high five. "Almost there," she whispers.

I think I made the right decision to go with her. Even though it's pretty hot here, it doesn't feel like hell. She's too nice. I must be in another dream.

We walk a little farther until we stop at a ladder leading up to an open window. She motions for me to follow, climbs the ladder, and disappears inside.

So… I do what any sane person would do in a dream. I follow her, totally unconcerned about what may be awaiting me.

CHAPTER 17

I'm a new girl

I jump into the room to find my monk standing next to another woman who's also bald and wearing the same orange robe. I'm guessing she's a monk, too. This room is clean, more well-lit, and better furnished.

My monk gives me a big thumbs-up. "We made it!" She looks to be in her early twenties like Malika, with golden-brown eyes and a spattering of dark freckles spotting her tanned face.

"Yes. You are almost safe," the other monk murmurs. She's older, like Mama's age, and her eyes are a chocolaty-brown. Her kind eyes wrinkle as she smiles at me. "I am Fah." She motions to the younger monk. "And you have already met Rinzen. What is your name?"

I don't answer right away. I want to say Lottie, but is that right? Maybe I'm really Aicha? Or the boy from Kabul? Or this Burmese girl?

"I really don't know," I finally answer, and that's the truth.

"Do you know who your parents are?" Rinzen asks.

I shake my head. I really don't. I thought Mama and Daddy were, but now I'm not so sure. What life, or dream, is really my own?

"Do you have any memories before this day?" Fah asks. Her voice is gentle and soothing.

Lots of them. Freaking out at Dillon. Mama being there for me. Berg crying. Mint tea with Malika. Daddy telling me Dillon was in bad shape. Malika's henna party. That sweet, dead, white kitten. Being buried alive in Kabul.

But I don't think that's what she's asking me.

I shrug. "Only that my mom sold me to that man to buy food for my baby brothers. And he brought me here to Bankok."

Fah nods, but her eyes look sad. "That is normal. I am very sorry."

I shrug again. "I don't think I care. I don't want to go back to them."

"Are you sure?" Fah asks.

I nod. "I don't think they can afford me anyway."

"Then you should come to the monastery with us!" Rinzen offers. "I always wanted a little sister."

Fah gives Rinzen a look.

Rinzen rolls her eyes. "I know. I know. We don't force anyone to do anything." She holds up her palms. "Hey, I didn't make her come with me. I gave her a choice." She looks at me. "Right, kid?"

I nod.

Rinzen grins and her freckles seem to dance with her excitement. "So, you want to come with us or what?"

I nod. Not like I have anything better to do.

Rinzen whoops.

"Are you sure?" Fah asks.

"As sure as anyone in a dream can be," I mumble. When they both give me a funny look, I add. "Yes, I am sure. I need a fresh start."

Fah nods. "Then it is settled. We can help you find your family if you desire in the future, but for now we'll help you with your fresh start. And a fresh start deserves a new name. Do you know what you would like to be called?"

I shake my head. I really don't. "Can you choose one for me?"

Fah bows. "Of course" She paces for a few steps then claps her hands together. "I got it! How about Pema? It means lotus flower, which is a symbol of rebirth, which I think is perfect for someone looking for a fresh start."

Something twitches inside me. I can't tell if it's a feeling of disbelief, but I know it should be. This lotus flower thing is following me.

I nod. "Pema is perfect."

Fah's smile fades a bit. "It will be easier to get you safely out of here and to the monastery if you look like us." She motions to a small electric razor lying on the bed. "Which means we must shave your head. But only if it is okay with you."

I instinctively reach up to protect my beautiful, long hair and remember I'm in this strange world where my hair could be blond or black, or short or long. I have no idea what I look like on the outside right now, even though I still feel the same on the inside. My hair feels short and greasy, and I'm pretty sure it hasn't been washed in a really long time.

"It's okay," I say.

Fah smiles and motions to the bed. "Would you like to sit then? It may be more comfortable than standing."

I sit down on the clean white quilt. The room is about the same size as the one I just left, but this one has a side table with a bright lamp, and freshly painted walls in a light blue just like my old room.

Fah turns on the razor. The buzzing is loud in my ears and the razor tickles my head as I watch my jet black, greasy hairs blemish the white comforter. The buzzing stops.

"All finished," Fah says.

I reach up and rub my bald head. It feels smooth and kind of prickly. I've never been bald before. I wonder what I look like.

Rinzen brings over a pile of orange material and sits down next to me. "You look good as a baldy, kid."

"Rinzen!" Fah scolds.

She raises her palms. "What? She does."

"Yes, but some people may not like nicknames that make them feel self-conscious."

Fah's right. Nicknames can be hurtful. Like calling my boyfriend a freak because he loves a boy. That was cruel. I was cruel.

"Sorry," Rinzen apologizes.

I shrug. "It's okay." And I mean it. I really don't care that she called me baldy. Or even that I'm bald. I don't mind anything right now.

Rinzen sticks her tongue out at Fah.

Fah sticks her tongue out at Rinzen.

I can tell these two are close. Almost like a mother and daughter. I should feel happiness, but the thought skitters away, and I feel empty again.

"Okay, kid, shaving your head was the easy part," Rinzen says. "Figuring out how to put on these robes may take you all night."

Fah grins. "Or you could teach her how you worked around it."

"Hey, don't diss my hack," Rinzen laughs. "When you have to get up at the crack of dawn, cutting five minutes off dressing time is heaven."

Fah rolls her eyes. "This girl will do anything to get more sleep."

Rinzen winks. "Stick with me, kid. I know all the secrets." She holds up the robe. "Would you like me to help you put it on?" She gestures to my skimpy clothing. "You can leave that on underneath."

"Sure." I had forgotten that I'm basically sitting here in my underwear. I guess this is nothing after strutting my boobs around the hammam with a bunch of strangers.

Fah pipes up. "If you're at all uncomfortable with this, we can find another way." Her eyes look concerned, like Mama's did that day she found me at the lake. Funny that thinking about that doesn't hurt at all right now.

I shake my head. "No, it's fine."

Rinzen twists the robe around me, and Fah adjusts it to completely cover all of my body and both my shoulders. It's almost like the jilbab, but this fabric feels heavier.

Rinzen grins. "Now, you look like a monk."

Fah hands me a pair of flip-flops like the ones they're both wearing. "Sorry, I should have given these to Rinzen earlier so you didn't have to traipse across the roof in your bare feet."

I look down. Huh. I didn't even notice I wasn't wearing shoes.

I slip on the flip-flops. "Thank you."

Rinzen claps her hands together. "Okay, here's the plan. We all walk out of here together. You look and act like a monk, and no one should recognize you."

Act like a monk? Should I chant and sing? Do I bless people when I walk by? I have no idea.

"How exactly do I act like a monk?"

Rinzen shrugs. "It's easy, kid. You just be yourself."

But I don't know who that is.

Fah sits next to me. "We may look different on the outside because we wear robes and shave our heads, but inside we are just like everyone else, trying to be the best person we can be." She gestures to Rinzen. "Do you believe she is a monk?"

I nod.

Rinzen beams. "Awesome! Cause I've only been at the monastery for six months!"

Fah smiles. "She is a young monk, just like you."

I interrupt her. "How young?"

"I'm twenty-five," Rinzen says.

"How old do you think I am?" I ask.

Rinzen looks at me in disbelief. "You don't know how old you are?"

"I don't know how much time has passed. I was fifteen. I may be sixteen now. What day is it?"

"April 7," Rinzen answers.

I almost killed Dillon on April 3. I wonder if I've been dreaming for four days, or if dream days are different.

"You said you may be sixteen," Fah asks gently. "What day is your birthday?"

"April 17." I brace myself for the answer to my next question. "Do I look fifteen?"

Fah puts her hand on mine and squeezes. "I will be honest with you, Pema. On the outside, yes, you look like a fifteen-year-old monk. On the inside, though, I think your soul has experienced things that make you much older."

A strange thought pops into my head. "You said I look like a monk on the outside. What does a monk look like on the inside? Do you have an extra heart or something?"

They both erupt into such joyous laughter that I think I should laugh, but the feeling never arrives.

"You are so delightful, Pema," Fah chuckles. "Physically our bodies are the same as yours. We do not have an extra heart." She grins. "Although that would make chores so much easier." Fah stands. "Now, if you're ready, we better leave so we can meet the others in time to collect alms."

Rinzen motions to Fah. "Cause this old broad may not be able to scurry across town as fast as us young things."

Fah grins. "Just keep thinking that, baby girl. We'll see if you can keep up with me today. We all know who planted more in the garden last week and who almost passed out from the heat."

Rinzen frowns. "You're never gonna let me live that down, are you?"

Fah's brown eyes twinkle. "Nope."

Rinzen cracks open the door and peeks into the hall. She turns back to us. "Looks clear. Let's get outta here."

Fah slips out the door. I follow, and Rinzen brings up the rear, closing the door behind her. Fah leads us down the hallway and into the stairwell. We scurry down six flights of stairs and stop in front of a door at the bottom.

"Ready, kid?" Rinzen asks.

"I guess so." I have no idea what I need to be ready for.

Fah smiles at me. "Remember, Pema, just be yourself."

Myself? If only I could.

Rinzen must think I'm scared, so she links her arm in mine. "Don't worry, kid. I'll be right beside you all the way."

Fah opens the door, and we follow her outside. The sun is just rising, but Bangkok looks like it was awake all night. As we walk along the crowded sidewalk, I'm assaulted by loud noises and pungent smells and smothering heat. Horns honk, and beep, and toot. Scooters and tuk tuks zip past. Two policeman directing traffic are wearing surgical masks to protect against the exhaust lingering in the air. I smell crisp curry, and bitter gasoline, and sweet jasmine. I spy two women wandering through traffic, dressed in long pants and long sleeves, their arms loaded with brightly colored strands of flowers.

"What are those for?" I ask Rinzen, who still has her arm looped through mine.

"Daily offerings for the spirit houses."

"What's a spirit house?"

Rinzen pulls me across the busy street, narrowly avoiding a tuk tuk swerving in and out of traffic.

"Thais believe spirits live everywhere- in nature and in buildings, in the city and in the country. So, we construct spirit houses like that one to keep the spirits happy." She points to what looks like a doll-sized Thai temple built on a concrete pedestal. Pillars surround the square base of the tiny temple and soaring peaks fly up from the pyramid roof. "The flowers, candles, and bottles of water and soda surrounding it are all offerings to the spirits," she adds.

Fah has scurried around the corner so Rinzen and I hurry to catch up. We pass a mall, a hotel, and more street vendors than I can count selling everything from meat-on-a-stick to beads to flowers to fried crickets.

We pass a complex of buildings with peaked roofs and soaring spires of gold stretching up towards the sky. A row of colorful tuk tuks are lined up in front.

"This is the Grand Palace and Wat Pho," Rinzen says.

"Wat What?"

She laughs. "Wat Po is how you pronounce it. It's a temple that houses many chedis and a big, reclining Buddha that's over 45 meters long."

I try to think of that in American terms. Forty-five meters is almost 150 feet, or about half a football field. That's one big Buddha.

"What's a chedi?"

Rinzen doesn't seem to mind all my questions. "A chedi is a memorial built to house the ashes of a loved one or a revered person. Usually it's a bell-shaped tower more than ten stories high, topped with a finial, and ornately covered in mosaic and flower-shaped tiles. They're really very pretty."

I try to see them through the gate but only catch a glimpse of colorful tiles as we hurry past. Fah really is a fast walker, and I'm having a hard time keeping up. I'm hot and tired, and Fah still seems fresh and spry. It's a good thing Rinzen is still holding on to me because I need her support.

Rinzen must notice I'm dragging. "We're almost there, kid." She squeezes my arm, and whispers, "Hang in there. You're doing great."

The crowds start to thin, and when we round the next corner, the street is deserted except for a line of monks wearing the same orange robes and sporting the same breezy haircut. Fah hurries to fall in line behind them. Rinzen unhooks her arm from mine and gently pushes me in front of her.

"Just walk behind Fah and do what she does," she whispers.

The monk in front of Fah turns and hands her what looks like three plastic cauldrons left over from Halloween. Fah takes one, and then holds the other two out to me.

"This is your almsbowl," she explains. "Please give the other one to Rinzen."

I almost drop them when she hands them to me because they're so heavy. They must not be made out of plastic after all. Rinzen grabs hers and helps steady mine.

"Hold it against your belly like Fah."

I turn back around. Fah's head is bowed, and she's holding the almsbowl close to her belly with both hands, so I do the same and luckily that gives it more support.

I follow Fah and the line of monks around another corner. I can't believe how far we've walked. No cars or tuk tuks pass us on this street. I don't even see any people. Just low concrete buildings, and our line of orange, shuffling slowly forward in our flip-flops.

I keep my head bowed, soothed by our slow, rhythmic walking. It's nice to just walk and not worry about anything. To just be.

We round another corner and I almost run into Fah when she stops. I look up. People are coming out from their houses and lining the road.

"Just do what Fah does," Rinzen whispers.

Fah approaches a gray-haired woman standing next to a large basket. Keeping her head bowed, Fah opens the lid to her almsbowl. The old woman places a small, plastic baggie inside Fah's almsbowl and then folds her hands to her chin in prayer. Fah closes the lid, murmurs something to the woman, and then continues on to the next person who is holding a bottle of water. The older woman reaches into her basket, and holds out another baggie.

Rinzen nudges me.

I don't move.

She gives me a little shove.

I just stand there.

Rinzen walks around me, approaches the older woman, and opens the lid of her almsbowl. The woman drops the baggie inside, and

Rinzen closes the lid. Rinzen twists her head around so the older woman can't see her and mouths, "Your turn, kid."

The older woman looks down at her basket and pulls out another baggie.

I can do this. Rinzen and Fah said I look like a monk, and I should just act like myself. I walk up and open my lid for the woman. She places the baggie inside. Wafts of jasmine and curry tickle my nose.

"Smells totally awesome," I whisper to the woman, and she snaps her head up, eyes wide.

Rinzen swoops in, murmurs something that sounds like a prayer, and then pulls me away.

"Ok, kid, a little piece of monk advice," she giggles as we hurry to catch up to the other monks. "Just take the food and don't worry about saying anything."

I wonder if I should stop acting like what I think is myself, but Rinzen just seems tickled, and when I glance back at the older woman, she gives me a big, gap-toothed smile.

CHAPTER 18

I think I know you

I follow Rinzen's advice and graciously accept whatever is put into my almsbowl without adding any colorful commentary. But soon I'm sweating and starving, and my almsbowl is so heavy that I lean over to set it down.

Rinzen nudges me in the back. "Hold on just a little longer, kid. The monastery's just around the corner and then we get to eat."

I trudge forward, wondering if my arms will fall off before we get there, but surprisingly not really caring whether they do or not.

Soon Rinzen is nudging me again. "We're here, kid," she whispers. "You made it!"

Thank God. Or Buddha. Or whomever a monk thanks.

We've stopped in front of a ten-foot-tall, bright-blue gate connected to a brick wall that extends on down the block. I briefly wonder if I'm headed into a prison but as soon as I walk through the gate, I think this could be heaven. Lush grass cradles acres of trees whose thick branches wing out over the shady paradise. The other monks continue into the monastery but Rinzen stops to lock the gate, so I wait for her.

"You did it, kid!" She grins so wide that one of her cheeks crinkles into a dimple. "You're safe now." She gestures to the beautiful grounds. "Welcome to the monastery. Welcome home."

I try to drum up some relief, or happiness, or even thanks, but I still can't seem to find any emotion. I just feel empty.

She frowns. "You must be exhausted and starving. Who knows when you've last eaten. I'll give you the tour after we eat. Come on."

As she leads me deeper into the trees, the canopy of green leaves above us block out the hot sun and rustle a song of greeting in the breeze. The thick grass cushions my steps and tickles my toes. After the crowded streets of Bangkok, this monastery is a beautiful oasis. It should make me happy, but I feel nothing.

We cross a small courtyard where a thirty-foot tall, golden Buddha is perched high on a concrete pedestal, smiling happily down at us. A spirit temple decorated with fresh flowers and a water bottle stands in front of a larger, people-sized temple with soaring peaks and finials.

Rinzen leads me around the Buddha and into what looks like an open, two-story house. The entire bottom floor is tiled and empty of furniture, and the back wall is completely open to an outdoor garden blooming under more trees. Rinzen gestures her head to where the other monks are sitting quietly in the garden.

"Monks eat a little differently," she whispers. "We use our hands to eat directly out of our almsbowl. No one speaks. And this is the only meal of the day. We're not supposed to be greedy, but you should eat until you're full." She winks at me. "And don't worry, kid. I always have a secret stash of food if you get hungry later."

She leads me into the garden, and motions for me sit on a straw mat. She opens her almsbowl and starts eating, so I do the same.

I'm so hungry that I inhale the first baggie I grab. It's some type of sweet, sticky rice dotted with flecks of mango, and it's delicious. My fingers are still tacky when I open my next baggie, but I don't mind. It's a different way to eat- with no utensils and no talking. It feels a bit animalistic, but at the same time very quiet and meditative as I focus on the flavors I put in my mouth. I try a little of every baggie- fragrant jasmine rice, a savory meat curry, tangy coconut, sweet mango- until I'm stuffed.

I've just opened a water bottle when Rinzen elbows me gently, mouths "Let's go," and then stands. I notice she's holding her almsbowl, so I grab mine and stand up, too. She leads me away from the house and deeper into the garden. We pass jasmine vines, colorful flowers, and rows of herbs until we reach a tall, chain-link fence. Rinzen opens the gate and motions me through.

"Feeling better?" she asks as I pass by her.

I know I should tell her yes, and thank her for helping me, but for some reason I don't want to lie. I shrug. "I honestly don't know. I mean, my tummy's full, and I'm safe, and this robe's not as hot under the trees here, but I feel nothing. Not better. Not worse. Not sad. Not happy. Just… nothing."

Rinzen nods, but doesn't say anything, and I like that. She's not judging me and she's not trying to fix me. She's just here with me, listening. Which is perfect because I didn't want her to tell me how or why to feel better. I just wanted to tell someone the truth.

She closes the gate, and leads me into an area that is more dirt than grass but is still covered with shade trees. She points to a humongous, grey elephant scratching its shoulder on the trunk of a tree.

I feel like I should be afraid, but I don't feel any fear. "Should we go back?" I whisper.

Rinzen chuckles. "Not unless we want her to chase us."

I arch an eyebrow.

She just laughs. "Our job is to feed her, kid."

The elephant must have heard or smelled us because it lets out an exulted trumpet of joy it and barrels towards us, its floppy ears and gray wrinkles flapping up and down. Before I can even think to run and hide, Rinzen steps in front of me and barks out a command. The elephant slides to a stop ten feet away, swinging its trunk back and forth as a dirt cloud rises around it.

Rinzen sets her almsbowl on the ground, and calmly walks up to this enormous animal that's twice her height and at least fifty times her weight. She taps the elephant's knee. The elephant kneels down, and Rinzen launches herself up onto its back, nestles in behind those huge ears, and rests her chin on the elephant's head.

She grins at me. "This is Kammoon." She scratches the elephant behind its ears. "And Kammoon, this is our new friend, Pema."

The elephant extends its long trunk out to me. I look up at Rinzen.

"She wants to shake your hand," she laughs.

"Um, okay." I set my almsbowl on the ground and take a few tentative steps forward. "Um, hello," I say and shake the elephant's trunk.

Rinzen grins. "Now she's your friend, too."

"Does she live here?"

Rinzen nods. "Yep. My uncle was Kammoon's mahout for fifty years. When he died last year, I took over as her mahout. Kammoon and I begged on the streets for a while, but then Fah found us, and brought us here."

"So Kammoon is your pet?" I ask, thinking about how I always wanted a dog, but Berg was too allergic so I never got one.

Rinzen shakes her head. "Nope. She's my best friend. I feed her and care for her and bathe her in the river every day." When Kammoon's ears perk up, she laughs. "That's our favorite part of the day." She frowns. "My uncle was forced to use her for logging when she was younger, but as her mahout, he dedicated his life to caring for her needs, and he refused to let her be used in any shows. I promised him I would do the same."

"How old is she?"

"Fifty-three," Rinzen announces proudly. She wraps her arms around Kammoon's neck in a hug. "And hopefully she'll be with me another thirty years and live longer than any other elephant in the world." She gently grabs Kammoon's ear, and slides her belly down the elephant's side until her feet touch the ground. Rinzen barks out another command and Kammooon follows her over to where she set her almsbowl on the ground. "She lost all her teeth a few years ago, so I have to feed her by hand." She glances over at me. "Want to help?"

Feeding an elephant. That surely will break me out of this nothing mood and shake up some emotion.

"And don't worry, Kammoon hardly ever eats girls," Rinzen jokes.

That almost makes me smile. "Very funny."

Rinzen pulls two tennis-size balls of rice out of her almsbowl. "Kammoon loves mango sticky rice. It's her favorite." She hands me one of the balls. "Squish it a bit onto your hand like this so it sticks."

I watch her mash the ball flat onto her palm and then do the same. It's warm and sticky and full of specks of mango just like what I ate earlier.

"Now flip your hand upside down, and rub it onto her tongue like this."

Rinzen sticks her entire hand into Kammoon's open mouth, smears the rice mixture on the elephant's huge tongue, and then pulls her hand out. Kammoon's eyes close as she manipulates the rice with her tongue and then swallows it. The elephant open its eyes and looks at my hand.

"Your turn, kid."

I should feel nervous. My entire head could easily fit inside this elephant's huge mouth. But I still feel nothing. I wonder if this girl has buried her emotions so deep they're officially gone.

I take a step closer. Kammoon's huge eyes are gentle and kind, framed by long, black eyelashes and surrounded by wrinkles. The light filtering in through the canopy above is just enough to illuminate the brown flecks of light in her irises. Kammoon opens her mouth. I wipe the sticky rice over her tongue and quickly pull out my hand. Kammoon pushes the rice deeper into her mouth with her trunk, gums it a little and then swallows. She looks back at me and I swear she's grinning. I exhale a long breath and a deep peace settles over me. Kammoon has to be one of the sweetest animals I've ever seen.

Rinzen and I feed Kammoon the rest of the sticky rice in Rinzen's almsbowl, and then give her a few of my leftovers. When we're finished, my hands are sticky and full of elephant slobber, but I don't care one bit.

Rinzen taps Kammoon's leg and jumps up onto her shoulders again. "I need to take her for some water, but I'm supposed to take you to the meditation garden first. Do you want to ride?"

I shake my head.

She laughs. "Just let me know when you're ready, and I'll teach you that, too."

She and Kammoon lumber ahead of me through the trees. I follow a safe distance behind, watching Kammoon's tiny tail wag against her huge bottom. I almost feel a bubble of laughter, but then it skitters away.

Rinzen and Kammoon stop at a dirt path.

"This leads up to the garden," Rinzen whispers. "I'm supposed to tell you that if you follow this path to Buddha you will be exactly where you need to be."

I glance down the path. It's a few feet wide with a row of trees forming a low canopy over it. At the end of the path, I can see a huge, marble Buddha reclining on a pedestal and a tiny monk sitting on a mat in front of it.

"Who's that?" I whisper.

Rinzen bows slightly before answering. "That's the Venerable Bhikkihuni Songkhandro. But we all call her Venerable Bhik. It's easier."

Something twitches inside me. I think I know that name.

"She's the head of our monastery," Rinzen continues. "And she's been sitting there in a meditative trance for four days now."

My eyes widen. "I don't want to disturb her."

Rinzen shrugs. "I doubt you will, kid. Just walk up there as quietly as you can." She gives me a smile. "Good luck. And I'll definitely see you later." And with that promise, she waves goodbye and the two of them lumber off.

I stand there for a moment debating what to do. Rinzen said I'm supposed to follow the path to the Buddha, but I don't want to get too close to this venerable person and bug her. What if she's going for a world record trance-thingy, and I trip on a rock and wake her up? I bet she'd be pretty peeved. And if she's head of this joint, she could throw me out.

But… maybe it's a magic path, and something will whisk me away before I even reach the monk. That seems to be happening to me a lot in this never-ending dream.

Well, here goes nothing.

I walk down the path, both eyes on the monk and wary of what may be about to happen. The trees are still and there's absolutely no sound. I keep walking. I'm on my tip-toes not ten feet away from the monk when I realize that she's really still.

Almost too still.

Is she even breathing? I watch her shoulders. They're not moving. Oh, I hope she's not dead. But if she were dead, she'd fall over, right? Or what if she's dying, and I'm supposed to follow this path and save her, and I'm taking so long that now she is dead and she just hasn't fallen over yet. They all welcome me into their monastery, and I kill their leader. That's not going to make me very popular.

I hurry over to the monk. She's sitting tall but her shoulders aren't moving. I guess she could still be breathing and maybe only her chest is moving. Can you be dead when you're in a meditative trance? I should've asked Rinzen.

I tiptoe around and kneel in front of the maybe dead monk. I watch her chest. It is really still. I swear she's not even moving a muscle. She has to be dead.

And that's the last thought I have before her eyes pop open and she cries, "It's about time, Lotus!"

I suck in a startled breath and fall over in a dead faint.

CHAPTER 19

I think my soul is crazy, or it may just be me

My body feels so warm and cozy that I know I must finally be back home snuggled under my comforter. In my bed. In my real life. With Mama, Daddy, and Berg.

I open my eyes. I'm lying flat on my back under the reclining Buddha staring at someone with muted green eyes. With pupils full of swirling, teeny, white stars.

Wait a minute.

It's her. I know it is. But who is she? Rinzen called her the Venerable something. But she has the same eyes as the woman who bandaged my arm and died on me. And the henna artist. And my counselor Ms. Foofaraw. Are they all the same person? Is this my real life then?

"Hiya, Lotus!" she squeals in a happy, high-pitched voice that doesn't at all match her brown, wrinkled face.

"Who are you?" I ask.

She leans back and grins, exposing her crooked teeth. "I am me!" she cries extending both arms out wide.

I prop myself up on my elbow and face the reclining Buddha as if I was a mirror image. "Then who am I?"

"You are you!"

Ok, this is not getting me anywhere.

"If I'm me, then I think I'm Lottie. But why am I'm in Thailand and not in Colorado?"

She bows her head. "You are right where your soul wants you to be. That has always been the case."

I arch my eyebrow. Oh-kay.

She plops down in front of me, crosses her legs, and sets her hands palms up on her knees. "Okie dokie. I am ready for your questions now. Ask away."

I don't know whether to laugh, or cry, or run away screaming with my hands in the air. I really don't know what to feel.

She frowns. "Actually, you don't know how to feel."

How did she know I was just thinking that?

She grins. "I know more than you think. And that is why we are both here." She pokes my head. "Because you have forgotten how to feel." She glances up at the sun. "Now I must eat before noon, and since I have been following your soul around for four days, I am starving." She leans close to me and grins. "So, get on with the questions."

My eyes widen. "What?"

She claps her hands. "That is a question! Good! We are making progress. What about why?"

I shake my head. "Huh?"

She shrugs. "That is not why, but it is close." She smiles like a mother prodding her child to talk. "Now why are you here?"

I frown. "You mean why am I stuck in this dream?"

"Why do you keep saying this is a dream?"

I snort. "Because it has to be. I was a girl in Morocco, and then I was a boy in Afghanistan, and then I died." I arch an eyebrow. "And you did, too. I thought we both died, but obviously we didn't because now I'm sitting here in Thailand with you." I pause, remembering something Rinzen said when I first met her about not being in hell much longer. "Maybe I am dead." I glance around. "Is this heaven?"

She answers my question with a question. "What do you think?"

"I think I'm in a crazy dream that just won't end."

"Then why don't you just wake up?" she cries.

"I've tried. I can't."

The monk nods her head a few times. "Yes, I can see why you think that." She yawns. "But, you are wrong. You are not in a dream. Try again."

I sit up. "Excuse me?"

"Yes, you are excused." She leans closer until we are nose-to-nose, and then grins. "You are not in a dream."

I pull my head back. "That's impossible."

"Nothing is impossible." She reaches into her robes and pulls out a wrench. She looks confused and then laughs. "That is not what I was looking for. Although this will be useful when I must fix the sink later." She holds up her index finger. "One moment." She returns the wrench to her robes, and rummages around again. I'm thinking that she's pretty tiny to have anything else hidden in there, when she proves me wrong and pulls out a kitten.

A teeny-tiny, white mewing kitten. A white kitten that looks exactly like the one that was rejected by its mother in Morocco. The same one that I found cold and dead.

But this one is very much alive.

She holds the kitten out to me. "You are as alive as your friend here."

I cradle the kitten close to my body. It's warm, and soft, and so very tiny. It looks up at me with brown eyes and squeaks out a mew. I look closer. It sure looks like the kitten from Morocco. It even has the same black spot shaped like a butterfly on its forehead. I stroke its tiny head, and it closes its eyes and purrs.

I look up at the old woman in disbelief. "This can't be the same kitten."

She nods. "But it is."

"Then this is definitely a dream."

"Nope. Not a dream."

I shake my head. "If this isn't a dream, then how in the world is this possible? This kitten was dead. I was dead. You were dead. But now we're all alive?"

The monk shrugs. "Depends on how you define dream and how you define reality." She grins. "And how you define alive."

I shake my head, thoroughly confused. "What do you mean?"

"Our souls are very powerful. Way stronger than our feeble, animal minds. Way stronger than death." She arches an eyebrow. "And capable of so much more than just going to heaven or hell." She strokes the kitten's head and its purr grows louder. "Lotus, do you believe this kitten is alive?"

I don't understand how, but I can see that this little, white, fluff ball swatting at my fingers is very much alive. I have to nod. "I guess so."

"Then you must believe that you are alive and real."

"Real? And not dreaming?" I shake my head. "Nope. I can't be."

"Then how are you speaking Thai with me? And you spoke Duri in Kabul. And Arabic in Morocco."

I shrug. "I'm in a dream. You can do anything in a dream."

"But you are not dreaming. You are as real as your kitten."

I shake my head. "That's impossible."

The old monk smiles at me, like Mama would do when she knows something I don't. "But it is possible, Lotus. Tell me, do you feel any emotions right now? Holding this precious life in your hands. Do you feel anything?"

I look down at the kitten, its tiny belly breathing in and out, vibrating my hand with its purring. I should feel happiness, and calmness, and a tinge of sadness remembering that it was dead. But I don't feel any of those things. I still feel empty.

The old monk places her hand on mine. Her skin is rough and papery, but very warm. "Don't you find that odd?" she asks me in a soft voice.

I look down at the kitten, searching for any emotion, but feeling nothing.

The monk sticks her face under mine. "You are empty, right?"

I jerk my head away. This chick has a lot to learn about personal bubbles.

She arches an eyebrow. "Right?"

"Well, I don't feel sad or angry, and that's perfectly okay in my book. I've been trying not to feel that crap for years anyway." I pause and frown. "But then again I don't feel happy or excited. I guess I just feel… blank."

"And you have always felt emotions very strongly, right? Especially those that caused you pain?"

I nod. "Yeah. But I hated that."

"Well, guess what?" She widens her eyes and splays her lips into a huge grin.

I don't think I really want to know, but I ask anyway. "What?"

She claps her hands together. "Hooray! And now we have come full circle to your very first question. What!"

I give up. "Okay, what?"

"Remember what I told you about the soul being very powerful?"

"Yes."

"Older souls are much more powerful than new souls. Some have been around for a millennium or even longer and they have experienced so much that they feel emotions more strongly. They know how it is to feel way more than happy, but they also know how it is to feel so very brutally sad or angry. They know life is all these emotions." She leans closer. "The problem is that our human body longs to be happy and worries that pain and sadness may someday take over. This sounds like you, yes?"

I nod, remembering how many times I couldn't handle all the painful emotions and just wanted to close my eyes and disappear. "I hated feeling that way. Worrying all the time. Worrying about too much. It was a curse."

She vehemently shakes her head. "No, Lotus. No. Not a curse. It is a gift! To feel so strongly is to truly live life to its fullest."

I feel like I've heard this before.

She grins. "You now understand, right? I can go eat?"

She looks so thrilled that I almost say yes, but I'm just as confused as before.

I shake my head. "Sorry, but I don't understand. If I'm not dreaming, then why am I here in this body, and not in my real Lottie body?"

She sighs. "A soul can only take so much. Your powerful soul was drowning in the unhappiness and pain you kept burying that it had to break free from your Lotus body. It is now searching for a body where you will allow it to feel every emotion." She raises one pale grey eyebrow. "Both the good, and the bad."

Huh?

"So, you're saying that I'm not dreaming?"

She nods.

"And I'm as alive as this kitten?"

"Yes!"

"And because I buried all my pain, my soul is upset with me."

She claps her hands. "You got it!"

I raise an eyebrow.

She raises hers.

This old bat is loco.

She grins. "True. I am a little crazy because that's what makes life fun, but I am also telling you the truth. You just have to choose to believe it."

I sigh. "Okay. I'll join you in your hippie fairyland for a second and believe that I'm not dreaming and I'm not dead. But my soul being upset is beyond crazy. You're talking about my soul as if it's a living thing."

"It is! Your soul is more alive than the body you are in now."

I have a horrid thought. "If my soul is in this body, then is someone else's soul in my real Lottie body in Colorado?" I make a face. "That's just gross. That's like wearing someone else's underwear."

She presses her palm against my heart. "You don't understand. Your soul is your real body. It doesn't matter the shell. Your soul is you."

I have a good thought. "So, I can go back to being Lottie?"

"Maybe you can," she arches an eyebrow, "or maybe you will choose not to."

The sudden realization that I may never see Mama, Daddy, and Berg ever again shoots a pain through me that's worse than being hit by that bomb shrapnel. A feeling of utter despair grips my heart and squeezes the breath out of me.

"Yes!" the loony monk cries.

I glare at her.

She quickly shakes her head. "Sorry. But you are feeling sad, right?" She wipes a tear from my face and holds it up to me like a prize.

I nod slowly. "Yes. I was thinking about never getting back to my real family."

She whoops. "This is good! You are feeling again!"

She's crazy, but she's right. I feel that pressure build in my chest and my face feels warm. But along with my sadness I also feel despair and hopelessness, and that makes me mad. Anger starts to bubble up inside of me. "Who cares that I'm feeling again! I don't want to be in this body. I want me and my soul to go back to my real body!"

The monk looks at me blankly. "Your soul is still in that body."

I groan. "What? How can that be if my soul is in this body?" I drop my head into my hands. "I'm so confused!"

She gently lifts my head until I'm facing her again.

"Lottie, your soul is you." She lays her wrinkled hand on my heart again. "Wherever you are."

I'm about to whine that I still don't understand when she holds up a finger.

"Let me finish, impatient one. Your soul has a shell that it considers home, so it is sad to leave a shell that it loves. That you love. Since you are one and the same."

I feel a sliver of hope. "So, my soul is here as Pema, but it's also back in my Lotus body?"

She waves her hand in the air. "More or less. Your soul is you and you are your soul, but in your case, your soul is old enough and strong enough that, yes, it left an essence of itself back in your Lotus body."

My spirits soar. "That means I can go back? This is great! No more waking up in bodies, not knowing who I am, or what I may find." I shiver thinking of the horrors I saw in Kabul, and know I never want to go there again. "So, if my soul is me then I can just tell myself that I want to go back to my real life?"

She arches her eyebrows. "Well yes…"

I sigh. "There's a big old 'but' coming, isn't there?"

She laughs but it sounds more like a hacking giggle. "I guess you could say it that way." Her eyes grow serious. "Do you really want to go back to your Lottie life in Colorado?"

"Yes!"

"To the pain of Dillon choosing the boy over you?"

"Yes," I answer a bit more quietly.

"Where your brother is disappointed, and your Mama thinks you are selfish?"

"Um, yes… I think so," I whisper.

"To the consequences that will come with almost killing your boyfriend?"

I open my mouth to explain that I didn't mean to hurt him and she holds up a hand to stop me.

"Whether it was an accident, or not."

I close my mouth.

She nods. "If you want to return to that life, then you can. All you have to do is stop burying your pain and sadness. You must re-awaken all of your emotions, and feel everything that life offers you. Only then will your soul believe you can return."

Crap. I don't like the sound of this. "All of my emotions?"

"Yes."

"Even the bad ones that really should be buried?"

She frowns at me. "Do we have to start at the beginning again?"

I sigh. "No. I get it."

I think I finally understand, and I don't like it. I worked really hard as Lottie to bury all my bad emotions so that I could have a perfect, happy life. And then I saw Dillon kiss that boy, and I felt so angry that I lashed out at him, and I screwed it all up. Then because I allowed myself to feel pain, I broke my promise to Berg. And because I felt sadness, I disappointed Mama. I hurt so many people because I allowed those negative emotions to win. How could that be good in any way?

"I wondered if you still might feel that way," the old monk whispers, even though I didn't say anything out loud. She frowns. "There is another option."

Hope flares in me. "What is it?"

"You can choose to continue on this path of burying your emotions and disliking your true self. You can try to never feel anger, pain, or sadness, but your soul will continue to flit around the world, trying out different bodies and different lives. It will be a struggle between your soul hoping you will feel everything again and you fighting to bury your feelings."

"Well, that doesn't sound so bad," I murmur.

She shakes her head.

"No?" I sigh. "Why not?"

The stars in her pupils seem to fade a bit. "If you do that, you may never go home again."

CHAPTER 20

Buddha may have the right idea

The old monk leaves me. I think her exact words were, "You ponder. I'll nosh."

Part of me still believes I'm stuck in a dream… but the other part of me is in shock and awakening to the possibilities that the old monk just opened. I don't want to give up my old life as Lottie, but a life without any crappy emotions sounds darn good.

"I thought I might find you sitting here."

Fah's voice surprises me, but I don't jump. I guess I'm not totally feeling every emotion yet. I turn around and find her standing on the path behind me.

"May I join you?" she asks

I nod.

She folds her hands in prayer, bows to the Buddha, and then sits down next to me. She chuckles. "Moments alone with the venerable old gal can be mind-numbing, right?"

"You have no idea," I mutter.

She snorts, which totally surprises me given her calm demeanor. "Oh, yes, I probably do."

That makes me wonder what secrets she may be hiding. I doubt they are as ludicrous as mine, but she doesn't ask me, so I don't ask her.

She motions to the reclining Buddha. "Do you know this statue symbolizes Buddha's last moments on earth, right before he entered Nirvana?"

I shake my head. "I thought he was just tired and about to take a nap."

She laughs out loud. "That's almost exactly what Rinzen said." A soft smile forms on her lips. "There are many ways Buddha can be depicted. This reclining Buddha represents the moment Buddha left earth for the final time and entered the state of enlightenment known as Nirvana. By doing so, he escaped the endless cycle of birth, death, and rebirth, and was set free from the confines of human misery and pain." She bows her head and whispers so quietly that I wonder if I'm supposed to hear her. "I hope to be set free someday, too,"

I gaze at the Buddha. His eyelids are half-closed, and he does have a very relaxed look on his face. Kind of like the purring kitten snuggled up in my lap. If I never had to feel human misery and pain again I wonder if I would look the same? All content and totally chilled-out.

Fah raises her head and grins. "Okay, then. Monk lesson over. Rinzen and I have another rescue, and we thought you might want to join us." She raises her eyebrows. "Or you can stay here until someone fetches you to help with the laundry. We hand wash all the robes, and trust me, that is a very smelly task."

CHAPTER 21

Can we keep him?

Rinzen grins at Fah. "Don't you think this rescue is way cuter than our last one?"

I know she's joking, but I have to agree. There's no way I could ever be cuter than a baby elephant.

We're standing in the tiny backyard of this tiny house, where this not-so-tiny baby elephant takes up almost all the yard. The baby is probably three times the size of a great Dane, but so stinking adorable that I want to put it on my lap and hug it close.

A young woman who introduced herself as Jampa found the baby elephant.

"I named him Kam-Tong," Jampa says. She looks to be about Rinzen's age and is wearing a bright yellow skirt, a white blouse, and black pumps. "I found him wandering the street last week. I've asked around, but no one seems to know where he came from." Her eyes narrow. "Although someone obviously wasn't taking very good care of him."

She's right about that. His ribs look ready to break through his gray skin.

Jampa sighs. "I've been trying to care for him around my classes, but I just can't do it all. I know he needs a proper home with space to run, and play, and grow up." She lowers her eyes. "Plus, I'm still living with my parents and they won't let me keep him any longer."

Rinzen pats Jampa on the shoulder. "I'm happy you called. We have plenty of space for him at the monastery."

Jampa smiles shyly. "I heard that you have another elephant there?"

"Yep." Rinzen smiles. "And I bet she'd love to call this little guy her own."

Jampa clasps her hands together. "Oh, that would be so wonderful for him."

Rinzen motions to Kam-Tong. "May I approach him?"

Jampa nods. "Of course. But I think he's blind in his right eye, so approach him on the left."

"Good to know. Thanks."

Rinzen walks slowly towards Kam-Tong. The baby elephant raises his ears. She approaches from the left like Jampa suggested, murmuring as she grows close. Kam-Tong raises his trunk out in front of him.

"He's trying to catch her scent," Jampa whispers to Fah and me.

Kam-Tong watches Rinzen approach with his left eye, but he doesn't move. The skin on his back twitches when Rinzen places a large rope over his neck.

"He's very docile," Rinzen announces. She leans against him, and Kam-Tong closes his left eyelid. Rinzen grins. "And super sweet."

"I know," Jampa sniffles, wiping a tear from her cheek. "I'm really going to miss him."

Fah places her arm gently around Jampa's shoulders. "There's no need for you to miss him. You live close, and you are always welcome to come visit."

Jampa's face lights up. "Really?"

Fah laughs. "Of course." She winks. "You must be able to see your baby."

They start discussing visitation details so I walk over to join Rinzen and Kam-Tong. I approach him the same way Rinzen did, but instead of raising his trunk, he just watches me.

Rinzen points to his tail swishing back and forth. "That means he's happy. I think he likes you."

I grin. My heart feels full and warm. The old monk is right. I am getting my feelings back. And I like feeling happy again.

We say goodbye to Jampa, and Rinzen leads our new gentle giant out onto the sidewalk. We are only a few blocks from the monastery, and Kam-Tong walks quietly the entire way, until Fah reaches out to unlock the gate and our sweet baby suddenly comes to life. He waggles his head, swishes his tail, and bumps into Rinzen just hard enough that she falls into Fah who falls into me. We all tumble to the ground like a bag of spilled apples. Then Kam-Tong rubs his baby tusks on the ground and dumps himself upside down right next to us.

Fah and I quickly jump up to avoid being squashed by the baby steamroller, but Rinzen just sits up and laughs.

"It's okay. He's playing."

She's still holding onto his rope, but Kam-Tong is writhing all over the road, looking very much like a dog getting in a good back scratch. His legs are high in the air as his body wriggles all around. He looks so silly and happy that I actually burst out laughing.

My feelings are definitely coming back!

Fah straightens her robe. "I think this little rascal knocked us over on purpose."

Almost as if he understands her, Kam-Tong stands up, starts wagging his tail, and nudges his head gently into Fah's shoulder.

Rinzen beams. "I think he's apologizing."

Fah smiles. "Clever fellow." She nudges Kam-Tong back, and he closes his left eye. They both look really happy.

"He's clever, and spunky," Rinzen says like a proud mom. And I can tell she's already fallen in love with him.

Fah smiles at Rinzen. "And a whole lot of sweet like someone else I know."

Rinzen blushes. A look of love passes between them, and that makes me miss my mama. A twinge of sadness wants to burble up, but I tamp it down. I'm not ready for sadness yet.

Fah walks over and opens the gate. "Welcome to your new home, Kam-Tong."

Rinzen leads Kam-Tong through the gate, and I follow. Fah locks up behind us.

"I'm going to show him the grounds, and introduce him to Kammoon," Rinzen says. "Do you two want to tag along?" Her grin grows mischievous. "Or I'm sure there's still laundry to be done."

Fah raises her eyebrows at me. "Oh dear. What a difficult decision."

I tap my chin. "Yes. Washing stinky robes, or playing with the cutest baby elephant in the world?" I purse my lips. "How will we ever decide?"

Fah sighs. "I know laundry is your favorite activity, Pema, but I strongly feel that we must go with our dear friend, Rinzen. She obviously needs our help."

I sigh. "Yes. I think you may be right."

Fah laces her arm through mine. "Laundry fun must wait. Rinzen needs us."

Rinzen snorts. "Just what we need. A kid and an old broad getting in our way." She looks at Kam-Tong. "Should we let them come?"

Kam-Tong nods yes, his ears flapping, and that makes us all laugh.

Rinzen leads our elephant parade around the side of the house and into the trees. Fah and I walk arm-in-arm behind Rinzen and Kam-Tong. Being so close to Fah brings me such comfort, and watching Kam-Tong swish his tail back and forth across his cute bum makes my heart feels so light. I open my heart to the peacefulness and love and happiness, and I embrace it all.

Suddenly, Kam-Tong stops, and raises his trunk in the air.

"Kammoon's close," Rinzen whispers. "You two go behind that tree, just in case…" she trails off.

Fah leads me over to the tree. "I don't think we want to know how she was going to finish that sentence."

I raise my eyebrows. "I think you're right." I feel a little afraid. I guess that's good, and bad. "Will Rinzen be okay?"

Fah nods. "Oh yes. Elephants are Rinzen's world. She knows exactly what she's doing."

Kammoon approaches at a trot. Her trunk is in the air, and her ears are pricked forward. Rinzen barks a few commands, and Kammoon slows to a walk. When I don't see either elephant wagging their tails, which I now know means they're happy, I find myself holding my breath.

Kammoon walks right up to Kam-Tong. She reaches out her long trunk and explores every inch of Kam-Tong's body. Kam-Tong stands very still, one ear listening to Rinzen's murmuring and one ear pointing toward Kammoon. Suddenly, Kammoon raises her head in the air and trumpets loudly.

I'm wondering if Fah and I should climb up the tree when something beautiful happens.

Kammoon wraps her long, grey trunk around Kam-Tong's back legs, and squeezes him close. She caresses Kam-Tong with her trunk. First, around his belly. Then, over his shoulder and under his neck. She touches his mouth. Comforting him. Loving him immediately and accepting him without any regard to his past. Just like Rinzen and Fah did with me.

Rinzen grins as wide as Kammoon. "She wants to be his mother."

"She will be a very good mama," Fah murmurs.

Mama. Just hearing the word brings a shot of sadness into my heart.

Fah must see it in my face. She pulls me close to her, and envelops me in a hug. A warm, loving hug. I melt into her, not realizing how much I longed to feel someone comfort me until she held me.

"You are safe now, Pema," she whispers. "And you can stay here with us for as long as you want."

I like the sound of that.

She holds me tight for a few moments before releasing me. A grin spreads across her face as she says, "And I mean that with both of my monk hearts."

I giggle at how silly I was asking that question, feeling my sadness dissipate. I give her another hug. "Thanks. I needed that."

Fah's face lights up. "I just had the most wonderful idea. Maybe you would like to help Rinzen care for the elephants? Now that there are two, I am sure she would welcome your assistance."

Rinzen nods. "Yeah! That would be great! I can teach you what to do. You can be Kam-Tong's mahout."

"Me?" I laugh. "I've never even had a dog. There's no way I can care for an elephant that's going to be bigger than most SUVs and live another 40 years." I nudge Fah. "I think you should do it."

Fah inhales very slowly. I think maybe she's contemplating it, but then she exhales and tears fills her eyes.

"I cannot."

"Why? You're so sweet and caring. You would be a perfect mahout." I glance over at Rinzen expecting her to back me up, but I see tears in her eyes, too. She quickly turns away and presses her face into Kammoon's side.

Rinzen is crying?

Fah gently takes my hands in hers. She tries to smile, but it doesn't look like she feels it. "Pema, I would love to learn how to be a perfect mahout, but I will not be here long enough."

I feel panic rising. Another emotion back, and not a good one.

"What do you mean?" I ask. "Where are you going?"

"I have pancreatic cancer," she whispers through a haze of tears. "I will likely die in a few months."

My chest constricts. A ball of rotten acid grows in my stomach, and huge tears of sadness and anger and pain swell up in my eyes.

And I. Hate. It.

I hate that I've gotten to know her, and that I like her so very much, and that I had fun with her, and felt comforted by her. And now I'm feeling all these painful emotions. It aches so much to know that she's dying. And I don't want to feel this way! I don't want to hurt. I don't want to feel Fah's pain, or Rinzen's sadness, or my anger.

I don't want to feel anything.

So, I run. As fast as I can. As far as I can. I close my eyes, run, and wish myself far, far away.

CHAPTER 22

Home is not where I should be now

"Are you sure she was there?"

Is that my mama?

"I don't know."

And my daddy?

"What did he say?"

Yes! That's my mama's voice! I'm home! I'm about to cry out with joy when my daddy answers.

"He said Lottie must have pushed Dillon down the stairs."

Oh. My. Crap.

I don't say a word. I don't move a muscle. I'm assuming I'm Lottie again, back in my room at home, but there's no way I'm opening my eyes to find out. I am in deep trouble. They think I can't hear them, and I don't want them to know I can.

My daddy continues. "Today was a better day for Dillon. Since we brought him out of the coma this was probably the best day he's had so I allowed him a few visitors. I was standing outside his room reading his chart, and I guess his family must have gone to the cafeteria because there was only a young man standing next to the bed crying. He asked Dillon why his girlfriend did this, and Dillon said something I couldn't hear, and the young man angrily responded that he knew Lottie was there and pushed him down the stairs."

I'm dead. I'm so relieved to hear that Dillon is better, but I'm definitely dead. I need to open my eyes and come clean. I need to tell them what really happened. That I freaked out. That I lost my cool. That my Oh my GAD reared its ugly head and destroyed me. And that I hated that I was mean and ugly and terrible, but that I did not push him down the stairs.

I hear my mama start sobbing. "Do you really think she could have?"

What?

My heart rate skyrockets. My chest constricts. My stomach crumples in on itself. I can't believe it. My mama thinks I hurt Dillon on purpose. My mama thinks I could have done that.

My own mama thinks I'm a monster.

I don't even hear what my daddy replies because I've already wished myself far, far away.

CHAPTER 23

I make a decision

I'm fighting the tears that are bullying their way into my eyes. This can't be right. I must have misunderstood my mama. She didn't say I pushed Dillon. Surely, she didn't mean that I did. Surely, my daddy doesn't agree.

I hold my breath and listen. But I don't hear anyone. I only hear… trees… and they're rustling.

Oh, geez! Now, where am I?

I take a big risk, and peek open one eye. I sigh. I'm back in Thailand. I don't know how I got here, but I find myself face to face with the reclining Buddha in the meditation garden. I remember Fah telling me that she is dying, and then running away. I wanted to forget. I wanted to forget the despair I saw in her eyes.

And now I want to forget what my mama and daddy said.

I want to be somewhere else. Somewhere far away. Out of this dream, or whatever the heck it is! The old monk is convinced this is all real. That my soul is so pissed at me for burying my pain that it broke free from my body. And as hard as that is to swallow, I think I now want to believe it. Because if this is real and not a dream, then at least I have options. At least I have some control. And I like the sound of that.

The old monk said I have a choice. If I choose to feel everything again- including this god-awful misery, I might go back to my old life as Lottie. But if I choose to bury my pain, my soul will flit around the world trying to make me feel everything. I laugh at that. I'm pretty good at burying my feelings. I think I could win that struggle. And think of the new adventures I'd get to have. I always did want to travel the world.

But that would mean I may never go back to being Lottie. Which would mean never seeing Mama, Daddy, and Berg again, and that makes my breath hitch with sadness. But that also means I wouldn't be the lunatic with Oh my GAD anymore, and I would love that.

Holy crap. My mind is about to explode.

I stare at the Buddha in front of me. His content face, immortalized in his happy moment of enlightenment, seems to mock my tortured one. Maybe Buddha had the right idea. He left this dreadful world with all its pain and suffering. He got the heck out of dodge and went towards the light.

Something rubs against my leg. I look down and see the white kitten parading around, tail high in the air, mewing at me. I pick it up, and hug it close. It purrs, and I feel happiness overcoming the pain.

Happiness. That's what I want. That's what I've always wanted. I just want to feel happy.

The more I think about it, I don't know why I want to go back to my life as Lottie. I hated who I was anyway. And now everyone there hates me, too. I almost killed Dillon. God knows what crap I'm going to face over that. Berg and Mama are pissed at me. And what if someday my mama or daddy get cancer and die just like Fah? Why go back to all of that when I have the chance to escape all that misery, see more of the world, and just be happy.

I suddenly find clarity. I know what I'm going to do. I'm going to pull a Buddha. I will escape this endless cycle of misery and sadness and anxiety. I will transcend all pain and suffering, so that, finally, I will be set free.

I kiss the kitten on top of its head, set it down on the ground, and give it a little pat. I whisper, "Goodbye," as it scurries into the trees. No more getting attached equals no more pain.

And I'm beyond ready for that.

It feels so good to have made a decision that I inhale one of the deepest breaths I've taken in a long time. I salute the Buddha statue. "Thanks for the help, big guy."

"You have decided then?"

Without turning around, I know it's the old monk. I recognize her voice, and before she finishes her question, she's standing inches away from my face. I forgot to talk to her about my personal bubble.

I take a step back. "Yes, I have. I'm not going back to being Lottie." My voice is strong and happy, and I know I've made the right choice.

She raises her eyebrows. Her galaxy eyes look dull. "Are you certain?"

I nod. "Yes."

"Absolutely one-hundred-and-infinity percent?"

I snort. "Yes. Absolutely one-hundred-and-infinity percent."

She takes a step back. "Then now it is my turn to ask why?"

I shrug. "I'm so sick of feeling sad and angry. I hate being anxious. I hate losing my temper. I hate feeling everything so strongly that I just don't want to hurt anymore." I motion to the Buddha. "Just like him, I'm choosing to escape the misery of human life and live in my happy enlightenment. I choose only happy. I choose Nirvana."

The old monk tilts her head. "You believe only feeling happy will be Nirvana?"

I roll my eyes. "Um, yeah. How could it not be?"

"Hmmm…that is the question, isn't it?"

I shake my head. "Nope. There's no question. It will be."

"Are you sure?"

I wink. "Yes. Absolutely one-hundred-and-infinity percent."

She slowly nods her head. "This is your decision to make, and you have made it." She glances down, and gestures to the white kitten that has returned and is rubbing its head all over my robes. "Would you like to take your kitty with you? I can arrange it."

I shake my head. "Nope. This time I'm on my own."

She nods. "Okie dokie. As you wish." She picks up the kitten, bows her head to the Buddha, and grins at me. "Goodbye, Lotus. I hope I will see you again very soon."

She starts walking down the path, and I have an epiphany.

"Venerable Bhik, you sent me the postcard didn't you?"

She turns and grins. "Maybe."

"So… I'll probably run into you giving me a henna or sending me another postcard?"

She shakes her head. "Sorry, not this time. As you said, you are on your own."

"Then can I ask you a question?"

She raises one pale eyebrow. "You can always ask."

"You moved your soul, didn't you? While you were meditating, you moved your soul into Ms. Foofaraw and the henna lady and the woman in Kabul so you could be with me?"

Her galaxy eyes twinkle. "Maybe."

I roll my eyes. "Well, if you did, then can you teach me to control my soul?"

She answers me with a question. Of course.

"If you are your soul, aren't you always in control?"

I sigh. "Yes, I get that. We're one and the same. Blah, blah, blah. But can I choose where we go? Is there a trick to this soul-wandering thing? Cause I'd hate to go someplace like Kabul again. I mean, who could possibly find happiness there?"

She raises both eyebrows. "Yes. Who could?"

I shake my head. "I'm guessing no one. That was misery at its finest, and I'm burying that memory so deep archaeologists won't even be able to find it."

She purses her lips. "I see. And have you thought about where you think you will find happiness?"

I grin. "Not yet, but there are so many happy places out there. The beach. The mountains. A palace in Versailles." I clap my hands together. "That's it! Paris! That's where I need to go to find happiness." I waggle my eyebrows. "It is the city of love. And being in love is always happy."

The old monk nods. "If you believe you will be happy there, then maybe your soul will believe it, too." She gives me a wide grin showing off her crooked teeth. "Well then, this is goodbye for now, soul wanderer. I hope you find what you need."

And as she walks away, I swear she's humming "Happy Birthday."

CHAPTER 24

How does this darn thing work?

I can't believe it. I'm going to Paris! Paris!

I wish the Buddha statue au revoir and close my eyes. Time for a huge heart to heart with my soul. Where I may have to stretch the truth just a teensy- tiny bit.

I'm you, and you're me, which means I'm in charge. I refuse to feel any more awful emotions so it's time for us to move on. And we're going to Paris.

I take a deep breath, close my eyes, and picture the Eiffel Tower all lit up in sparkling lights, just like on the postcard on Lottie's great-grandmother's desk.

I slowly open my eyes. I'm still standing in front of the Buddha.

The old me would be frustrated. The new me isn't allowing that emotion anymore.

Just so you know. I calmly tell my soul. I refuse to feel any negative emotions here, so we might as well move on and head to Paris. I cross my fingers as I lie. Maybe I'll feel them there.

I close my eyes again. I picture the postcard.

We're going to Paris.

I open my eyes, and… I'm still standing in front of Buddha.

It's okay. I can figure this out. What was I doing when my soul left Colorado? I was angry and didn't want to be, so I was trying to disappear to protect myself from feeling all that pain. And in Morocco I was really sad because Mama rejected me and I found the dead kitten. Then in…

"Pema!"

I gasp. It's Fah.

"Where are you, kid?"

And Rinzen.

I don't want to see them! I don't want to talk to them! And most of all I don't want to feel their pain.

So, I close my eyes, and wish myself far, far away.

CHAPTER 25

Is this really Paris?

The air shifts. Something compresses my lungs, squeezing my breath like when I want to cry but have to struggle to hold it in. My body twists, and I feel like I'm on a roller coaster as my stomach flops, then flips, and then drops. My body feels like it's turning inside out. I want to scream, but then the pressure slowly eases and my stomach settles.

Well, that was super uncomfortable.

I'm afraid to open my eyes. I'm hoping my soul and I jumped because I really don't want to see Fah or Rinzen. I listen. It's quiet. And hot and sticky.

I dare to peek open one eye. I don't see Buddha, or Fah, or Rinzen. Did I actually do it? Did I actually move my soul into another body?

I open my other eye and look around me. I'm definitely not in Bangkok anymore. I'm standing in the middle of some sort of grassy area and… OH MY GOD! Is that the Eiffel Tower?!

I jump up and down. I can't believe I did it! I'm in Paris!

I take a moment to check out my new body. I'm wearing denim cutoffs, a white strappy tank, and pink cowboy boots. I feel my head. And I'm not bald anymore! I have hair! And it's long enough that it's up in a ponytail. Yes!

I feel so happy.

And so free.

I wipe a trickle of sweat racing down my face, shield my eyes from the sun, and gawk at the Eiffel Tower. Wow. Just wow. I can't believe I'm standing in front of the world-famous Eiffel Tower in Paris, France. My heart races with joy and that feels so good.

I tilt my head. Huh. It looks smaller in real life than I thought it would be. And why is there a giant, red cowboy hat on top of it? I stare for a moment. Maybe it's part of an art exhibit? Like when Lottie's parents went to Versailles and that artist had a giant pink balloon dog in one of the ballrooms. Parisians are always doing something outrageous and cool like that.

A deep voice interrupts my thoughts.

"Excuse me, ma'am."

I tear my gaze away from the Eiffel Tower and drink in the man standing behind me. This body must be a lot shorter than Lottie, or he must be really tall, because I have to tilt my head back to look into his dusty blue eyes. His chin is scruffy, like when Lottie's daddy wouldn't shave over the weekend, and he's wearing a button-down, chambray shirt, jeans, and a black cowboy hat.

And he's grinning at me with the cutest, dimpled grin I've ever seen. My stomach does a happy flip-flop.

Lottie's mama would probably think he's too old for me, but I don't care. I grin back. Maybe I'm older in this body. I've never changed ages before, but I'm pretty new at this soul wandering stuff so maybe this time I did.

Cute Dimples extends his hand. "I'm George."

"Nice to meet you. Are you the artist?"

Oooo! My voice sounds velvety smooth. And obviously I can speak French!

George tilts his head in the most adorable way. "Excuse me?"

My belly feels warm, and I suddenly feel shy. "Well, since you're wearing a hat and the tower's wearing a hat, and not many people in Paris wear cowboy hats, I thought you made the hat, because I didn't even know it even had one, or at least on postcards it never did, and I didn't know about the art exhibit."

Oh my god. Stop talking. You're babbling like an idiot.

A funny look crosses his face, but then it's gone and he smiles all dimply and cute. "Maybe we should get out of this heat. Would you like to join me for a cold drink?"

My heart pitter-patters. I feel my cheeks heat up. Cute Dimples is asking me out? And I'm old enough to drink legally? Paris really is the city of love.

I giggle. "I'd love to."

He tips his cowboy hat, and holds out his elbow. I slip my arm through it, and waves of happiness knead through my muscles until I'm more relaxed than limp spaghetti. I knew I would find happiness in Paris.

George leads me away from the Eiffel Tower and down the sidewalk. We stop at the street to let a battered, red pick-up truck pass by, and George points to the red brick building across the street.

"We're heading over there. If that's okay?" he asks.

I can see there's a little café in the bottom half of the building. A large, black-and-white sign above the door reads The Paris Bakery.

"That would be lovely," I purr. I am on a date with a handsome Parisian. I must try to sound older and more sophisticated.

George leads me across the street. "They have the best croissants in town here. Although, that's pretty easy to do because no one else makes them," he laughs.

I find his comment a bit odd in a city known for its croissants, but when he opens the door, I forget all about it as I'm swaddled by heavenly smells of butter, cinnamon, and yeast.

The bakery is crammed with people. A long line winds past a glass case filled with goodies, and every metal-topped table is full. George leads me to a long, black bar jutting out from the windows. He points to two open barstools.

"Why don't you sit down, and I'll get you a croissant and a drink."

I nod, and flash him what I think is a flirty smile. "That would be lovely. Thank you."

He tips his hat and ambles over to the counter. My heart flip-flops again. He's polite, and sweet, and tall, and lean. Yay! And his bum looks awfully cute in those jeans.

George bypasses the line and slips behind the counter. He hugs an older woman ringing someone up at the cash register. She's wearing a white apron and her hair is up in a tight, grey bun. They speak briefly and then he points to me. She looks over, gives me an ear-splitting grin, and waves. I wave back, and find my heart filling with happiness.

A few minutes later, George returns with two, red plastic glasses, and sets them on the bar in front of me. "Here ya go. Nice and cold."

I smile. "Thank you."

I can't believe it. I'm about to have my first alcoholic drink in a real restaurant. Legally! Lottie's parents used to give her sips of their wine at dinner, but this is so different. This is a drink date. I'm a little nervous, but I like it. It's a good feeling, full of excitement and joy.

I take a small sip from the straw. It's sweet but also bold with hints of smoke and lemon. "This is delicious!" I announce. "What's it called?"

George raises his brown eyebrows. "Sweet tea," he says slowly.

I take another big sip. It's so refreshing I want to drink the entire thing, but I know I need to be careful. I have no idea how much alcohol this body can handle.

"What's in it?" I ask.

He wrinkles his brow. "What's in tea?"

I nod, and take another sip. I rack my brain trying to think of alcohol names. I don't want him to think I'm not sophisticated. "Does it have vodka or wine in it?"

A look of concern crosses his face, and he shakes his head. "No, ma'am. It's just tea, sugar, and water."

"Just tea, sugar, and…" I pause as my brain finally kicks in. "Oh my god," I giggle. "This is just plain, old, iced tea!" And without worrying what anyone thinks, my giggles transform into full-blown, belly-shaking laughter.

A huge dimpled smile grows on George's face. "I think you may have been standing out in the sun too long," he chuckles.

And that just makes me laugh harder.

The older woman with the grey bun bustles up and plops a china plate with two croissants on it down in front of me.

"Now y'all just have to tell me what's so funny," she drawls in a sweet voice, a smile warming her wrinkles. Her blue eyes are bright with amusement, or maybe they just look that way because of the electric-blue, eye shadow covering her lids. She wipes her hands on her apron. "I just love a good joke. I can always use a new one to share with the customers."

I stop laughing. I don't think this is a joke I want her repeating.

George shakes his head. "Sorry, Gran. It wasn't really a joke." He winks at me. "Or at least one I want you telling customers."

My heart stutters. Wow. He's cute, and protective of my feelings.

She nods. "Understood." She extends her hand. "Howdy! I'm Rita Regina, but everyone just calls me Gran. I see you've already met my grandson."

I shake her hand. "Nice to meet you."

"And what's your name, darlin'?" she asks with a warm smile, still gripping my hand.

I pause. What is my name? I'm not Lottie anymore. Or Aicha. And god knows I don't want to be Boy. It's odd that I'm not getting anything off this body at all.

Wait.

"Swan," I reply. Yes, I think that's my name. I nod. "Yes, my name is Swan."

And it appears that I've run away from home. Interesting.

Gran tilts her head to the side before nodding and releasing my hand. "Well, nice to meet you, Swan. You're as pretty as a peach, but I don't recall seeing you around here before. Do you go to George's high school? Are you a sophomore, too?"

Well, that answers that. I guess I do look fifteen.

"Gran," George groans. "Please, not the questions."

She frowns at George, plucks his cowboy hat off his head, and hands it to him. His cheeks blush pink as he takes it from her and sets it on the windowsill behind him.

Gran turns back to me and chuckles. "Boys. They don't like me meddling in their business." Her blue eyes sparkle as she grins. "But I know a good'un when I see her." She winks, "And you could be a good'un."

George groans again.

Gran waves him off. "Okay, okay. Message received loud and clear. I'm leaving." She winks at me again. "You're in good hands here. A cold drink, a buttery pastry, and a cute boy can go a long way in healing anything."

"Gran!" George cries.

She just laughs and leans over to hug me tight, making my insides feel warm and cozy. "You stay as long as you need, darlin'," she whispers in my ear before straightening up and hustling back to the counter.

George runs his hand through his messy waves of brown hair. His dimpled mouth turns up into an apologetic grin. "Sorry. Hope she didn't scare you."

I shake my head. "Not at all. In fact, I like her."

And you. I like you. Especially when your hair is all disheveled like you just woke up, and you're blushing, and looking at me like that.

I grin. And he grins back. And my stomach feels all gooey and happy.

He gestures to the croissants. "So, I'm dying to eat one of these, but my Gran would never let me hear the end of it if I had one before you. So please tell me you're one of those girls that eat?"

I laugh and nod. "I am."

"Then, ladies first."

I tear off a piece of the warm pastry, and pop it into my mouth. Crisp, buttery flakes melt on my tongue and bliss overcomes me.

"Oh, yum," I moan. "I can see why they're the best in Paris!"

I reach down to tear off another piece right just as he does, and when my fingers brush his I feel a zing of electricity flow through me. His eyes widen, and his adorable, dimpled cheeks turn pink. But he leaves his fingers touching mine, sending zings of joy straight to my heart.

"I like you," I hear myself say out loud, and almost clamp my hand over my mouth at my boldness.

And I like this girl. She ran away to see the world, and says what she thinks. I like her spunk!

I mean, I like my spunk.

A grin melts into his dimples. "I like you, too," he murmurs. He slowly envelops all my fingers into his big hand and squeezes them tight. His hand is warm and a little sweaty. My heart pitter-patters overtime.

We sit in silence for a few seconds, grinning crazily at each other, the best croissant in Paris forgotten. I'm admiring his full pink lips and wondering what it would be like to kiss him, when he breaks the spell.

"Swan, can I ask you something?"

I nod. Excitement flares in my belly. Please ask me out!

"Are you, um…." He clears his throat. "Well, I was wondering if you're dating anyone?"

I shake my head no, not trusting myself to speak.

He inhales a deep breath. "Then would you like to go out to dinner with me sometime?" he asks in a rush of expelled air.

Woohoo! Yes! I want to jump up and down! I want to leap up on the counter and tell everyone that Cute Dimples just asked me out! I want to sing with joy! I want to kiss him!

I love setting my happy emotions free again, but I don't want to be that crazy girl and scare him off with too much excitement, so I grin and answer calmly. "That would be lovely."

His denim eyes brighten. "Really? Wow. That's great. I mean, really." He pauses and then asks shyly, "Well, are you free tonight?"

"As a matter of fact, I am." Tonight, and tomorrow, and forever. I am finally free.

His smile stretches so wide that I can't help smiling, too.

"Great! I just got my license. I bet Gran would let me pick you up." He squeezes my hand and glances at me under his lashes. "If that's okay with you?"

I giggle. "It's more than okay."

"Let me grab my phone and get your address." He tries to wriggle his phone out of his pocket using only one hand, but he can't, so instead he pulls our entwined hands up to his lips and kisses my knuckles. "Never mind, I'll get it later."

I melt into a pile of happy goo.

His brow furrows. "I'm not keeping you from something right now, am I?" he asks, wrapping his other hand around mine.

I shake my head. "Nope. I really don't have any plans yet. Although, I would like to see the Louvre while I'm here."

George gives me a goofy grin. "We don't have a Louvre here."

I nod. "Well, I know the Louvre's not here. But it can't be that far away." I smile coyly. "Maybe we could go together?"

He swallows, and gives me a funny look. "To the Louvre?"

I nod. "Yeah."

He loosens his grip on my hand. A trickle of sweat dribbles down his face. How weird that he got so nervous when I mentioned the Louvre. Maybe he had a bad experience there? Maybe the Mona Lisa's smirk bugs him? Or the Sphinx gives him the willies?

"Um, we'd have to get on a plane and fly to the Louvre, Swan," he says, lifting one of his hands off mine to wipe the sweat from his face.

"We have to fly? Huh. I thought the Louvre was pretty close to the Eiffel Tower. I had no idea Paris was so big."

He furrows his brow. "Swan, you know the Louvre is in France."

I nod. "Yep."

"And we're in Texas."

My eyes widen. "What?"

He tilts his head. "We're in Texas."

"Texas?"

He nods.

"I'm not in Paris."

He shrugs. "You are in Paris. But this is Paris, Texas. Not the Paris in France."

I sigh. "Then I guess I'm not speaking French."

He shakes his head. "Not to me."

"And that's not the real Eiffel Tower?"

"Not the one that's in Paris. This one is a replica." He frowns. "That heatstroke really did a number on you, didn't it? Why don't I get us some more iced tea?" He kisses my knuckles again, and gazes at me with a caring look. "I'll be right back," he promises before releasing my hand.

The minute I lose contact with his fingers, he takes his warmth with him. I feel cold. And empty. And sad. Like how this body felt when she left her family in Dallas. No one was even home from work yet when I ran away.

Um. No. Good try, Soul. I know I've chosen not to be Lottie anymore, but I refuse to feel whatever pain this girl is dredging up. Not happening.

I shove away the feelings of sadness that start to sweep over this body, and I go back to the joy and giddiness and first-love-crush feeling I feel with George. I think of his dimpled smile. His sweet voice. The way his hand feels in mine. My heart speeds up. My stomach flips. And suddenly I feel like the sun is shining all over me. I love falling in love. It's happy and wonderful and sweet… until you fall out of love. And he wants to move on with someone new. Like that boy did to Swan. Like Dillon did to Lottie.

And just like that my joy is tainted with a dash of melancholy.

I sigh. I know what I have to do, and it sucks, because I really like George. I'd love to go on a date with him and his cute dimples, and see what it's like to kiss him, but I know I can't. I'm happy now, but what happens when he breaks my heart? I just met him, and I already feel sad when he walks ten feet away. I can't imagine how agonizing it will be when I start to love him and he does something to shatter my heart.

Nope. Getting close to someone means having to feel. And having to feel eventually involves sadness and pain. And I don't want any of that.

I straighten my shoulders. Besides, I'm not even in France! Which means my soul is still calling the shots. I need to quit flirting with boys and figure this out.

George returns with our glasses and a smile so bright and full of promise that I almost change my mind.

But I can't.

"Where's the bathroom?" I ask before he can say anything.

"Other end of the bar," he tells me, unaware that he's sending me away forever.

"Thanks." I start to walk away, but something I can't control stops me. I find myself turning around, leaning towards him, and placing a soft kiss on his lips.

Heat rushes to my belly, and a whirlwind of emotions flutter throughout my body like a swarm of golden fall leaves flying off their trees. Elation. Love. Tears.

NO!

I pull away. "I'm so sorry," I stammer.

His sweet lips open to say something but I don't wait around to hear what it is. I dart across the bakery, and fling myself into the bathroom, locking the door behind me.

Why did I do that?

I bang my head against the door, hoping to scare the tears away. Exhale sadness. Inhale happy thoughts. Of a new body. Of a new adventure. Hopefully seeing the real Eiffel Tower.

By the way, Soul, real funny.

I walk over to the mirror, and take a first and last look at this body. My front teeth and my nose are both too big, but my eyes and hair are both a pale, almond brown. I guess George thought I was attractive, but that doesn't matter because I'm leaving. It's a bummer to have to run away from happy feelings, but I'm also running from the pain that is bound to come sooner or later. Love just doesn't exist without feeling all the emotions. It just can't. And I don't want to feel bad emotions anymore, so I guess love is not going to be for me.

Did you hear that, Soul? I'm not falling for this again. No love for me. Only happy feelings. And Paris, Texas? That was a dirty trick.

I narrow my eyes.

I get it. You think you're still in charge and you choose where we go. But not this time. This time I choose. I choose somewhere happy. Somewhere fun. And with cute boys that I don't want to fall in love with.

Then I close my eyes, and wish myself far, far away.

CHAPTER 26

Time for an adventure

The air warms and cools around me. My lungs contract, but not as tight this time, and my stomach only flips once before it drops.

I blink my eyes open. I did it! I'm not in the bathroom in Texas anymore. And I'm must be getting better at this jumping bodies thing because this time was less upside-down, out-of-control roller coaster, and a little more tilt-a-whirl.

But where I am?

I'm sitting in the front passenger seat of what must be a Jeep because it says so right on the glove compartment. I glance out the windshield. The sky is overcast and gray. Everything in front of me looks like flat, empty pasture where cropped patches of brown and green grass swirl out in an endless pattern until they meet the horizon. There are no buildings or houses as far as I can see. I look out the side windows and don't see any cars or people either. Weird. It's like I dropped into a grassy moon.

No matter. If don't like it here, I'll just have my soul move along. Wander on to the next body and experience the next thing. I grin. This is so cool. I get to avoid feeling pain, and I'm getting to see new places. Like a cowboy hat on top of the Eiffel Tower! I laugh. That was definitely something I never thought I'd see.

I doubt I'm in hot Texas anymore because this body is wearing black ski pants and a white wool sweater with some type of navy, zigzagged Nordic pattern around the neck. I pull down the visor and check out my new self.

My dark-blond hair is divided into two shoulder-length braids. The color is kind of like Lottie's hair color when she got highlights. I have pale skin, a perfectly nice nose, and icy blue eyes just like when Lottie wears her contacts. I look a little German. Or maybe Swedish?

I see people in the mirror approaching the back of the Jeep. Maybe I know them! Time to jump right into my new character. The new me for today!

I open the door, and a gust of frigid wind greets me. Whoa! Wherever I am, it's really cold. And Lottie was from the mountains of Colorado, so she knew cold. I grab the red wool hat poking out of my pocket and tug it over my braids before I jump out of the Jeep.

What I see behind the Jeep takes my breath away. While the land in front is flat and endless like the moon, behind the Jeep is like a fairy-tale, mountain paradise. An imposing range of jagged mountains iced with green moss rise up from ground. A wide waterfall slices through the mountains, diving off the rocky cliffs and spraying mists of glistening rainbows as it crashes into a frothy pool two-hundred feet below. I have never seen anything more beautiful in my life. Part of me wants to sigh with joy, but this body must have seen this before because I feel like I belong here in this wild, rugged scene.

I tear my gaze away from the waterfall and focus on the approaching group. Two girls and two guys. Well, maybe I should say two women and two men because they're definitely older than high school. Maybe college-aged. Although it's hard to tell because they're bundled up in waterproof jackets and pants, and they're sopping wet.

The girls start sprinting towards me. One is thin and tiny, and leaps like a ballerina. Her curly, black hair is plastered to her cocoa cheeks and sticking out in all directions. The other girl is much taller and more athletic-looking. Her bright, red hair is piled on top of her head in a messy bun, and a long scarf blows out behind her.

"Blimey, I'm freezing!" Curly Hair says in a thick, British accent when they reach me.

"I don't think I've ever been this cold," Red Hair laughs in what sounds like a German accent.

"Or wet!" Curly Hair adds. She grins at me. "But you were right, Gunna, it was brilliant."

Red Hair nods, opens the back door of the Jeep; and they both jump in.

Gunna. Yes. I know that's my name.

I turn my attention back to the guys. They're both tall, and really cute. One guy has neatly cropped, brown hair. The other has shaggy, dark-blond hair cascading down to his shoulders. And they're both wearing huge, melt-my-knees smiles.

"I should have listened to your advice, Gunna," Cropped Hair laughs. He has a German accent like Red Hair.

"Aw, don't tell her that," Shaggy Hair scoffs. He doesn't have an accent. "She'll get a big head over it, and never let you forget it."

Cropped Hair grins even wider, exposing the tiniest dimple above one of his hazel eyes. "Oh, I doubt she would give anyone a hard time."

My heart speeds up. I think Gunna likes this boy.

Shaggy Hair winks at me. "That's just what she wants you to think."

My heart speeds up, again. Wow! Two gorgeous guys! Oh, darn. Poor me. I almost giggle out loud at my luck.

"Now boys," I scold with a smile. I don't have an accent. But my voice is smooth and a little husky. "I would never steer you wrong."

Cropped Hair folds his hands together and bows. "So true, 'o wise one."

Shaggy Hair claps Cropped Hair on the shoulder. "Oh, come on, Nils. Did you really think she was joking when she told you the Seljalandsfoss waterfall has some wicked spray?"

Nils is Cropped Hair.

"Wicked spray?" Nils snorts, pointing to his soaked clothes "I don't think I would be quite as wet without a little help from Bjorn here."

Shaggy Hair is Bjorn. And I suddenly know I have really strong feelings for him. Wow. Am I in love with him?

Bjorn raises his hands, palms up, his bright blue eyes crinkling mischievously. "I have no idea what you're talking about."

"Riiiight," Nils laughs.

Bjorn waggles his eyebrows at me. "And you, poor Gunna, missed all the fun staying in the Jeep." He dips his head down and shakes his long hair, spraying water all over me. "Can't have you missing out," he laughs.

The water is freezing cold and quickly numbs my face, but I could care less. Bjorn makes this Gunna body so happy. Maybe he's flirting with me?

I giggle. "Gee thanks, I feel so lucky."

Nils interrupts our love connection. "And I'll be so lucky if Bjorn would turn on the heat before we freeze to death."

Bjorn lifts up his palms. "Okay, okay. I guess since you're paying us to show you around our beautiful country, we really shouldn't turn you into popsicles."

"It may give Iceland a bad name," Nils laughs and jumps into the back of the Jeep with the girls.

I'm in Iceland?

Yes! This Gunna body grew up here. Iceland is her home.

Oh my god, so awesome! I'm in Iceland!

Bjorn turns to me, smiles, and shakes his head. "Tourists." He walks over to the driver's side and opens the door. "Where are those extra sweaters Father told us to pack for them?"

Father?

"Our father?" I ask.

Oh my god. It's all coming to me. Bjorn is Gunna's brother.

Bjorn tilts his head. "Um yeah. Do you have another father I don't know about?"

I shake my head. Not anymore.

"Let's get this show on the road then," he laughs, and climbs into the Jeep.

I can't believe I thought my brother was flirting with me. Ew. Although I guess that explains why I have such strong feelings of love for him. Like Lottie did with her brother, Berg. She would have done anything for him.

Even though I royally messed up that day and wasn't there when Berg needed me.

No! Stop it! I'm not thinking about that. I'm here now. As Gunna. Not Lottie.

Bjorn yells out his door. "If you're not here, let me know. Otherwise off to the glacier caves we go."

I pause. Do I want to go with them? I could jump bodies again, or I could stay. I've never seen Iceland before. It would be really cool to explore it. And I could spend more time with that cutie Nils. I don't want to fall in love. I just need to know that I can still attract a boy. I know I left Lottie behind, but the sting of Dillon choosing that boy over me still lingers. Was I not good enough? I know George liked me, but Swan's body was dredging up painful memories so I needed to take off. Plus, I did choose this path because I wanted adventure. What better place to find adventure than in Iceland?

I take one last look at the striking waterfall, grin, and jump into the Jeep.

CHAPTER 27

Cheesy puffs, I've missed you!

"I can't believe how bloody cold the waterfall spray was!" Curly Hair says when I climb into the Jeep. "My jacket was soaked!"

Her name is Bridgit, and she's from London.

"Aw, come on," Bjorn laughs as he pulls the Jeep out of the dirt lot and onto a small country road. "That wasn't cold. That was like bath water."

Bridgit shivers. "You Icelanders must take bloody cold baths then. We have this thing called hot water in the U.K.."

Red Hair nods in agreement. Her name is Camille and she's from Switzerland. The details of Gunna's memory are coming more easily to me now!

Wait.

Camille and Nils have the same Swiss accent. Does that mean they're in Iceland together? Are they dating, or just friends, or… oh my god…are they married? They do look older than me.

Camille unravels her hair out of its bun. The color is a dramatic, copper red that falls in perfect waves all the way down to her lap. Her high cheekbones and thin nose are splattered with light freckles that look perfect against her pale skin and big, violet eyes. Even with this smoking hot Gunna body, there's no way Nils would go for me over her.

"Nils didn't think it was that cold," Bjorn teases.

Nils shrugs. "It was cold but not nearly as cold as that time I jumped into that snowdrift in Zermatt with Camille's father." He shivers. "Now that was cold."

Camille laughs. "That was because you were only wearing bathing trunks!"

"Blimey!" Bridgit exclaims. "Why would you do that?"

"We were playing cards, and we lost," Nils explains.

"Man, that's harsh!" Bjorn chuckles.

Camille nods. "Yes, but it's a family tradition. Every time we get together for reunions, the losing team has to jump in the snow."

Nils raises an eyebrow. "I'm pretty sure your father lost on purpose."

She shrugs. "It was your first game, and he is your uncle. I think it's like a right of passage or something."

Wait a minute! Her father is his uncle? So that means…

"You two are cousins?" I ask, trying to hide my glee.

Camille nods. "Yes. My father is Nils' father's older brother."

I grin and want to fist punch the air. Yes! This is totally going to work out. Nils is mine! Woohoo!

Bridgit faces Nils. "So, you're saying this waterfall wasn't as cold as jumping in the snow?"

Nils waves his hand. "Not even close."

She grins. "Is that why you ran through so fast you almost knocked me over?"

Nils mirrors her grin. "I was only running because someone decided I might be cuter when wet."

Bjorn inhales a sharp breath. I don't think anyone else heard him, but I notice his cheeks are pink. Seeing Bjorn's embarrassment makes this body's heart warm, although I have no idea why. A fuzzy thought nudges at my consciousness, but Bridgit's squeal scares it away.

"Oh, Bjorn!" she exclaims. "There are some ponies! Can we stop? Please!"

"Sure," Bjorn answers, his cheeks fading back to normal. "But Icelandic horses are a proud breed and will bite the fingers off anyone who calls them ponies."

Camille gasps.

Bridgit frowns. "Really?"

"He's totally kidding," I laugh. "He doesn't like when someone calls them ponies instead of horses. They may be short, but they are horses."

It's weird. It's like I arrived with no idea of who I am in this body, but gradually bits and pieces are becoming crystal clear. It's almost like I'm plugging my brain into a computer and downloading what I need to know about Gunna when I need it.

I twist around in my seat. "Do you want to feed them?"

Everyone nods but Camille. She's biting her fingernail.

"Is that safe?" she asks.

I nod. "Oh sure. You just have to make sure your palm stays flat." I lay my hand out as an example. "Just keep it like this and even if they nibble your fingers, it won't hurt."

"But it may wreck your nails, Camille," Nils chuckles, shooting an adorable wink my way.

Camille examines her geometric nail art, and then shifts in her seat. "Well, perhaps, I'll just stay in the car to be safe."

Bridgit links her arm through Camille's. "Oh, blimey, girl, you're on vacation. You have to experience it all! Just put on your gloves and you won't have to worry about the ponies nibbling anything."

"They're horses!" Bjorn yells.

Bridgit giggles. "Right. Sorry. I mean you won't have to worry about the big, humongous Icelandic horses nibbling anything."

Bjorn pulls off the road and onto a dirt shoulder. About ten feet down a sloped hill lies a barbed wire fence guarding a pasture filled with brown grass, the occasional jagged rock, and a group of shaggy horses. They see us pull up and trot over to the fence. A light, misty rain is falling but with their wooly coats and long tangled manes, the horses don't even seem to notice.

A chestnut horse with a shaggy, blond mane hanging over its eyes catches my attention. "Look, Bjorn, it's your long-lost twin," I joke.

He waggles his eyebrows. "Ah yes, it's baby bjorn."

I chuckle. I like being Gunna. This is fun.

Bjorn kills the motor and turns around in his seat. "Okay, then, everyone out for the finger nibbling." He motions to the backpack sitting near my feet. "Grab those cheesy puffs out of my pack just in case the horses want something other than fingers."

Cheesy puffs? Lottie loved cheesy puffs. My mouth immediately starts watering. Maybe Gunna loves them, too.

I rummage through his backpack and pull out the orange bag. They call to me like a long-lost love. Like an addict needing a fix. I'm the addict. And I need the fix.

I wait for the girls and Nils to climb out of the Jeep before I hug the bag to my chest. "You can't feed these to the horses!"

Bjorn gives me a funny look. "Okay, fine. But why can't I?"

"Because I want them!"

His eyes widen. "You want to eat cheesy puffs?"

I nod. "Yeah!"

He snorts. "Since when do you eat cheesy puffs? You're allergic to them, and you hate them. I believe you described them once as 'vile toxic waste never before seen in nature.'"

I twist my lips. "Oh yeah. I do hate them."

Huh. How weird. Gunna despises cheesy puffs but Lottie loved them. What does that mean? Am I still Lottie? Only one delicious way to find out. I rip open the bag, pop one in my mouth, and let that tart, fake-cheese coat my tongue for a second before biting into that crispy cloud of puff.

I moan. "So good." And I don't feel sick. Gunna sometimes pukes. Some allergic reaction to the dye or something.

Bjorn's eyebrows draw together. "You feel ok?"

I don't answer. I'm not sure how I feel. I thought I left Lottie behind? I thought choosing this path meant I was no longer myself. I was no longer Lottie. But then why do I love cheesy puffs?

"Gunna?"

"I think I'm fine." I grin. "But let's really test it." I stuff a handful of cheesy puffs into my mouth, like a squirrel loading up with nuts, and savor every little bite. I swallow and wait.

No reaction. Just happy taste buds.

I laugh. "This is awesome! I still love cheesy puffs!"

Bjorn chuckles. "I didn't know you ever loved them, but I'm guessing by your reaction I'm going to have to share from now on."

I nod and stuff another handful in my mouth. He reaches to grab a few and I slap his hand away.

Bjorn puts up his hands, and laughs. "Okay. Okay. You can keep your bag of orange candy. You have a lifetime of dye to catch up on." He grabs crackers from his bag. "Hey, I know you were joking before about the horse being my hair twin, but really, does my hair look okay?"

His blond hair is now peeking out from the bottom of a gray woolen beanie. I think it makes his blue eyes pop, and looks way better than when his hair was wet from the waterfall and sticking-out-in-all-directions.

I nod. "Yeah. I think it looks cool."

His mouth turns up into an embarrassed smile, and it makes me happy. The reason why I'm happy is right at the tip of my brain, trying to break through... but I can't quite reach it. Maybe I'm feeling this way because this reminds me of Lottie's brother dressing up for his girl crush? Bjorn must like Bridgit or Camille!

Bjorn climbs out of the Jeep, so I set down the bag of cheesy puffs and follow. Lottie may have let her brother down when he had a crush, but that's not going to happen here. I'm Gunna now and I'm going to help Bjorn impress his crush any way I can.

Camille and Bridgit are huddled in the misty rain at the back of the Jeep. Nils is already at the fence, petting a very short, bulbously fat, black horse with a blond mane.

"You gals ready?" I ask.

"They really like lady fingers." Bjorn jokes as he strolls past and heads over to join Nils at the fence.

Camille frowns. "I think I'm going to pass."

"Why?" Bridgit asks.

"You heard what he said."

Bridgit sighs. "He's just being cheeky." She glances at me and rolls her eyes. "I think your brother is scaring her."

Oh! I bet Bjorn likes Camille and thinks teasing her is like flirting. I shake my head. I better fix this.

"My brother's just trying to be funny. They really won't nibble your fingers off."

Camille blushes. "I know."

She's blushing? Oooo... maybe she likes him, too!

Camille leans against the Jeep. "Horses just aren't my thing. I prefer watching them from a distance."

"But you're in Iceland," Bridgit says. "Don't you want to experience it all?"

"I'm experiencing exactly what I want," Camille answers.

And I know what she means. I chose this soul jumping thing for the same reason. I only want to experience some things, like happiness and joy, and I will happily ignore pain and sadness and melancholy from a distance.

Camille waves a gloved hand toward the fence. "You two go on. I'm totally fine right here. Really."

"You sure?" I ask.

She nods and grins. "Completely."

Bridgit and I walk down the hill to join Bjorn and Nils. The black horse Nils was petting is now leaning so far over the fence that it's blond mane is touching the ground and it's roly-poly body looks like it just might topple head first right over the fence.

"I've never..." Bjorn is laughing so hard that he can't finish his sentence. He motions us closer. "You've... got to... see this," he manages to say between guffaws. He points to Nils. "Watch."

Nils grins at us. "Ladies! Are you prepared to see something so amazing that your lives will never be the same?"

I almost laugh out loud. I have seen many something amazings and my life is no longer the same. But I don't say that. I just nod along with Bridgit.

Nils looks the black horse in the eye. "Blackie, catch," he commands, and tosses a cracker into the air.

The horse snaps up its head, follows the cracker's descent with its long nose, and then catches the cracker in mid-air just like a dog catching a treat.

Bridgit claps. "Smashing, Blackie! Do it again!"

Nils pulls another cracker from the box, tosses it up, and the horse catches it again.

"That's awesome!" I gush, all flirty-like. "Can I try?"

Nils hands me a cracker. I immediately feel a zing when our fingers touch and wonder if he does, too. I like the feeling, but then my stomach tightens. Nils is charming and cute, and I really like him, but I still don't want to get too attached. I need to be ready to leave whenever I want.

"Here Blackie," I say and flip the cracker up into the air. It soars up… and careens down, right past Blackie's muzzle and onto the ground.

I arch my eyebrow at Nils. "Well-trained, you say?"

He laughs, a gleam in his hazel eyes. "I taught him that trick, too. It's called Oopsie daisy."

I giggle.

Nils tosses up another cracker and Blackie catches it. He grins at me, with that little dimple melting my heart. "It's all in how you throw it."

"Then maybe you'll just have to teach me," I coo.

I just know Nils would have scooped me up into his arms and told me how much he'd love to teach me if Bjorn didn't interrupt us just then. Brothers!

"The others are getting jealous," Bjorn says, pointing to the mob of shaggy horses straining against the fence trying to get closer to the food.

"We're about to have a mutiny on our hands," Bridgit says nervously.

"It's okay." Nils says. "I'm on it."

He tosses a cracker at a chestnut-and-white paint squashed next to Blackie, but the cracker just falls to the ground and the other horses almost trample the paint and Blackie trying to find it.

Bjorn laughs. "I don't think the rest of them know that trick yet."

Nils shakes his head. "Nope." He glances over at Bjorn and grins. "I guess there can only be one special horse in everyone's life."

I really hope he's referring to me, and not to Blackie.

"How do I feed the others so I don't lose my fingers?" Nils asks.

I don't even have time to offer my help before Bjorn flattens Nils' hand, places a cracker in it, and pushes him towards the paint. "Just keep your palm flat."

Nils takes a step forward and extends his hand. The paint gobbles the cracker up before his next-door neighbor can.

"That tickles!" Nils laughs. He looks down at his hand and frowns. "And that's a lot of slobber." He looks up, grins mischievously, and wipes his goopy hand right on Bjorn's jacket.

Bjorn howls and jumps out of reach, dropping the box of crackers. Nils sprints after him, chasing him around the Jeep like a couple of little boys.

I pick up the box of crackers and look at Bridgit. "Guess it's up to us to feed the others."

Bridgit starts at one end one and I take the other. It only takes a few minutes to empty the box, and I offer the last cracker to the chestnut mare with the frosty blond mane that I joked was Bjorn's twin. The horse greedily slurps it up and then peers up at me. Her coarse mane is such a dense curtain that I can't even see her eyes.

"No need to hide, little one," I murmur, gently combing aside her mane and exposing warm brown eyes framed by thick, reddish-brown eyelashes.

She snorts, and her eyes widen, almost as if she's fearful of what she can now see without her mane blinding her.

My heartbeat slows. I know how she feels. I was once only Lottie. I thought the worst thing ever was the pain and anxiety I felt. Then my soul pulled my mane back and shoved me into all those bodies trying to get me to feel and see everything. Like Mum's pain in Morocco. And the bombing in Kabul. And my captor in Bangkok.

For a moment, I wish my mane had never been pulled back. I wish I had never seen all those horrible things, and that I was Lottie again.

The mare quickly shakes her mane back over her eyes, drops her head, and exhales a sigh.

"You're right," I whisper, caressing her velvety nose. "It's better this way."

Camille's voice brings me back to the present.

"Is it snowing?" she asks.

She's standing a few steps behind me, and I was so lost in my thoughts that I didn't hear her approach or see the white flakes falling softly around us.

"Looks like it," I reply, and raise my chin to the sky, hoping to catch snowflakes like Lottie always did in Colorado.

"But snow in April?" Camille asks in disbelief.

I laugh. "Yep."

"But it was sunny like twenty minutes ago."

I chuckle. "Well, you know how they say 'If you don't like the weather, just wait a few minutes and it will change'?"

She nods.

I grin. "Iceland invented that phrase." I notice one more cracker hiding in the box. I pull it out and hold it out to Camille. "One left. I'm pretty sure this sweet girl won't hurt you."

Camille shakes her head. "No, thank you. No offense to Bridgit, but I really have no desire to experience it all."

"No offense taken," Bridgit laughs behind us.

Camille blushes. "Sorry, you weren't supposed to hear that."

Bridgit waves it off. "Didn't offend me, but won't you be sorry if you don't try it?"

Camille shakes her head. "Nope. The thought of it makes me so anxious that I know doing it will frighten me, and I don't like feeling scared."

I get that. I hated feeling anxious. No. I meant, Lottie hated feeling anxious.

"But if you've never tried it, how do you know how you'll feel?" Bridgit prods.

Camille shrugs. "I don't. But at least I won't be scared."

I understand, and that's why I'm here. I may be missing out on experiencing some things, but I'm choosing to live in happy bodies so that I don't have to experience any anxiety, or pain, or sadness. And right now I'm exploring a new place, meeting new people, and hopefully will be kissing a very cute, Swiss boy soon. So far missing out on the bad in order to be happy is all good!

Bridgit heads back to the Jeep and I feed the last cracker to the sweet mare.

"They're really cute together, don't you think?" Camille murmurs.

I nod. "Especially this time of year when they haven't shed their coats yet. I think they look like big, well-loved teddy bears."

"What?"

"Well, they still have their winter hair. That's why they're so shaggy."

She bursts out laughing. "Oh! You're talking about the horses."

I arch an eyebrow. "Um, yeah. What are you taking about?"

"Them." She nods her head towards the Jeep where Bridgit, Bjorn, and Nils are all leaning against the Jeep.

Them? Bridgit is standing next to Bjorn, laughing at something he said, and Nils is standing next to Bjorn, grinning. Oh! She must mean Bridgit and Bjorn. I'm wondering if Bridgit told her that she likes Bjorn, but before I can ask, Bjorn motions to us.

"We better get going," he says.

I give the sweet mare one more pat and follow Camille up the hill.

"Want to me to drive?" I offer when I reach the Jeep, and then suddenly realize that I'm only fifteen in this body and I can't drive. Oops. Guess that download didn't hit in time. Wonder what else I'm missing?

Bjorn snorts. "I don't think so. You still have two more years, sister."

Two years?! Am I'm only fourteen?!

"At least you can drive here when you're seventeen," Nils laments. "Camille and I had to wait until we were eighteen in Switzerland."

Oh, okay. Whew. I am fifteen.

Wait a minute.

"You're eighteen?" I marvel, suddenly feeling butterflies in my stomach. An older guy likes me. V-e-r-y cool.

Nils laughs. "Yeah. Five years ago."

Gulp. A much older guy.

Bjorn tilts his head. "You're twenty-three like me?"

Nils nods and grins. "Just like you."

Bjorn's cheeks pinken again, and that fuzzy thought dashes through my brain, but I'm too busy watching Nils' cute bootie climb into the Jeep to pay attention.

CHAPTER 28

Haven't I been here before?

The sun is playing peek-a-boo with the snow clouds, but it doesn't matter. The scenery outside my window is spectacular.

We're driving on a road that looks like a snake slithering between snowcapped mountains on one side and the dark sea on the other. Black volcanic rocks surround us. Massive boulders on the mountainside of the road grow increasingly smaller on the other side until they dissolve into black volcanic beaches plunging into the cold sea.

It's funny that this stark scenery takes my breath away because I know this body has seen this all before. You'd think Gunna would be bored by the same old thing, but maybe she's a little like Lottie. No matter how much time Lottie spent at Conifer Lake, she still thought it was one of the most beautiful places on earth. Maybe Gunna thinks the same thing about Iceland. Which I guess is good because I'm Gunna, not Lottie.

I point to a hill of ice jutting out of the mountain like a massive frozen waterslide.

"That's one of the glacial tongues of the Vatnajökull glacier," I explain.

"It's huge!" Bridgit exclaims.

"Yeah, it is. It's probably as wide as one hundred Jeeps, but the entire glacier is 8,100 square kilometers. Which is like a million Jeeps! So, this tongue is really just a teeny baby tongue on a massive dinosaur."

Bjorn rolls his eyes. "I don't think it's a million Jeeps."

I shrug, and grin. "It's probably close. Anyway, Vatnajökull is the largest glacier in Iceland, and one of the largest in Europe. Which is why we've been driving for over thirty minutes and we still haven't passed all of it."

Bjorn makes a left onto a small, dirt road that will lead us up to the icy tongue.

"Settlers back in the 11th century found forests and great soil in Iceland," I continue. "Then the glaciers started growing during the ice age, and the glacier tongues basically gobbled up all those farms." I turn in my seat. "Did you know glaciers can sometimes move over teo-hundred meters a week?"

"And that's like a million Jeeps!" Bjorn pipes in with a laugh.

"Maybe even two million!" Nils adds.

I grin. "Funny, you two. I think it's more like twenty-five Jeeps."

Bridgit whistles. "Blimey. That's still a long way for what seems like an inanimate object to move in just a week."

I nod. "That's because glaciers are a perfect example of the natural process of growing and changing. Strong rivers run beneath the glacial tongue, and those rivers constantly change the landscape so much that Iceland even has movable bridges."

"And those same rivers also like to sweep postmen into the sea to their deaths," Bjorn adds in a creepy voice.

"Whaat?" Camille stammers.

Bridgit rolls her eyes. "He's just trying to scare you again."

I bite my lip. "Actually, this time he's telling the truth. Jökulhlaup is an Icelandic word we use to describe a glacial flood. These days we know that jökulhlaup happens every year or two, mostly in the spring or summer, but long ago they didn't know…" I trail off, not really wanting to go into any sad details. I don't do sad anymore.

Bjorn unfortunately continues my thought. "Our glaciers are on top of volcanoes. When the volcano erupts, tons of water rushes down the glacier drowning everything," he lowers his voice, "and everybody in its path."

Bridgit's eyes grow big as saucers. Camille gasps.

I punch Bjorn. "Quit scaring everyone!" I turn back to the girls. "That's not going to happen today. The part of the glacier we're going to is very safe."

"Well, maybe I'll just stay in the Jeep anyway," Camille murmurs. "No sense asking for trouble."

"And I better keep her company," Bridgit adds.

Uh oh. I don't like the fear that they're feeling. Maybe it's time for me and my soul to take a first class ticket out of here. But I really don't want to leave yet. I need to see if I can get Nils to like me.

"You took it too far," I hiss at Bjorn, quiet enough that only he can hear me. What is it about boys that they think scaring girls will suddenly make a girl fall in love? Geeesh!

Bjorn quickly glances over at me, sees I'm not kidding, and immediately looks chagrined. "Gunna's right," he quickly says. "Sorry if I scared you. I personally guarantee that we are safe here. I promise."

"Do you promise on Nils' life?" Camille asks.

"Hey!" Nils says. "Why my life?"

Camille shrugs, but winks at me.

Bjorn doesn't even hesitate. "Most definitely."

"Okay," Bridgit says, sounding more relaxed. "I believe you. I'll get out at the glacier."

Camille still looks a little nervous, but she nods her head. "Okay. Me, too."

I sigh in relief, happy that the mood is light again. It would have been a bummer if I had to leave before kissing Nils.

Bjorn pulls into a dirt parking area that hugs the base of the glacier. The landscape here is surreal. The glacial tongue looks like a wavy, blue carpet of ice filling the valley between two, snow-capped mountains. Although this ribbon of ice looks short compared to the towering mountains, the tongue is taller than a five-story building and wider than most downtown cities.

Bjorn cuts off the motor and turns to face our passengers. "This is where you will all learn how to walk on ice, so meet at the back of the Jeep to get your crampons."

"And be sure to dress warmly," I add. "The sun may disappear behind the mountain before we're back, and that makes it feel even more cold."

Bjorn and I hurry to the back of the Jeep. I hand out the poles and axes, while Bjorn helps everyone put crampons over their snow boots. Once everyone is fitted with gear, I slip on my crampons and lead the group over to the edge of the glacier.

"While we wait for Bjorn to lock up, I'll teach you the basics of walking with crampons," I announce. "Think of it as having four-wheel-drive for your feet, which means you must walk differently than you normally do." I pick up my foot and plant it firmly on a patch of icy snow in front of me. "You must keep at least one foot on the ice with all the crampon spikes, called points, on the ice at all times. And shorten your steps so that you keep your center of gravity over the points that are in contact with the ice. Now everyone try walking, but stay here on the ice that's covered in snow."

Nils and Bridgit are gung ho to try it. Bridgit gets the hang of it after only a few steps, but Nils is lifting his knees all the way up to his chest and then slamming his points into the snow so hard that slivers of ice explode underneath his feet. I rush over.

"You're doing great, Nils, but you're so strong that if you keep slamming your foot into the ice like that, you're going to crack it." I give him what I hope is a flirty smile.

His forehead furrows. "Really?"

I giggle. "Sorry. No, not really. But try walking a little more softly and don't lift your knees so high." I raise my foot and push it into the snow. "More like this."

"It doesn't seem like they're going to hold me," he says. "I feel like I'm going to slip if I don't cram them into the ice."

I nod. "I know it feels that way, but these points are so sharp, they'll grip even the slickest patch of ice." I point to a patch of ice without any snow. "Why don't you try it there? And if you want, you can hold on to me until you feel more comfortable."

He looks relieved and grabs my arm. I feel a sizzling zing that makes me shiver all the way to my toes. I really like it, but this is how Lottie felt when she used to hold Dillon's hand, and I know how that ended.

No! Get a grip on your memories. I've left that life behind. I'm not anxious, or in pain, or suffering from Oh my GAD. I may still love cheesy puffs, but I'm not Lottie anymore.

I smile at Nils. "Ready to try it again?"

He nods, focuses on his feet, and takes a few steps. After a few more tries, he's walking on his crampons with no problems.

"You got it," I say proudly, hoping he's so grateful for my help that he'll fling his arms around me and give me a well-deserved kiss. Instead, he let's go of my arm.

"Now I'm okay?" he asks, his hazel eyes bright with excitement.

I grin. "Yep. You look like you were born to walk on ice."

He hugs me, and I feel searing warmth spread everywhere as a little butterfly does a happy dance in my stomach.

"Thanks so much for helping me!" He glances around us, and his cheeks pinken when he whispers, "I would have hated to make a fool of myself in front of Bjorn."

What?

And then all of a sudden that little fuzzy thought I've been missing becomes crystal clear. Nils likes Bjorn. Bjorn likes Nils. Because my brother, Bjorn, is gay.

 I stumble away from Nils. This may not be a surprise to this Gunna body, but I am shocked to my core at this déjà vu.

Nils doesn't like me. He likes Bjorn. Dillon didn't like me either. He liked that boy.

My heart starts racing. I can see Nils' moving his mouth, but all I hear is the blood rushing through my ears.

CHAPTER 29

Everyone deserves to be loved

I see darkness. And those little black and grey swirly things that always appear when you close your eyes. My soul must have jumped bodies again.

I'm wondering why I felt so nauseous the last time my soul jumped and not this time, but then I hear Bjorn call my name.

"Gunna! Can you hear me?"

Crap. I'm still here in Iceland. I debate faking sleep, or possibly my death, until I can get my soul to jump, but then I feel something really cold on my forehead and my arm instinctively jerks to wipe it off.

"The magic of snow," Bjorn chuckles. "Come on. Open your eyes."

I really don't want to. I would rather not deal with being rejected by a boy again. Nothing happy is bound to come out of that. I fake stillness again.

Okay, Soul. Time to scram-o. Get outtta town. Vammooose!

"Bjorn, stop it! That's really cold!"

Oh crap. I'm pretty sure that was me yelling.

Bjorn laughs. "It's snow. It's supposed to be cold. But it's working. Are you going to open your eyes, or do you want another?"

I know Bjorn's just going to keep smothering my face with snow until I open my eyes, so I groan and just do it. Bjorn and Nils are kneeling on either side of my head while Camille and Bridgit are standing behind them, their faces drawn with worry.

I can't deal with Nils just yet, so I focus on Bjorn. He's holding a fist full of snow and it's headed toward my face. I growl, grab his fist, and smash the snow into his face.

Bjorn just laughs. "At least I know you're feeling better. Sorry, I was just trying to wake you. Do you want to sit up?"

I nod. "Yeah."

Bjorn slips his arm under my shoulder. I feel Nils slip his arm under my other shoulder, but I ignore the zing of electricity and keep my attention focused on Bjorn.

"What happened?" Nils asks. "I was walking up when you keeled over. Nils thought maybe you passed out or something." He glances over at Nils.

I don't glance over at Nils.

"One minute we were talking," Nils explains, "and then your eyes rolled back and you started falling. Luckily, Bjorn ran up behind you and caught you."

I don't have to see Nils' face to hear the affection in his voice. Oh yay. Bjorn is his hero. How wonderful. Let me just rejoice in my rejection and be happy for you. Or… NOT!

"But Nils is the one who stopped you from falling," Bjorn adds. "He grabbed your arm, slowing your fall just enough that I could get over here and catch you." He gives Nils a look I've seen before. A smile full of affection just like Dillon had for his boy. The one that sent me over the edge that day.

I brace for my anger to rear its ugly head… but it doesn't come.

Weird. I should be upset. I just found out that the cute guy I like and I thought liked me, doesn't. But instead of freaking out, my sadness is dissolving. And now I feel sort of happy. Which I guess makes sense. Lottie would be angry because of her past, but I'm Gunna now. And Gunna would be very happy for her brother.

I bat my eyes at Bjorn. "You're my hero," I coo, and my silliness brings more happy into my heart.

Bjorn smiles. "You know I'm always here for you, Sis."

And I do know that. Bjorn has been there for Gunna her whole life. I see flashes in my memory. Bringing her a cupcake when she failed her science test. Picking her up from school because she didn't want to take the bus with the school bully. Giving her hugs, just because.

Gunna is one lucky gal.

I stand up. "Well, let's get on with our trek then."

After I assure everyone a million times that I feel fine, Bjorn leads our group onto the glacier. I don't like to lead. It's too stressful. Glaciers are living organisms that must be respected and revered, and you have to really pay attention to where you walk. Trekking on a glacier is not like mindlessly hiking in the park. The ice shifts and changes daily depending on things like heat, or snowfall, or the water running below the ice. And what looks like ribbons of ice from the parking lot, are actually crevices that can be thirty feet deep and twenty feet across.

Most glacier ice is a brilliant light blue. Some sections are cloudy, some have air bubbles, and others are speckled with volcanic rock. It just depends on what was there when the ice was formed. We pass a section of ice that looks dirty because of all the volcanic rock trapped inside, and I suddenly feel like I'm the volcanic rock, trapped here in Gunna's body. Did my soul bring me here to force me to relive Lottie's pain with Dillon?

I walk a little farther and the ice is clear again, but scattered with bubbles suspended in a frozen dance. This also feels like me. I'm a light, airy bubble dancing from body to body, trying to be happy, but still frozen in space with the same memories.

Bjorn stops everyone at the edge of a deep crevasse. I peek over the edge at the river of water gushing between the sapphire ice thirty feet below. This is a rare glimpse of the mighty river raging underneath the glacier. The river controls the glacier, and the glacier must change with the river. It must be willing to change. Or it will no longer exist.

Maybe I'm like the glacier. Maybe my soul is the river, and I must change to survive. I must learn to feel everything again, or I will no longer exist.

I shake my head. Whoa! Let's reel in the deep thoughts for a while. How about we just walk, and enjoy, and be happy? That's why I'm here, right?

The sun has set, so Bjorn leads our group back to the Jeep. We collect everyone's gear, and I secure it in the back. Bjorn's already got the heat cranking and giving instructions for our next stop when I climb into the front seat.

"Go ahead and keep your coats on," Bjorn advises. "It's only a couple minutes to our next stop." He glances up through the front windshield. "And I think it's going to be a good night for the lights."

"The Northern Lights?" Bridgit asks excitedly.

"Yep." Bjorn turns on the headlights, pulls out of the lot, and leaves the glacier behind us.

"What causes them?" Camille asks.

Bjorn glances at her in the rearview mirror. "Well, they really depend on the sun. When there are storms on the sun, charged solar particles hurtle across space and strike atoms in the earth's atmosphere. This collision is what creates the lights."

Camille sighs. "Amazing that something so far away can affect what we see here."

"I can't wait," Bridgit squeals. "I've never seen them, and it's one of the main reasons I came to Iceland."

Bjorn grins. "Good. Because it's time to see them. Welcome to the Jökulsárlón Glacier Lagoon."

He pulls into another dirt lot, and the headlights illuminate the surreal landscape in front of us. This Gunna body knows that the lagoon is usually sapphire blue in the daylight and spotted with chunks of light blue ice. But at night, the water is inky black and the ghostly chunks of ice almost glow. Some chunks are as tall as two-story buildings, but they all eventually melt smaller and smaller until they finally turn into water in the lagoon. It's basically an ever-changing pot of glacial soup.

Bjorn cuts the lights. "Everyone bundle up, and grab your cameras." He smiles. "And just for Nils, I'll even keep the heat on until everyone's ready."

"Aw, thanks," Nils sings out from the back.

That's sweet, I think to myself. And then don't quite know what to do with that, so I immediately bury anything I'm feeling and pull on my hat and gloves.

Bjorn gives more instructions. "Once we get outside, it may take a few moments for your eyes to adjust to the dark. But don't worry, the sky looks clear and the lights are supposed to be pretty strong tonight, so everyone should be able to see them."

Bjorn is true to his word and waits until everyone is ready before turning off the motor. The girls and Nils climb out, but Bjorn stops me when I reach for my door.

"Hey. Are you really okay? You've hardly said a word since you fell."

He really is a caring brother. Even if this body didn't already know that, I would.

I nod and smile, feeling really happy that he likes me, or Gunna, so much. "Yeah, I'm fine. I'm just feeling a little reflective, that's all."

"Ok." He smiles. "You know I love you, right?"

That warm feeling spreads through my body again, thawing my tension, like when the sun finally appears after a long dark winter. Lottie felt this way when Berg loved her. She was pretty lucky to have that. Just like Gunna.

I grin. "Yep, I know. And I love you, too." I nod to the sky. "Looks like it's going to be a magical night."

He glances past me out the window. "I sure hope so."

I'm pretty sure he's not talking about the lights, but I swallow that thought, open my door, and step outside. The air is cool on my exposed face, but there's no wind. I close my eyes for a moment to let them adjust to the dark, and when I open them again, the sky is plastered with a million, tiny, iridescent stars. It looks like someone took glow-in-the-dark paint and splattered it all over an inky black canvas.

It's so beautiful. I feel my heartbeat slow, and I soak in the happiness.

Camille grabs my arm and tugs me away from the others.

"Everything okay?" I ask.

"Oh yes!" she whispers. "More than okay! This is just breathtaking."

I can barely see her face, but she sounds happy.

"I need to ask you a question and I didn't want anyone else to hear," she whispers.

"Okay."

"Please don't think I'm being forward, but Nils is my favorite cousin and I love him with all my heart, and I would do anything for him." She pauses. "His last boyfriend really shattered his heart, and Nils has been so sad since then that I can't believe he's happy again. So, I just need to know. Is Bjorn a good guy?"

I answer immediately. "Yes. A million times yes. He's one of the best." And I know in my heart that it's true.

She exhales. "Good. Good. I figured he was. And is he… Well, Nils is looking for a relationship. Someone who will be his friend. Someone who will be there for him in both the good times and the bad. He's not just looking for a good time. He's looking for love."

Love?

I glance over and see Bjorn slip his hand into Nils' hand. Then Nils leans over and kisses Bjorn. On… the… lips.

I gasp. Oh my god. I've been here before. I've seen this. The boy I love kissing another boy.

I get ready to bolt. I don't want to feel this pain. That's why I chose this path. I get ready to fight the anger and pain and heartbreak… but it never comes. My heart doesn't break. It squeezes. With joy. Pure, happy joy.

And I suddenly see everything this Gunna body has seen over the years. I know how hard it's been for my sweet, thoughtful, funny brother to find someone. I know how many times he cried on my shoulder about how alone he felt. I know he's been searching for someone to share his life with. To share his deep love.

And now it looks like he might have found that.

And it doesn't matter that it's with a boy. Bjorn is happy. And isn't that what everyone deserves? To be happy.

Isn't that what I'm searching for?

I know I shouldn't, but I think of Dillon. When I saw him kissing that boy, I freaked because all I thought about was myself. I didn't think about how Dillon felt, or about how he deserved to be happy. I only thought about me.

How awful for Dillon or Bjorn to have to stay away from someone they like just because others don't approve. Or worse, to stay with someone you hate, like that devil man in Bangkok, because that's what you feel you have to do. Like Dillon staying with me, even though he loved someone else.

I'm suddenly very ashamed. Dillon didn't hate Lottie. He didn't fall in love with that boy to hurt her. He was just looking for happiness.

I inhale.

"Bjorn is looking for love, too," I tell Camille.

She glances over at the two men that we both love so deeply and murmurs, "Then I'm happy that they found each other."

I nod. "Me, too."

And suddenly the northern lights are here. A shimmering wave of green dances across the sky, bouncing among the stars with glee until it flickers and fades into darkness. I know this body has seen them before, but I never have, and they are utterly glorious. I watch another flickering curtain paint triumphant streaks across the starry sky, and I smile.

Well, I didn't get the boy, but I got to see some amazing things. And I think maybe I even understand a little bit why Dillon chose that boy over me. We can't make ourselves love someone. It just happens. Whether it's a boy loving a girl, or a boy loving a boy, or a girl loving a girl. It just is.

Okay, Soul. It's time to get on the road again. I'm ready for more happy. And I'd still love to see Paris. The one in FRANCE that is! But if that's just way too much trouble for you, at least take us somewhere warm.

And then I close my eyes, and wish myself far, far away.

CHAPTER 30

Pain, true love, and a wedding

I hear laughter. Happy laughter.

Okay, Soul. So far so good.

I'm not cold anymore and my stomach is rolling a bit, so we must have jumped bodies. I hope for the best and open my eyes.

I'm lying on a bed, staring up at wispy pink veiling and drowning in orange and purple pillows. The room is painted a bright teal blue, the ceiling is covered in ornate metallic tiles, and red and purple bejeweled lanterns hang under arched doorways in every corner.

I can't believe it! I'm back in the bedroom I shared with Malika! I jump up, race over to the pale pink wardrobe, and look in the mirror. And I'm Aicha, again!

I hear someone singing. "Wow! Wow! Wow! I'm getting married today!" and I totally recognize that sweet voice singing the goofy song I made up. That's the voice that started this whole, crazy, soul-jumping adventure. That's my sister, Malika. And today must be her wedding!

Right on, Soul! This is a happy place!

I follow Malika's happy song across the courtyard and into our mother's room. Malika is sitting on a purple, cushioned stool in front of a small dressing table and mirror. Auntie is curling her hair and Malika is beaming from ear to ear.

"Happy wedding day!" I sing.

Malika sees me in the mirror and purses her lips.

I grin. "Are you beyond excited?"

She doesn't respond.

Why is she mad at me? What did I do the last time I was here? I can barely remember with everything that has happened since then. Let's see. We were having fun at her henna party. She was happy and showing me her henna… oh. And then I left.

No problemo. If there's one thing I've learned, it's that no one can stay mad at a happy girl who spreads happiness. And I'm still not doing mad. Only happy.

I grin at Auntie. She's seen my boobs. I've seen her boobs. I feel like we have a connection now. "May I please take over?"

Auntie raises her eyebrows so high that they almost disappear under her headscarf.

I grin wider. "Pretty please."

No response.

Okay. Time to pour it on thick. "But it's my only sister," I pout. "I've dreamed my entire life about how I would curl her beautiful hair for her wedding day. I practiced on dolls. And made charts. And took classes. Well, not really classes. More like practiced on other girls, like at homecoming and stuff." Now I'm rambling. And I don't even know if they have homecoming in Morocco. "I can't wait to make this day extra special just for her."

Auntie looks at Malika, who rolls her eyes and shrugs. Auntie smiles and hands me the iron.

Success! Auntie likes me again. Look at me spreading my happiness.

"Thanks so much!" I squeal. As Auntie leaves the room I call after her. "Don't worry, I'm going to make this a day she'll always remember."

"Really?" Malika mutters. "That must be why you slept so late."

"Now, now, sassy sister of mine," I chuckle. "I'm not that late to the party."

She turns to glare at me. "Really? It's already seven-thirty. At night. Our guests start arriving in thirty minutes."

Uh oh.

"I'm so sorry." I gently turn her to face the mirror again. I grab a section of her hair and slide it through the curling iron. "Why didn't you wake me?"

She shrugs. "After the way you've been acting, I really didn't think you cared."

She tries to grab the iron out of my hand, but I bat her hand away. I release the curl and it falls into a perfect spiral on her shoulder. I set the curling iron on the table and kneel down next to her. I grab her hands and squeeze them tightly between mine.

"I do care," I insist, surprised at how much I truly mean it. "I really do. I want you to be happy on your wedding day, and I promise I'm going to do everything I can to make it the happiest day of your life."

Malika sniffs like she doesn't believe me. And she has good reason. Last time I was here, I tried to steal her blue jilbab, went shopping instead of going to the hammam, and then I selfishly skipped out on her henna party. And now I've missed the entire day of wedding prep. I have not been a very good sister. But I refuse to feel sad and guilty. That's all in the past. I need to let it all go. I'm here now, and I'm going to make it up to her by making her happy.

I stand up and bow. "My stunning sister and wedding day queen, please forgive me. And pretty, pretty please with a cherry on top allow me to bring you happiness by asking me to do anything!" I make a face. "Unless you ask me to eat pickled squid. That I won't do. Even for you."

A grin tugs at her lips.

I roll my eyes. "Okay. Okay. I'll eat your slimy squid. You happy now?"

That makes her snort. "Oh, Aicha, you're crazy."

I shrug. "Only if you won't let me help you."

She welcomes the grin onto her face. "I can never stay mad at you. You're my favorite sister!"

Now it's my turn to grin. "I'm your only sister."

She waggles her eyebrows. "Exactly."

She reaches out to hug me and I eagerly let her. My stomach fills with butterflies of happiness.

She pulls away first. "I love this, but I have to get ready. Want to help me put on my first dress?"

"I'd love to!" I squeal, and I really mean it.

She grabs my hand and pulls me over to Mum's bed. It's drowning in colorful dresses and gobs of gold jewelry.

"Girls." Mum's voice drifts in from the doorway. Her cheeks are flushed, and her eyes are wide, but she looks lovely. She's wearing a scarlet-red kaftan dripping with elegant, gold appliques and cinched at the waist with a golden belt trimmed in silver crystals. She gestures to the three women standing behind her dressed in identical cream kaftans. "The neggafate are here."

I'm already tuned into Aicha so I know Mum hired the neggafate to help Malika change into her dresses and jewelry over the next eight hours of the wedding.

I want to speak privately with Mum and apologize. I don't want her to be mad at me either. So as the women descend upon Malika, I sidle up to Mum.

"Are you feeling better?" she asks, her face a beautiful mask.

I nod. "Yes, thank you." I inhale a deep breath. "I know I was being selfish before, and I'm really sorry. But now I'm going to do everything I can to make this day happy."

Mum's red lips swell into a smile. "I know you will, Aicha. You are an amazing sister, and I love you. I love every part of you, the good and the bad. And I always will."

Wow. I didn't expect her to say that. She loves Aicha despite all the crap I've done. I wonder if Lottie's mama would do that, too. After everything she did.

Not that I should care about that anymore. I may never be Lottie again.

"And I will love you even more when you are dressed!" Mum scolds with a grin. She hugs my waist and motions to one of the neggafate. "Please help her. She must go up before her sister." She presses her forehead against mine. "Promise you'll come up to the roof as soon as you are ready?"

I smile. "I promise." I'm so happy that she's so happy that I might burst.

"That's my amazing girl," she says, and kisses my cheek before leaving the room.

One of the neggafate introduces herself as Aya and hands me my kaftan. I know Mum had this one specially hand-made for me for the wedding, and I'm so grateful. It's really stunning. It's made of a deep blue silk with a tiny wave of purple and orange flowers cascading down one side. Gold embroidery trims the neckline and a wide gold belt cinches it all together.

I add a few curls to my long, black hair; and when Aya places a delicate gold tiara on my head and drapes a gold necklace dripping with deep blue crystals around my neck, I get positively giddy with happiness.

"I feel like a princess!" I gush to my reflection in the mirror.

Malika hugs my shoulders. "You look like a princess," she coos.

She's only wearing the sheer white gown that goes under her first kaftan, but she's glowing and grinning, and looks more lovely than I've ever seen her.

I bow to her. "But I'll never be as beautiful as you, oh best-sister-ever who didn't make me eat pickled squid!"

She giggles. And that makes my heart burst with even more joy. I feel full of happiness and I want to spread it!

I grasp her hands in mine. "You truly are as beautiful and kind on the inside as you are on the outside." And without even thinking about it, I say her name just like Lottie always did with Berg. "I love you, Big M."

Malika's eyes fill with tears. "Oh, Aicha. You haven't called me that since before I tried on my henna dress!" She squeezes me in a hug, and sniffles, "I thought you were angry with me, because I'm getting married and leaving."

One of the neggafate glares at me before wiping Malika's eyes with a tissue.

I squeeze her hands tighter. "Oh no! I've never been mad at you. I'm so very happy for you, and I just want you to be happy." This time I'm not just saying it make her happy. This time I mean it, and it feels good.

"I love you, Little A," she says, pulling me into a hug. "You're the best sister ever."

I hug her tight and breathe in the happiness and joy. This is love, too. A strong, amazing sibling love. A love like Gunna and her brother had. Like Lottie and Berg had.

Aya clears her throat. "I'm sorry to interrupt, but we really need to help the bride get ready. The wedding is about to begin."

I give Malika one more squeeze and then pull away. If I can't go back to Berg, then I'm happy I will have her to love.

I grin. "Now you need to get ready for your big day, and I need get upstairs before Mum comes searching for us!" I kiss her on the cheek. "See you up there, Big M."

I dash out of the room and take the stairs two at a time, which is hard to do in the tight kaftan. I somehow make it to the top without ripping anything, and when I walk out onto the rooftop a gorgeous scene of happiness and color greets me.

The billowy white tent is still overhead, but the roof is now filled with round tables draped in soft-pink tablecloths and topped with ornate, white lanterns. Giggling children are chasing each other around the tables while smiling women and men are mingling and chatting like old friends.

Half the men are wearing long, cream robes while the other half are donning crisp, dark suits. The women add striking splashes of color to the dark night. I see kaftans in rich crimson, deep purple, pale peach, dark pink, and even deep blue like mine. A few women are wearing colorful headscarves, but most have their hair flowing free.

Auntie greets me. "Aicha, you look stunning!" She hands me a glass of milk. "For love," she explains. Then she hands me a date, and winks. "And for fertility."

I know this is typical to give wedding guests, but hearing my aunt say "fertility" makes me blush. I hope she doesn't expand on what she means, and luckily, the band begins playing and saves me.

"Your sister is arriving!" Auntie announces. She grabs my hand and tugs me to the front of the mob that's suddenly crowded near the dance floor. Mum floats out of the mob to stand beside me.

She smiles warmly. "You look beautiful, my darling."

My body hums with happy.

The door opens, and Malika's soon-to-be husband, Youssef, leads the lavish procession onto the roof. He's dressed elegantly in a dark suit, his black hair short and cropped, and his grin huge. Behind him, four men are holding up a throne called an amaria. Each man is dressed in a long, avocado-colored robe trimmed in gold, and wearing a red fez on their head. The amaria is elaborately adorned with gold and pearls, and has four white pillars holding up a thin roof.

My beautiful sister is sitting on a pillow under the roof. Her silk kaftan is the palest pink and finely beaded with gold and silver. Her dark hair is flowing down from a golden tiara, and she's waving to everyone and grinning with such elation that her eyes are nearly closed. All the guests clap and cheer as the procession makes its way across the rooftop, and I make certain I'm whooping the loudest.

The men set the amaria down. Youssef extends his hand, helps Malika up from her perch on the pillow, and leads her to sit on a purple velvet couch. This is the meet-and-greet part of the wedding where the guests can congratulate the bride-and-groom. Mum and I hurry over so we can greet them first. Youssef is holding Malika's hand tight, and they are both grinning like crazy.

I lean over to give her Malika hug. "You look so happy and so beautiful," I burble. I don't know why but I feel tears in my eyes, and I don't want them. I shake them off and laugh. "Tell me that ride was as fun as it looked?"

Malika only has time to nod before Mum gently pulls me to stand beside her as the mob arrives. The guests greet the bride-and-groom, and we greet the guests. It's a whirlwind of talking, and laughing, and flashes of light that goes on and on, but I love every second of being surrounded with so much love and joy.

When Malika leaves to change outfits, Mum motions to the dance floor. "Go have some fun, Aicha."

"Are you sure?" I ask. I want to make sure everyone is happy tonight, and that includes Mum.

She nods. "Yes, I'm absolutely sure. I need to check on the dinner preparations."

"Do you need my help?" I ask, secretly hoping she says no. Dancing sounds way more fun.

She shakes her head, kisses me on the cheek, and smiles. "No, thank you. I'm fine. You deserve to be happy tonight, too."

I like the sound of that so I make my way over to the dance floor, feel the music and just let go. Almost immediately a group of my cousins join me, and soon we're all jumping around like lunatics together. Crazy, dancing lunatics! And I don't care one bit what I look like. Cause I'm happy.

The music slows and couples start to pair up. After the Nils fiasco in Iceland, I'm not feeling particularly romantic, so I excuse myself from the group and find Mum standing by the door.

"Perfect timing," Mum says. Her red lips spread into a huge grin as she nods to the stairway. "There's the beautiful bride now."

Malika walks onto the rooftop wearing a violet kaftan embroidered with bright silver swirls. Her hair is twirled into a low bun at the nape of her neck.

I clap my hands together. "I take back what I said earlier. Now you are even more beautiful!"

Malika laughs. "Spoken by the best sister ever."

I'm about to give her a hug, but her face lights up at something over my shoulder. I turn to see what she loves more than her sister and am not really surprised to see Youssef rushing to her. He caresses her cheek and whispers something in Malika's ear that makes her blush and grin even wider. A memory of Lottie's Dillon pops into my mind so fast that I can't stop it.

They were ice-skating on Conifer Lake around Thanksgiving. The sky had turned dark, threatening a snowstorm, so most people had gone home and Lottie and Dillon had the lake all to themselves. They skated hand in hand, around and around, in a peaceful rhythm that Lottie never wanted to end. But then Lottie hit an uneven chunk of ice, completely lost her balance and pulled Dillon down with her. They both laughed so hard. Then as big, fat, fluffy flakes floated down all around them, Dillon leaned close, caressed her cheek and whispered, "I love you, Lottie." It was the first time he ever said it, with the snow falling gently around them, cocooning them in a moment of warmth.

They had only been dating a month. But they both knew.

Or she thought they did.

My heart races, and my palms grow clammy. That memory should make me happy, but it doesn't. That moment was happy for Lottie. For me. But it was followed by terrible pain when Dillon fell in love with someone else. I was right to leave Lottie behind. To leave George in Texas. Love can be joyous, but it's also so very painful, and I just don't understand how joy and pain can co-exist. It would be like mixing cheesy puffs and strawberry milk. It may seem like a good combination at first, but it's bound to make you sick.

As Lottie knows.

I feel Mum's hand on my shoulder. "Are you okay?" Her eyes are concerned. "You suddenly look so pale."

Everyone around us is singing and laughing, and I want to be happy with them so I shove that memory down deep, and force a smile. "Yes, I'm great. I'm even better than great. I'm so great."

Mum frowns. "I think you need something to eat." She grabs my hand and leads me over to the table where Malika and Youssef are already seated and feeding each other pastillas.

Mum sits next to Malika and pulls me to sit next to her. She places a pastilla on my plate. "Eat," she orders.

The pastilla smells like cinnamon and makes my mouth water. Maybe I am hungry. I bite into the flaky pastry and moan with happiness. It's hot, and the filling tastes like chicken mixed with almond. This will definitely make me feel better.

Lottie's mama used to say she got angry when she was hungry. Hangry she called it. She always gave Lottie a snack and a hug whenever she was hangry. She was always there for Lottie.

No! Stop thinking about that. That's behind us. Think of something funny.

Hangry. That's a funny word. Macadamia. That's another funny word. Flabbergasted. Gobsmacked. Blubber. Brouhaha. Doozy. Kerfuffle. Flatulence. Fart. Fart. Fart.

I giggle.

"Feeling better?" Mum asks with a smile.

I nod and take another pastille.

We spend the next hour feasting. We have steaming couscous mixed with delicate lamb and caramelized onions, an aromatic tagine of tender beef and sweet apricots, and a jumble of brightly colored fruits. I eat so much that my belly poofs out like a happy Buddha.

Malika leaves to change again so I head back out onto the dance floor. I focus only on the happiness surrounding me. The bright music. The cheery faces. The lively singing. I shut my mind to anything negative. It's after midnight, but I don't feel tired. I feel energized, and happy, and alive.

Malika and Youssef reappear together this time. They are each seated on their own cushioned platform carried by four men. Youssef has changed into a white, silk jabador- it looks like a fancy, floor-length hoodie. Malika is finally wearing the traditional labssa fassia. Her dress is a striking gold and forest green, and her golden headdress makes her look like a female King Tut.

Everyone sings and cheers as Malika and Youssef are paraded around the rooftop. They lead everyone in more dancing, and before I realize it another few hours have passed and Malika leaves for her last outfit change.

I finally feel tired. I find a seat by the stairwell door and just look around me. It's 4 AM, and all of the guests are still here, dancing and laughing and happily enjoying every second of this celebratory moment.

Mum plops into a chair next to me. Tiny lines have formed at the edges of her eyes, and her hair is a bit ruffled. She looks tired, but her red lips are grinning, and her eyes are still full of joy. "Are you having a good time?"

I nod. "An amazing time. This really is the best wedding ever."

She smiles. "I hope so. I just want Malika to be happy." She pauses. "That is what we always wanted."

I watch sadness cross her face, and know that when she said "we" she was talking about her husband. I start to panic.

"The way Youssef looks at Malika is the way your father used to look at me," she murmurs. Her smile is still bright, but her eyes glisten with tears. "I still love him, you know. After all these years, I still love him with all my heart."

I watch a few tears escape her perfectly lined eyes and I just can't understand what's happening. Here it is again. Love is supposed to be fun and happy and warm butterflies in your stomach. Not tears and sadness. I didn't like feeling that way with George, and Lottie sure as heck didn't like feeling that way when Dillon moved on to someone new. Is love really worth this sadness? This pain? I just don't know. Bittersweet is meant for chocolate, not for love.

Mum squeezes my hand and gives me a soft smile. "And one day we will do it all for you, my darling."

Um, that would be a big fat, no thanks. Don't get me wrong. The wedding part has been super fun, but I don't think I want any part of this sad/happy roller coaster called love. I'm meant to be happy. That is what I've chosen.

"Is this Malika's last outfit for tonight?" I ask.

Mum wipes her tears, and nods. Her lips spread into a grand smile, wrinkles deepening the creases around her eyes that again fill with tears. "And there she is."

Malika and Youssef walk hand-in-hand onto the rooftop. Malika truly is glowing with happiness and love and life. Her white, silk kaftan is bejeweled with luminescent pearls and shimmering, silver beads. Her dark hair is loose and flowing. She looks just like an angel.

Mum hurries over to greet them, but I stay seated and just watch.

Youssef, still in his dark suit, leads my beautiful sister out to the dance floor. Right now they both look beyond happy. I truly hope this feeling lasts forever for them… but who knows what the future may hold.

It's funny. Even though I'm only borrowing Aicha's body, I feel like the Lottie part of me has really come to love Malika like a sister. Unconditionally. Without wanting anything in return. I smile. It feels nice.

And Mum really loves Aicha, despite her flaws. Just like Lottie's mama. She probably would have forgiven me for everything I did. If I gave her the chance.

But I don't think I'll have that chance.

Well, this wedding has been a blast. Malika's happy. Mum's happy. And I'm really happy for all of them. But I've stayed too long and gotten too attached.

It's time for me to move on.

Yo, Soul! Wake up, big dude. It's time to say goodbye. I learned a lot. Really. I'll concede that real love may be worth the occasional pain for some people, but I'll pass for now. I still think happy all-the-time is the way to go. So, how about we continue this amazing partnership and head somewhere else happy? Comprendo, amigo?

I close my eyes, and smile.

CHAPTER 31

I choose to be me

I know I've jumped bodies again because now I'm so awesome at this.

Ha! Just kidding, Soul.

I know because the wedding music suddenly mutated into beeping horns; and exhaust and road tar assault my nose. I barely register any nausea this time, but my heart is racing and I do feel really sweaty.

I open my eyes.

Whooosh! BEEP!

I'm straddling my bicycle on the side of the road as cars and trucks whiz by me. I'm wearing tennis shoes and a long-sleeved, printed dress over jeans. I peek into the little bike mirror perched on my handlebar and see that I'm sporting wide black sunglasses and a bright blue headscarf over my deep black hair. Something clicks, and I know immediately who I am.

I really am getting the hang of this soul wandering thing!

I'm a fifteen-year-old girl named Zahra, and I'm part of one of the very first girls bike clubs in Kabul, Afghanistan.

Cool! How kickazz am I? Especially rockin' these awesome shades.

I pedal out into the road. A car honks at me, and a man inside yells at me in Dari, "You should not be riding!" But I don't care. I just pedal faster.

I know I risk my life every time I ride. Women are no longer banned from riding bikes, but many people still think it's immoral, and I'm going to change this taboo.

Besides, I love the freedom I feel when I ride. It gives strength to my voice. I feel strong and free and independent. Plus, I can now get to school and the market so much faster and safer.

I reach the market, and stop in front of my favorite stall that sells the best bolani. It also happens to be run by my brother, Hamid.

He wipes his hands on his shalwar kameez and grins at me. "Looking good, Zahra," he says with a sparkle in his walnut eyes. "I just know you'll make the Olympics one day."

My brother is my biggest fan. I smile. "Thanks."

Hamid is older than me, and always tells me that times are changing and women can do anything. In fact, he taught me to ride. He studies at the university when he's not selling bolani. We live in a four-room house on the outskirts of Kabul with our parents, our uncle and his wife, our five cousins, our younger brother, and our four sisters.

Wow! Fourteen of us live in a four-room house?

I also used to have a twin brother, but he died recently in a bombing.

I really am tuning into this body fast! Yay me!

Wait a minute.

My twin brother died in a bombing? I was here in Kabul just a few days ago as a boy. I was buried in rubble after a bombing, and then shot. Was I here as my twin brother? And now I'm back as his twin sister?

Okay, Soul. What's up with coming back here? What do you have up your sleeve, you sly fox?

Hamid hands me a bolani. I bite into the triangle-shaped, soft flatbread and savor the rich pumpkin and leeks that are in it today.

Hamid waves to someone behind me. "Tariq!" he yells.

I turn and see a guy about the same age as my brother. He approaches us, embraces my brother, and they kiss each other on both cheeks. I know this is not because they are lovers, but because they are friends and this is a common greeting here. But either way I don't mind.

Whoa, baby. Look at me. I have come a long way.

"What did you think of Professor Habibullah's lecture today?" Hamid asks, his eyes wide.

Tariq gestures excitedly. "That was by far the best he's given all year."

"And who knew crap could be so interesting?" Hamid laughs.

"Why is crap interesting?" I mumble as I chew.

Hamid explains. "You know those concrete ditches on the side of the road that hold all the poop and stuff?"

I nod. Ick. And double ick. They're worse than an overflowing port-a-potty. Although they do motivate me ride faster.

My brother's face is alive with hope. "Professor thinks our class can help build a sanitation system to replace them!"

"Crap will be a thing of the past!" Tariq jokes.

"It sure will make everything smell better," Hamid adds. He smiles at me. "And then maybe Zahra's class will solve our water problem."

His friend looks at me. "You are planning to go to university?"

I nod. "I hope so. I want to study engineering." I grin. "After I win the Olympics, of course."

Tariq grins back at me, his excitement palpable. "That is wonderful news!"

The two friends return to their discussion about the lecture. I snatch another bolani, and take a moment to look around. I realize I'm back in the same market that was bombed less than a week ago. That day I was smothered by smoke and fire. I faced dead bodies and grim faces. And I gulped in a crapload of fear and pain. The ghosts of that bombing are not only in my memory, but also still visible near the bombing site. Armed police officers cradling their massive machine guns guard the crumbing building that buried me. The tower of rubble and burned stalls are now surrounded by razor wire and scorched dirt.

But as I look around, I notice that the market is back to business as usual. Here in Kabul, the living thrive. We mourn and move on. That day the explosion happened, I grieved my twin's death when I went out for a ride.

I watch a vendor carefully arrange plump, purple eggplants, juicy, red grapes, and crisp, green apples in piles taller than me. In the next stall, another vendor is selling spices. Yellow cumin, green cardamom, brown coriander, and red cloves spill out of their burlap sacks and create a rainbow of color.

There's no wailing or crying today, only the bustling voices of vitality. The living are still here today, and it doesn't matter that they are surrounded by memories of death. They are choosing to move on, and to live.

I spy a young boy's smile as he kicks a handmade soccer ball into an imaginary goal. I study the grim look of determination in the policeman's jaw as he protects what he loves. I watch the faces of my brother and his friend light up as they plan the future.

And I get it.

Well done, Soul. Well done. I still definitely prefer happiness, but I get what you're trying to show me.

This is life. Joy and pain living together. Sometimes in harmony, and sometimes not. But they make it work. Just like here in this market, and in this country. There is the constant pain of war, of a country trying to find peace among numerous tribes and ethnic groups with different cultures and languages. But then there is the joy of fresh fruits and vegetables, of loving families and special friends, of feeling the wind in my face when I ride, and of knowing that we will rebuild.

This Zahra body embraces who she is. A girl who loves to ride. She knows riding her bike still brings great risk to her honor and safety, but she continues riding to hopefully encourage other girls to find their voice. And someday she hopes to make the national team, and then the Olympics. Even though many think she shouldn't ride and think she should be someone she's not, she chooses not to listen to them.

She chooses to be herself.

I wish I could do that. I wish I could just be me. But then I would have to be a girl with an anxiety disorder who feels everything. And I don't think I can do that. I understand how joy and pain can thrive together here in Kabul, and even in the love Mailka and Mum have with their spouses, but I'm not ready. I can't handle the sad. Or the pain. Or the anger. I still just want to be happy.

I gaze over at the snowcapped peaks of the Hindu Kush mountains. They tower over Kabul like a caring mother, spreading her arms wide in a protective way as she whispers, "Don't worry, my sweet child. After all we've been through, I am still here with you. Together, we will get through this. And together we will succeed."

And I have to close my eyes, murmur a silent prayer, and hope she's right.

CHAPTER 32

It's my birthday, and I want to be happy

I open my eyes to find hundreds of people staring up at me, chanting, "Make a wish! Make a wish! Make a wish!"

I've soul jumped again. I'm a little out of breath, and my belly quivers with what I think is excitement, but I feel more grounded than I have in days.

I'm standing on a stage above a large crowd. A marble table in front of me barely contains a gigantic, five-tiered cake, each layer a different color of blue. A girl sporting a neon-pink bob and cartoonishly-long eyelashes is grinning at me.

"Did you think of a good wish?" she asks above the chanting, tucking her arm into mine.

I pause before I answer. I'm not quite sure where I am or what's going on yet.

"Well?" she prods. "Do you know what to wish for?"

Wish for?

I see the candles blazing on top of the cake, and my brain kicks in. I grin a mile wide. It's finally my sixteenth birthday!

Blue and silver metallic ribbons hang from every inch of the ceiling. Bubbles float out of machines surrounding a blue-and-black tiled dance floor. A DJ is blasting tunes. And the place is jam-packed with very attractive, very hip people grinning up at me like they're having the time of their lives.

My name is Ling. I'm Indonesian-Chinese. I live in Singapore, and I'm celebrating my sixteenth birthday party at the Marina Bay Sands with two hundred of my closest friends. And this girl with the pink hair is my older sister, Huan, who just legally changed her name to Pinkie last year.

I inhale a deep breath and blow out all the candles. Pinkie jumps up and down.

"You did it! You have to tell me what you wished for." She stops jumping, and taps her chin. "No, on second thought, don't tell or it might not come true."

I grin. "Don't worry, it will."

"Oh my god! The pop are here!" Pinkie cries.

The pop? Who are the pop? And why don't I know this? I thought I was tuning into my new bodies faster.

Pinkie yanks me around so my back is to the crowd, but she does it so fast that I almost topple over.

Why I am so unsteady on my feet? I look down. OH… MY… GOD. I'm in love. I'm wearing the most insanely gorgeous, sky-high, Jimmy Choo sandals. They're powder-blue with white laces wrapped delicately around my ankles.

Pinch me now! This body has exquisite taste!

"I knew they'd come," Pinkie burbles, pulling out her phone. "I mean, your sassy sixteen party is like the hottest thing to happen in Singapore since that Insta guy moved here!"

Pinkie opens the camera and uses it as a mirror to check her makeup. She and I are both wearing skinny, black leather pants and silk tanks. Hers is pale-pink and mine is powder-blue. She hands me the phone.

"Your turn, birthday girl," she sings.

Pinkie is really pretty. I hope that runs in the family. I take the phone and look at my new body. My hair falls almost to my waist with streaks of blue dancing among the glossy black. My brown eyes are wide and angular, and I'm totally rockin' it with a bright-blue cat-eye. I grin. Awesome.

Pinkie peeks over my shoulder. "We look good!" she giggles. She purses her plump, pink lips and snaps a selfie. "Now let's give the pop our sexy sisters pose," she purrs, and tucks the phone into the waistband of her pants.

I can't help it. I'm still drawing a blank. "And who are the pop?"

She arches one of her black, pencil-thin eyebrows. "Really, Ling? Who are the paparazzi?" She rolls her eyes. "They've only been following us around since forever."

"They have?"

Why would the paparazzi follow this body? Am I famous? And again, why don't I know this? Why can't I get a feel for this body? Is it because I've been thinking so much about Lottie?

Pinkie tucks my hair behind my ear. "It's okay. Today's a big day. You turn sixteen, and suddenly you're an entirely different person."

You can say that again.

She grins. "Stick with your big sister. I'll take care of you." She links her arm in mine. "Ready?"

I nod, and she twists us around so fast that I almost lose my balance again, teetering on my heels. My sister squeals with joy as light bulbs flash in our eyes. She kicks her leg out to the side and flings one arm over my head. The flashes go crazy.

"What's wrong?" she mutters out the side of her mouth.

I smile at the cameras and mumble, "Nothing."

She lowers her leg. "Then why aren't you doing it?"

"Doing what?" I ask.

"Our sexy sisters pose!" She leans over, grabs my hand, raises it over our heads, and kicks her leg out to the side again. "Do your kick!" she pleads.

We do this all the time? I find myself blushing.

Pinkie raises her eyebrows at me, pleading, so I sigh, kick my leg out to the side like her, and the light bulb frenzy explodes like the grand finale at a fireworks show. After a few more seconds, she drops my hand and lowers her leg.

"That's all," she sings sweetly to the paparazzi.

Five, beefy men wearing black suits descend upon the pop, and corral them away from the stage.

She turns to me and pouts her pink lips. "What was that? I'm trying to make you look good, and you get stage fright?"

That was making me look good? Oh-kay. I get the feeling that this body despises that sexy sisters pose, but it's my birthday and I want everything to be happy. I'm about to apologize when she shakes her head and grins.

"Don't worry about it. The pop knows if they post anything unflattering Father will just close them down."

"Ling," a man's voice rises up from the crowd. "How do you feel about spending over a million dollars on a birthday party when your father just laid off most of Indonesia? Do you..."

I never hear the end of his question because more beefy men surround him in a cage of suits and lead him away.

I turn to my sister. "This party cost a million dollars?"

She suddenly looks serious and grabs my hands. "I know you told Father that was too much to spend, but I convinced him you didn't mean it. You know he only wants us to be happy." She motions to the crowd. "And look how much fun everyone is having! Look at how happy they all are!"

I glance around. She's right. Everyone looks pretty happy. They are all smiling. There's no frowning. No sadness. No anger. No pain. Just joy, and lots of laughing.

Just like I've always wanted.

I can't help but grin. This is the perfect body. Everyone is happy. I have a cool sister. And it's my birthday!

Thanks, Soul. Good choice.

My heart squeezes with delight, and oddly, a little hiccup of something I can't place. It's like something is missing.

It must be cake!

I search around on the marble table. "Where's the knife?"

My sister's eyes widen. "Why do you need a knife?"

I chuckle at her shocked expression. "How else can I cut my cake?"

She waves her hand in a vague gesture, and tsks. "Ling, we hire people to do that for us." She juts out her lower lip. "I'm tired of being up here. Come on, let's go dance!"

Dancing does sound like fun. I can eat cake later.

She grabs my hand and pulls me down the stairs and into the crowd. The first girl we pass is wearing the black-and-white Jimmy Choo sandals Lottie saw in Morocco. I screech to a stop.

"Oh my god! I love those!" I shriek at the girl wearing them.

"I know," the girl yawns. She's dressed in a slim, black dress almost the same color as her long, shiny hair. She gives me a crooked smile that definitely doesn't reach her eyes. "I got the first pair." She turns to my sister. "Um, nice hair… Pinkie."

I wait for my sister to get angry at the insult, but she just tilts her head to the side. "Oh, thanks." She pats her bob. "Javi said pink is what black used to be."

The girl's eyes widen, but then she composes herself. "When did Javi say that? I was just in his spa a few days ago, and I didn't hear that."

Pinkie nods her head like she's speaking to a kindergartener. "Oh, you were at his spa? That must have been nice. Ling and I never go there because Javi just comes to our house." She grins wide and leans in like she's sharing a secret. "Like he did this morning." She air kisses the girl on both cheeks. "Sooo good to see you," she gushes, and then links her arm through mine, and pulls me away. "Ugh," Pinkie whispers close to my ear. "I so wanted to smack her upside that botoxed face."

She leads me through the crowd of people I think must be my friends if they're at my party, but no one says hi or wishes me a happy birthday. Or really even looks our way. It's a little odd.

Pinkie sighs. "Too bad Father made us promise to be nice. Although, I heard her dad only made 2 bill last year which is peanuts compared to what Father made."

Two bill?! She can't mean two billion dollars?! Holy crap!

Her face suddenly lights up. "There's Father now!"

A man wearing tailored, black slacks and a crisp, white shirt strides towards us. His black hair is trimmed short, and carefully styled off his wide, smooth forehead. Their Father is quite handsome, but when he grins at us, he doesn't have any smile wrinkles like my Daddy.

I mean, Lottie's Daddy.

"There are my girls," Father gushes. He's just tall enough to place his arms over our shoulders and pull us both into a hug. His cologne smells of sandalwood, and musk; and his shirt feels like smooth silk. I feel safe and happy in his embrace like Lottie always did with her daddy. I exhale into him. I like this father.

He pulls back and beams at me. "And I know the birthday girl must be having a fabulous time?"

I grin. "Yes! It's so wonderful!" I'm just about to thank him for my party when someone bumps into me and spills what looks like icky, brown liquid all over my beautiful, blue-and-white sandals.

"Oh no," I cry.

Father leans into me. "Remember," he murmurs quietly through gritted teeth. "Happy image."

I look up, startled. What?

The man who dumped his drink doubles over and points at my shoes. "Thoth were blue before," he slurs. "But now they look slo much better." He hoots, obviously finding himself hilarious. He rights himself and leers at me. His dark hair is slicked back, and he's wearing a pale green shirt tucked into crisp, denim jeans. His dark eyes turn into slits as he purrs, "Well, hellooo there, thexy lady."

Me? A thexy lady? Um, I don't think so! First of all, you're like forty, and second of all, I don't go for drunken jerks. Especially one that Mama would tell me is waay too old for me.

"Stay happy," Father croons in my ear. "Remember our image." He grins widely at the jerk, extends his hand, and booms, "Hi, Philip! Glad you could make it."

Philip bobs his head back and forth, probably trying to get his drunken eyes to focus. "Oh, iths you!" he laughs. He shakes Father's hand. "Wouldn't mith a party thrown by your famous aths." Then he turns his attention back to me.

Lucky, lucky me.

Philip wraps his arm around my waist. "Now where were we? Ah, yeth." He strokes my cheek. "Thoth heels would look bether in my thuite."

My eyes widen. I know I want everyone to be happy and have a good time, but this is going way too far.

I shake my head. "No, thank you," I reply, trying to sound happy like Father requested.

Philip leans closer. "Yeth, please," he purrs.

Ew. And then an extra EWWW!

"Father, did we need to see to those details?" I ask, raising my eyebrows, hoping he understands that his daughter needs help.

He doesn't. Father just stands there, a smile pasted on his face. I can see his hands are fisted and his lips are pursed, but he doesn't do anything. Is he that worried about his freaking happy image that he can't even help his daughter? My daddy would have already kicked this drunk jerk to the door.

Guess I'm on my own.

"Well, thank you for coming to my party," I say politely, "but I must be going. Party details to attend to, you know." I try to wiggle out from under Philip's arm, but instead of letting me go, the drunken jerk grabs the back of my head, pulls me to him, and plants a slobbery, bourbon-laced kiss right on… my… lips.

When Philip's tongue punches into my lip, I remember the self-defense Daddy taught me and kick him square in his family jewels. He drops to the floor quicker than I did when I saw Dillon kissing that boy. I'm feeling proud of myself, but Father just gapes wide-eyed at me and Pinkie's mouth is stuck in a perfect, pink O.

The dance beat thumps in my heart, building and pulsing a little too fast until my heart starts racing and the pressure builds in my chest just like I'm back to my Oh my GAD days, embarrassed of what I did and who I am.

CHAPTER 33

Who am I really?

The beefy suits arrive and treat nasty Philip like a guest of honor while Father quickly leads Pinkie and me through my oblivious guests and into a corner. I hope he's going to congratulate me on sticking up for myself and tuck me into a hug to help me feel better, but instead he just grins at me.

"That was definitely not good for our image," he says. He's obviously angry with me, but he looks and sounds like he's delighted. His creepy, fake grin doesn't reach his eyes. His voice is calm. And he's even chuckling a little.

I feel my anxiety building, so I watch the bubbles float over my head and force myself to inhale and exhale. Inhale and exhale. It's okay. It's all going to be okay. I'm happy. I'm good. I can take care of myself.

"Ling," Father continues, "you need to remember our image. Our family must always be happy and having fun. We are never angry. We are never sad. We are only happy."

Hmmm… that sounds familiar.

He pats my arm. "Okay. I love you. When your party is over you can buy whatever you want to help you feel happy again. Now, let's all hug in case anyone is watching, and then…" he pauses. "Excuse me, please." He reaches into his pocket and pulls out his cell. Whatever he sees on the screen makes his eyes widen before he looks up at us with a real grin. "It is time!"

Pinkie jumps up and down. "It is?"

He sighs happily. "Yes." He squeezes my arm. "Enjoy your party. I'm sure Kim will be in labor for some time. You and your sister please come later to meet your new brother." He kisses us each on the cheek and strides away.

I grin at Pinkie. "We're going to have a baby brother?"

Pinkie shrugs. "Well, half-brother."

I'm going to have a baby brother! I adore my little brother, Berg. The thought of getting to have a little brother in this body makes my heart soar.

I'm grinning ear to ear. "This is so exciting!" I burble.

She shrugs. "I guess."

I tilt my head. "You guess? You're not happy about a little brother?"

She pastes on a fake smile. "I will be happy because that's what Father wants."

I don't understand why she doesn't want a sweet, baby brother, but I do understand wanting to make Father happy. I want to make everyone happy. When I was Lottie, I would have done anything to make Daddy happy. That's why I worked so hard to stop worrying. I would have done anything for Mama and Berg, too. Even though I screwed up and made everyone angry. IF I had chosen to go back there, I would have made it better. I would have made sure everyone was happy again.

Ugh. Stop thinking about the past. You made your decision. Think about the now. The happy, happy now!

I clap my hands together. "Well, I bet once you meet him you'll be happy!"

Pinkie shrugs. "Probably. But like Father says," she deepens her voice, "we must be happy in order to uphold our happy image. And life is better when you're happy all the time."

"So, true," I agree. That's what I always said. It's what I always strived for when I was Lottie. It's why I'm here now.

She sighs. "But a little brother means less time for us. Just like when Father married Kim." Her face droops a little and I think she's going to be sad, but she surprises me and pastes on a grin and wiggles her hips. "Let's go dance!"

Huh. I don't know exactly why, but watching her ignore her sadness bugs me a little.

She bounces up and down. "Come on, Ling! This is your night! Your sixteenth birthday party! It's barely eleven, and we're going to party until the sun comes up." She grabs my hands and squeals. "And then we'll go shopping! Father said you could buy anything. Maybe that new, quilted Chanel handbag? Or that pink, polka-dotted one from Givenchy?" She squeals again. "Or both!"

"But aren't we supposed to meet Father at the hospital?"

She waves her hand. "Nah. He'll be so focused on Kim that he won't even know we're not there. We'll just sneak in sometime tomorrow and tell him we've been there the whole time."

I raise an eyebrow. "I think he'll know if we aren't there."

She shrugs. "It doesn't matter anyway. He won't get mad. He can't." She makes a face. "It's not good for his image. Remember?"

His image. He can't get mad at us for missing our brother's birth because it's bad for his image? That's just wrong. We should be there. That's what family does. They are there for each other. In good times. And in bad times. And if we aren't there, then he should be mad.

Or disappointed. Like Berg was when I wasn't there for him. He had every right to be angry at me. And it was good that he told me how he felt.

No. Stop. I'm not thinking about that. I'm here. With this family. This family that is always happy. Or at least they try to be.

Are they really happy? Pinkie seems sad about not spending time with her Father. I wonder if she ever told him that? Or maybe she did and he didn't care. Maybe he can only care about his image. I mean, he and Pinkie both stood there and allowed grabby drunk to kiss me and never did anything. And they never even asked if I was okay! What does that say about them? That they care more about projecting their happy image than each other?

Or maybe they just forgot how much they care about each other?

Pinkie is singing in my ear. "Happy Birthday to Ling! Happy Birthday to Ling! I know what the night will br-ing. Let's dance now, come on, Ling!"

Yes. Dancing. It's time to stop all this thinking, and just enjoy my party, and be happy.

I follow her back into the crowd. We shake and shimmy and laugh. I try to let the music take over. I try to be happy. But instead I feel a little sad. And alone. I'm dancing with hundreds of people at my own party and I don't feel like I know anyone.

Especially myself.

I know happy and sad can co-exist, but I'm here in happy-land and I want to be happy, not sad. I try to bury all the negative thoughts whirling around in my brain, but they're bombarding me so fast that one sneaks past.

I'm sad. And I know why.

This is not how I imagined my sixteenth birthday party. It's clearly over the top cool, but I feel so alone. I'm not surrounded by my loving family who cares about me more than some happy image? Who love me no matter what I do, or who I am.

Are the people here really my friends, or are they just here for a free party? Do they like me because of who I am, or do they like me because I'm rich?

Stop it. Stop worrying. Just. Be. Happy.

I know! I need a little distraction-action. Like a cute boy! I glance around. There are definitely lots of options in this crowd. I can choose tall or short, well-dressed or hip, cute or cuter. But are any of them sweet boys? Like Dillon always was. Or even like George of the cute dimples in Paris?

Stop! Inhale. Exhale. Deep inhale. Deep exhale.

I spot Pinkie a few feet away, dancing with three, cute guys. One has a thick head of black hair, a thin mustache, and huge, brown eyes. One has shaggy, perfectly-dyed white hair, and almond eyes. And the third looks a little like a younger version of Pinkie's Father.

I dance my way closer, convincing myself that one of them is bound to be a sweetheart and a good kisser, and will fill my heart with happy. I tap Pinkie on the shoulder to get her attention.

She whirls around and jerks me to her side in a hug. "It's the birthday girl!" she shrieks. "Everybody, this is my sister, Ling. This is her party! Isn't it the best?"

No one answers her. Or says hello to me. Or even looks my way.

I try to engage them. "I'm happy you could all come!" I sing, all happy, and perky, and birthday-girl like. "Is everyone having fun?"

No one answers.

Mustache is swaying to the music with his eyes closed. Shaggy is head-banging. And mini-Father is staring into the middle-distance looking for who knows what.

I try again, louder and even more happy this time. "Is everyone having fun?"

Crickets.

I look at Pinkie. "Can they hear me?"

She shrugs.

"Are they deaf?"

She shakes her head. "No."

"Are they on drugs?"

She frowns. "No!"

I nod. "Got it. So, they're just being rude."

She looks at me sheepishly, and shrugs.

My heart drops. This humongous, million-dollar party is for me and my friends... who apparently aren't my friends after all. It's all a show. It's all part of the happy, happy image of this family.

And it's all a fake.

Just like me.

CHAPTER 34

This is not who I want to be

I'm a fake.

Lottie was a fake. I dyed my hair. I wore blue contacts. I hid my feelings. I tried to be an image. And it was all fake.

I suddenly realize I don't want to be here anymore with this fake life of happiness and all these fake people. This is my one and only sixteenth birthday party. I may be wandering the world with Miss Soul here, but time is still passing me by. I will never have another sixteenth birthday party, and I should be loving, and living, every second of it.

Not faking my way through it.

I could be hanging around with Malika who wanted to spend time with me, or laughing with Rinzen who rescued me and seemed to really like me, or even listening to that crazy, old monk who made me think. I bet Dillon would have even wished me a happy birthday and meant it, even after what I did.

But I must stop thinking about all of them. I would like to go back and fix everything, but I have chosen to move on. And since the loser-boy-trio is too worried about looking good for whoever may be watching them, I need to find someone else to help me celebrate and be happy.

Like my new brother!

Yes! What could be happier than a sweet, pudgy baby all pink cheeked and baby powder fresh?

"I'm going to the hospital," I announce to Pinkie.

She stops dancing, and raises her eyebrows. "You're leaving your party?"

I nod. "Yep."

Her mouth gapes open. "But why?"

My answer surprises even me. "Because life is too short to pretend to be someone I'm not with people I don't like." I nod my head. Yeah. I like that.

She tilts her head, but doesn't say anything.

I inhale a deep breath and exhale something that tastes very stale; and suddenly, I feel better than I have in a long time.

I grin. "Would you like to come with me?"

She looks at the boys who haven't even acknowledged that we stopped dancing, and then back at me. She starts to shake her head, and then very slowly, like she can't believe what she's doing, she nods. "I guess I do," she murmurs.

I laugh at her shock. I know exactly how she feels. Sometimes you don't understand exactly why you want to do something, but you just know it feels right.

Like getting the heck out of this lame-o party.

I link my arm in hers. "Okay, then. Let's blow this popsicle stand!"

I'm the birthday girl, the very reason for this party; yet, as I push through the crowd, I'm completely ignored and unseen. As if I'm invisible. As if I'm a nobody.

As if I'm a nobody…

A nobody.

I stop. The music thumps on. Bubbles float and pop around us. Bodies bump us from all sides. Everything and everyone is oblivious… to the nobody.

"What's wrong?" Pinkie whispers.

I'm about to confide in her when suddenly, deep in my soul, I know that it's not true. I'm not a nobody. I'm not.

I'm somebody.

I'm me.

I'm Lottie from Colorado.

Who loves cheesy puffs. Who cares deeply for her family. Who works hard to be happy. Who feels emotions way too strong. And who worries a lot. That's me.

And I've always been me. Even when I was Aicha in Morocco, and Pema in Bangkok, and even Swan in Paris. No matter where I was, and what I was doing, and who people thought I was, I have always been me.

Lottie.

I grin. And I have one more thing I want to do before leaving the only sixteenth birthday party I'll ever have. I want to eat my cake.

I tug on Pinkie's arm. "Come on."

"I thought we were leaving," she says as I lead her back into the crowd and up the steps of the stage. "What are we doing?" she squeals.

I stop right in front of my monstrous, blue cake and grin. "We're having my cake and eating it too!" I extend my finger towards the cake.

"Ling, you wouldn't?"

"I would," I chuckle, feeling happy way down into my soul. I run my finger along the top of the cake and scrape off a hunk of icing.

"Ling!" Pinkie exclaims, her eyebrows as high as I've ever seen them. "You can't do that! What will people think?"

I shrug. "I really don't care," I mumble as I lick the icing off my finger. I close my eyes. "Mmmm, buttercream. My favorite."

Pinkie looks like she wants to run and hide.

And I'm tired of hiding. Who I am. What I want. What I feel. I don't want to hide anymore.

I gesture to the crowd. "I don't care what people think right now. Besides, we're worrying what they're thinking about us, and they're too busy worrying what we think about them. So, if you think about, everyone is worrying for no reason because no one is seeing anything!" I dip my finger back into the icing. "And I'm not apologizing for who I am anymore. This is me. I'm the birthday girl who wants to eat her icing right off the cake." I waggle my eyebrows. "Are you sure you don't want to join me?"

Pinkie stares at me, her eyes wide. I have no idea what she's thinking. I don't know if she's about to call the suits to drag me away or call her Father and tell him I've gone cuckoo, but she doesn't do either of those things. She stares at the crowd until her face blossoms into a huge grin. A grin like I've never seen on her before, because this one is full of real happiness. She winks at me, jams her fingers deep into the cake, and scoops out a huge chunk.

"Everyone knows buttercream is best with cake," she laughs, and shoves the whole thing into her mouth, smearing icing all over the sides of her smile.

Laughter bubbles up and spills out of me like a waterfall. I laugh so hard that I feel all the tension and worry deep in my belly unravel. This is what a birthday should be. Silly, and fun, and happy!

And none of it fake.

Pinky points to one of the beefy suits walking up the stairs. "Uh oh. Now we're in trouble," she giggles.

The Suit is bald and wearing a deep frown. He's probably coming to stop us, so I scoop out a chunk of cake and offer it to him. "Want to join us? It's delicious!"

The Suit shakes his head, eyes wide. "No, thank you, Miss Ling."

Pinkie laughs and licks the icing stuck to the corners of her mouth. "Don't worry, Alberto. She is the birthday girl. If she says it's okay to eat the cake, Father won't care."

Alberto arches one thick, black eyebrow, wrinkling his forehead like a Shar Pei puppy. He looks over at the cake with a gleam in his eye, just like a Shar Pei who really, really loves cake.

"Go on," I whisper. "Dig in."

I can tell he really wants to dip his finger in it like a ten-year-old boy, but he doesn't crack. Alberto is all business.

"I'm sorry to disturb you," he apologizes. "But your father called and said to hurry to the hospital. Mrs. Kim is delivering soon."

"Really?" I cry, wiping my finger on the tablecloth. "Oh, Pinkie. We need to go!" I turn to Alberto. "What's the fastest way to get there?"

Pinkie claps her hands with glee. "Don't worry! I know!"

As she pulls me down the stairs, I glance back just in time to see Alberto swipe a finger along the icing and sneak a bite. A look of delight softens his strong jaw as he eats it, and that makes me heart soar. Everyone has layers. Sometimes you just have to choose to shed some of them to find the sweet one.

I follow Pinkie across the dance floor. She stops at a door leading outside. "You have to close your eyes."

"I do?"

She jumps up and down. "Please just do it. Father wanted it to be a surprise for your birthday."

"A surprise for my birthday?" I grin.

She nods. "And it's beyond good. Trust me."

She trusted me to eat cake with her fingers, so I close my eyes. She links her arm through mine and leads me outside. After being in the arctic chill of the air conditioning, the warm, humid air outside feels like a hug.

"A little farther," she says, guiding me. "One more step. One more. Okay. Stop." She giggles. "You can open them now."

I open my eyes to find a powder-blue, Ferrari Spider sitting at the curb, sporting a huge blue bow on the hood.

My mouth gapes open. "That's… my surprise?" I stutter.

She laughs. "Yes! Happy Sweet Sixteen Birthday!"

Oh… my… god.

Oh my god!

OH MY GOD!

I close my eyes and open them again. Yep. It's still there.

"It's your Happy Birthday car!" Pinkie sings. She giggles. "Are you surprised?"

Surprised? I'm way beyond surprised. I just got a Ferrari for my sixteenth-birthday! I'm in shock. But this is a good shock. Not at all like when I saw Dillon kissing that boy. Or got shot in Kabul. Although my body is reacting the same. My heart is racing. I feel like crying. And I can't even speak. I guess joy and pain can co-exist because they feel the same sometimes.

My first car is a… Ferrari!

A FERRARI!

"Father ordered it for you almost a year ago," Pinkie explains. "He wanted you to have one to match mine, but said it had to be blue since that's your favorite color and he wanted it to be special just like you. He even flew out there three times to make sure it was the right color."

Interesting. Maybe he does care about Ling. He just shows it in his own way.

"Since you have an international driver's license you could drive it now instead of waiting until you're eighteen, but…" she pauses and grimaces. "It's a stick. Father planned to teach you tonight, but then Kim went into labor, and…" she gives me a distressed look. "I'm so sorry, but will you hate me if I drive us there in your new car?"

My first thought is absolutely, because it's MY car. But then I think about the word hate. It's an awfully strong word.

I know I hated being killed in Kabul. And I hated being that Thai man's slave. And I hated knowing Fah was dying. Hate seems like a good word for those moments.

But I've also hated myself for so long because of my Oh my GAD, and now the word hate doesn't seem to fit anymore. I shouldn't hate myself for how I react. It's me. The emotional Lottie. And when I have a bad experience, I need to vent. I need to purge all that anger and sadness inside of me, and not bury it.

I do terribly regret calling Dillon names and really hurting him, both emotionally and physically. But I'm happy that I cried and got mad. I needed to allow myself those awful emotions so I could feel them, get over them, and then move on.

And moving on means no longer worrying about what others think of me, or my emotions, like I'm doing tonight. Moving on means just going out there, being myself, and living.

Yo, Soul. Is this what you've been trying to tell me all this time?

"Ling?" Pinkie interrupts my epiphany with a frown. "Please don't hate me if I drive."

I want to fake happiness and pretend like it's no big deal, but I decide to be myself and just be honest.

"I'm disappointed you get to drive my car first," I sigh, and her face falls. "But," I quickly add, "there's no way I'll hate you! It's not every day you get to see your baby brother enter this life, and we don't want to miss it." I smile and tears spring into my eyes. For the first time in a long time, instead of putting all my energy into stopping them, I remain in the moment and let them fall.

Pinkie reaches out and pulls me close. "I don't know what happened," she murmurs. "But I really like the new you." She squeezes me tighter. "And I like who I am when I'm with you."

She smells of vanilla icing, and that makes me remember the chunk of cake she grabbed and shoved into her mouth, and suddenly happiness overcomes my tears. All on its own. For real. No burying required.

I think I like who I am now, too.

I wipe my cheeks and pull back. "Okay, enough gushy sister stuff. We have a brother to see!"

Pinkie scurries around to the driver's side, and I open the passenger door. I pause and inhale the glorious scent of brand new leather.

Pinkie leans over the stick shift. "Come on, Ling! This thing's fast, but not that fast."

My leather pants barely whisper as I slide onto the soft, leather seat. It feels like sitting on a cloud. In a Ferrari.

IN MY FERRARI!

"Buckle up!" Pinkie squeals, and peels away from the curb.

I click in my seatbelt and glance at the three towers of the Marina Bay Sands as we leave. The towers must be sturdy and strong to hold up the ship that looks precariously balanced on top of them. If I were the ship, my three towers would be Mama, Daddy, and Berg. They are always there for me, loving me unconditionally, and holding me up.

"Look!" Pinkie cries as we race past the bay. "The laser light show has started!"

Beams of red, yellow, and green dance across the bay, weaving patterns of joy in their celebration of nothing other than the fact that today is another wonderful day. The image of a pale blue flower is illuminated on the metal petal walls of the ArtScience Museum next door, but it takes me until we've already passed the double helix bridge before I realize what I just saw.

"It's a lotus flower!" I cry out. "The ArtScience museum is shaped like a lotus flower! The symbol of rebirth and enlightenment. It rises out of the mud and muck, out of the sadness and anger, and it expands to open itself to whatever life may offer." I inhale, and whisper on my exhale, "Just like me, Lottie."

I lean my head out the window and the wind caresses my grin until Pinkie screeches to a halt in front of the hospital. She jumps out and tosses the keys to a valet who looks tickled pink to be handed the keys to a Ferrari. My Ferrari.

I suddenly get worried. And I don't try to bury it. I haven't let myself worry in such a long time that it feels a little strange, but I tell myself that it's okay to be worried. I mean, this is my new car. I should be worried about it.

I give my worry a voice. "Please be careful with it," I ask the valet.

He nods and grins. "Of course, Ms. Ling. And happy birthday." And surprisingly, he sounds like he means it.

I smile. "Thanks."

I follow Pinkie into the hospital. A nurse immediately greets us and ushers us down a white hallway sparsely decorated with photos of orchids. I notice her scrubs have birthday cakes on them, and that makes me smile. It's so appropriate! But I'm not even thinking about my birthday. I'm thinking about my baby brother, and that today will be his birthday.

The nurse leads us through a door into another hall where adorable pink babies adorn the walls. She stops in front of a set of locked doors and presses an intercom. "The sisters have arrived," she says. The doors buzz and she opens one with a smile on her face. "Congratulations." she says and motions us through.

I follow Pinkie into what I guess is a hospital room even though it looks nothing like one. An intricately carved, four-poster bed neatly made with dark blue sheets sits against one wall. A soothing waterfall trickles over another. And a mahogany bassinet draped with baby-blue veiling waits in the corner. The lights are dim, soothing music is playing, and a vase of colorful orchids sits on every table.

Father is leaning over a woman. She is sitting up in a smaller, hospital-looking bed in the center of the room, and her dark hair is messily piled on her head. She looks sweaty, like she just went for a long run, but she's smiling. I'm assuming this is his wife, Kim, but for some reason I can't place her. Suddenly, I'm drawing a blank. Like the book I was reading about Ling was suddenly slammed shut.

Pinkie's father hears us walk in and turns around. He's cradling something wrapped in a soft-blue blanket. "You made it!" he bellows, and grins so wide that I see happy wrinkles near his eyes. He gazes

194

down at what's in his arms. "You're just in time to welcome your baby brother into the world."

Pinkie and I both rush over. The baby's face is squished and blotchy red, but I think he's the cutest thing I've ever seen.

"Can I hold him?" I whisper.

Pinkie's father nods, and starts to hand him to me.

"Wait," I say, shoving my arms behind me. "Maybe I shouldn't." I take a deep breath and again give a voice to my worry. "I'm afraid I'll drop him."

He winks. "Trust me. You won't." He holds the baby in one arm and takes his other hand to pull my arm around and close to my body. He snuggles the baby into my side and wraps my other arm around him. "Now just hold him tight." He kisses my forehead, and smiles. "How lucky that your little brother joined us on your sixteenth birthday."

I grin. "Yeah. I am lucky." And I truly feel that way. I gaze down and love floods my heart. His chubby cheeks make me think of Berg wearing Daddy's cologne and yelling "I love you, Big L." His blue eyes remind me of Mama's. Bright, and full of unconditional love. His furrowed brow reminds me of Daddy. Always trying to make his little girl happy.

I allow this bittersweet thing we call love to engulf me, and I realize it's okay. Tears spring to my eyes, and I don't even try to stop them.

"This is the best birthday present I've ever received," I murmur.

Even better than a Ferrari.

I close my eyes, hug that sweet baby, think of my family, and happily let my tears fall. I feel the emotions washing over me – sad, happy, all of them - and this time I don't wish myself far, far away.

CHAPTER 35

Could it be?

Before I even open my eyes, I know my soul wandered. I'm still holding something warm, but I'm pretty sure it's not my baby brother.

Unless he knows how to purr.

I open my eyes, and want to leap with joy. It's my white kitten! The teeny one with the brown eyes and the black butterfly on its forehead. My heart overflows with such happiness that I probably resemble the big, reclining Buddha that's right in front of me wearing that lazy smile of contentment.

I'm back in Thailand!

My kitten kneads me with her tiny claws, and when it pricks my chest like tiny knives, I realize I'm not wearing thick, monk robes. I glance down and can't believe my eyes. I'm wearing my skinny jeans and my favorite blue sweater. It even has the mascara stains from wiping my eyes that day outside the school. I'm wearing my Lottie clothes! I touch my ears. And I'm wearing my lucky earrings! The small white circles with the painted blue lotus flowers.

My heart races. What does this mean? Am I Lottie again? But I didn't go back home.

"Quit being that way, and just let me help you down," an exasperated voice grumbles behind me.

I know that voice! I cradle the kitten to my chest and jump up to see Rinzen standing at the other end of the path. She's leaning against that darling baby elephant, Kam-Tong. Big Kammoon hovers protectively nearby with Fah sitting on her back.

Fah! She's still alive! My stomach flips with happiness. I set down my kitty, and rush down the path to greet them.

"I can't believe it!" I cry. "It's really you! I'm back and it's really you." Tears spring to my eyes and I don't care. I let them flow. "I missed you both so much. I'm so sorry I ran away."

Rinzen raises an eyebrow. "I'm sorry you ran away, too, but do we know you?"

I'm laughing and blubbering all at the same time. "Yes! Yes, you know me! Probably better than anyone." I reach up and touch my head. I'm no longer bald. I have long hair again. "Although, I think I'm Lottie now."

Rinzen gives me a look that says she's thinks I've been in the sun too long.

"What color is my hair?" I ask in a rush.

Rinzen tilts her head. "I'd say maybe blonde, but your brown roots are really showing."

"Rinzen!" Fah scolds, her voice more raspy than I remember.

Rinzen raises her hands in a palms-up gesture. "What? I'm not being rude. She asked and I'm just telling the truth." She turns back to me and shrugs. "It actually looks really cool that way."

I laugh. "I love that you are always yourself, Rinzen."

She squints her eyes and examines me closer. "I'm sorry, but how do you know my name?"

I laugh. "It's me. It's Pema!"

"Pema?" Fah says softly from her lofty seat.

"Yes, Fah. It's me." I sigh and smile. "And I can't tell you how happy I am to see you."

Fah tilts her head, gives me a funny look, and then nods to Rinzen. "I think I will let you help me down."

Rinzen taps Kammoon's leg, and the elephant bows down onto one knee. Fah slowly moves her legs together, lies on her belly, and starts to slide down Kammoon's side. Rinzen tries to guide her, but right before she reaches the ground, Fah starts to fall over.

I rush over and support Fah on the other side. My heart slows. "You're not well?"

She offers me a small grin. "Not today. Maybe tomorrow. But not today." She points to the reclining Buddha. "Would you please help me over there?"

Rinzen rolls her eyes. "Always has to be treated like a queen," she jokes, but I hear the catch in her voice.

Sadness creeps up on me, and this time I choose not to run away from it. It's hard because it hurts. Really hurts. But I know I have to take the pain of Fah's illness along with the joy of seeing her again.

Rinzen and I help support Fah as she walks down the path. Her gait is unsteady and she leans on my shoulder for support, but she jokes all the way there. We help her sit in front of the Buddha. Rinzen sits down next to her, and I plop down in front of them. Fah closes her eyes, and inhales deeply, like I use to do when I wanted to bury my pain. My stomach clenches. She's not well at all. Is she dying? I don't want her to die. I want her to live.

And that thought makes me want to run away.

But I don't. I choose not to run this time.

Fah opens her eyes, and a tear escapes down her cheek. "I'm so sorry," she sighs. "I'm so sorry you have to see me like this."

Rinzen drops her head into her hands, and her shoulders start to shake.

I'm ambushed by sadness, and long to escape it, but I choose to stay. It hurts. Really bad. Like Kammoon is sitting on my chest. But I don't want to leave. I want to stay with my friends. I want to share their sadness, so they don't feel alone.

I reach out, and grasp Fah's hand. "It's okay. Really, it is."

She looks up, startled.

I reach over, and grab Rinzen's hand. She flicks her head up, eyes red and wide.

"Do you two remember when you first rescued me?" I ask. I feel tears spring to my eyes as the memory forms. "I just woke up and found myself tied to the bed. I thought I had died and gone to hell. I thought that man who imprisoned me was the devil himself." I squeeze both their hands, and let my own tears leave trails of bittersweet happiness down my cheeks. "And then you two rescued me. You set me free." My breath catches. "And I ran away from you." I snort out a cry. My kitty doesn't seem to care about my slobbering snot fest and crawls into my lap, mewing loudly.

"Aw, pet her already, will ya?" Rinzen jokes, softening the emotional moment like she's so good at doing. "Besides, I need my hand to wipe off my face."

We all laugh, and I let go of their hands. I swipe the tears from my cheeks, and rub my kitty's soft fur. She immediately settles into my lap, closes her eyes, and turns on her purr.

"Pema, is that really you?" Fah asks. She stares into my eyes, searching for something.

I nod. "Yes."

A smile starts to form, like she wants to believe me but doesn't know if she can. "But how?"

Rinzen shakes her head. "You can say that again! I mean, you were bald when you left and then a few days later, you're back with brown hair?"

I arch my eyebrow.

She rolls her eyes. "Fine, blond hair. Whatever, kid." She laughs. "It must be you. I'd recognize that eyebrow anywhere." Her eyes grow wide as Kammoon's ears. "Did you die? Is this your reincarnation?"

I shake my head. "I don't think so because this is who I always was."

"About time you figured that out!" a familiar voice cackles from behind me.

I turn and see the old monk skipping down the path towards us, her robes billowing out around her. When she reaches me, she throws her arms wide.

"I'm baaack," she sings. She tosses me her best grin, crooked teeth and all, and then bows. "Welcome back, Lotus."

This sets off a whole series of bows that look like a comedy routine. I bow. Then Rinzen rises and bows to Venerable Bhik. Then the old monk bows back. Then Fah bows from her seat. Then the old monk bows again.

"Okay, enough bowing," the old monk laughs. "It's rattling my brain loose." She sits down in front of me, so close that she's almost on my lap. She places her hands on her chin, and leans forward, her eyes wide and eager. "So… whatcha been doing?"

I laugh. I missed this old broad.

"Well, right now I'm trying to figure out why I look like Lottie and not Pema."

The old monk looks down her nose at me, like an elderly schoolmarm. "Now, don't you backtrack on me, young whippersnapper. You know exactly why."

Fah chuckles. It's soft and short-lived, but it reaches her eyes.

The old monk shakes her finger at Fah. "Nuh uh. If you know why, you keep it to yourself, young missy." She nods to me. "Lottie here has to figure this one out all on her own."

Fah continues to smile, but nods her head. "Okay. I won't say anything about Pema accepting her true self."

"Gah!" The old monk squawks. "No hints either!"

Rinzen swivels her head back and forth between the two of them. "What are you all talking about? Who's Lottie? And why does Pema have to accept her true self?"

"Pema is Lottie," Fah explains.

The old monk's eyebrows fly up. "You two zip it!" she yelps. "No more talking."

Fah winks at me and smiles.

She's trying to help me. Fah said Pema had to accept her true self. Which is me. Which is Lottie. I think back to what I discovered in Singapore. That even though I've been all these other people, I've always been Lottie. But I just had to accept all of her. Oh…

I nod. "I get it. I've always been Lottie. Whether my hair was black or brown. Whether I was Moroccan, or Thai, or Afghan, or Icelandic, or Indonesian Chinese. Whether I was a boy or a girl."

Rinzen raises her eyebrows.

I wave her off. "Don't ask." I grin. "No matter who I was, I've always been Lottie. I just never accepted all of her. I mean all of myself." I nod. "But now I think I can. And that's why I'm me now." I point to my clothes. "I'm really Lottie."

The old monk rolls her eyes. "You figured that out with a little help from your friends," she mutters, but a happy smile grows on her lips and she giggles, "which is sometimes just what you need." She folds her hands in her lap. "When you left, you longed for the enlightenment that Buddha had found."

I nod.

"But you thought enlightenment meant running away from pain and sadness, and burying the bad parts of yourself?"

"Like my emotions," I add.

She nods. "But it doesn't. Enlightenment means you understand and accept your true self. Both the good and the bad. Enlightenment means you stop trying to control your nature, and simply be… who… you… are."

I nod. "I had to stop hating myself for who I am."

She grins. "Yes. And you had to accept anger and sadness, as much as you embraced joy and laughter. Or at least understand there is a reason they are a part of you." The old gal winks at me. "And that is what your soul wanted all along."

Hope pounds a fast rhythm in my heart. "Does this mean I can go back?" My breath catches. "Back to my real life, I mean. Back to my Mama, and Daddy, and Berg?" I feel the biggest smile I've ever had pulling on my lips.

She raises both eyebrows and shrugs. "I really don't know. Every soul has a different journey." She leans close, and stares at me with those bright, galaxy eyes. "But remember, Lottie. You are your soul and your emotions, and they are you. And who you are is who you will always be."

"I think that's from a song." I chuckle.

I can see she's trying not to grin.

"Shush now, Lotus. Close your eyes."

I do as she asks. She presses her forehead to mine and begins to chant something deep and serene. Her chant reverberates, and I feel my heart rate slow, and my muscles release like I'm just about to fall asleep.

"And now, you finally understand," she whispers, and pulls her forehead away.

I slowly open my eyes and grin, feeling more at peace with who I am than I ever have in my life.

She stands up and pulls a wrench from her robes. "Okie dokie, artichokie! Now, I must fix that sink, and Lottie must say goodbye." She winks. "For now."

I only have a chance for a quick goodbye before she skips down the path, her robes sailing out behind her, humming the happy birthday tune.

Fah reaches out for my hand. "I'm so happy for you, Lottie," she sighs using my real name.

Rinzen lightly punches me on the arm. "Yeah, me too, kid. Although to me you'll always be that scrawny little Pema who thinks curry smells 'totally awesome.'"

I laugh out loud, remembering when I said that to the woman who was graciously putting food in my almsbowl on that day they rescued me.

"Thank you both," I gush, tears forming in my eyes. "Thank you for being there when I needed you, and for accepting me for who I am." I extend my arms, lean forward, and embrace them both in a hug.

And as I feel their love hug me back, I can't help but close my eyes and smile.

CHAPTER 36

I'm baaaaack!

My body can still feel Rinzen's and Fah's warm arms around me, but somehow, I know they're gone. My soul has wandered once again.

My heart skips. I don't know where I am and I'm not quite ready to face it just yet, so I keep my eyes tightly closed. I do know that no matter what awaits me, I've changed.

I'm happy to live as my soul desires. I want to embrace my true nature. I want to explore and experience both my good and bad emotions. Because I know I need them all to make my life full and rich and vibrant.

The anger I felt at the devil man in Thailand and the drunk jerk in Singapore just made me happier that I had so many beautiful months of friendship with Dillon and met cute dimples George. The pain I caused Berg helped me realize the joy I could bring Malika by just being there for her. The sadness I felt when I discovered Fah couldn't care for the baby elephant, helped me find happiness when I knew I could help her.

I guess embracing all my emotions really is the blessing and curse of life. I need to see and feel the bad, so I can fully appreciate and love the good.

I start sobbing and laughing at the same time. I don't even care who sees snot running out of my nose and hears me hiccupping giggles. I don't care that I'm revealing what I'm feeling.

Because I'm not burying my emotions anymore.

I will try to embrace who I am – flaws and all – and accept that this is who I will be. I am Lottie, a girl who's sometimes blond and sometimes happy, but who still loves cheesy puffs and Jimmy Choo sandles. My Oh my GAD won't define me, just like all those other titles won't either. I am like the glacier in Iceland. Constantly growing and changing, and in my case, living.

It won't be easy. I know that. And I know I'll still dislike some feelings, but that's ok. That's part of being me. And I vow to never hate myself ever again.

I don't know where I am. Am I home, or is this another stop in my soul's journey? Am I here for a few moments, or for a lifetime?

Or was this all just one humongously-weirdo dream?

Whatever it is, I don't care. Because this time, I will live. I will allow myself to feel every emotion – wretched pain and miserable sadness, jubilant laughter and exuberant joy. Whether this is my reality, or this is my dream, I will savor every moment of today, and the next day, and the next dream, and the next reality.

Because no matter what, I am finally awake.

And I don't want to miss feeling anything ever, ever again.

So, I inhale a deep breath. I'm ready. It's time to open my eyes.

TWO MONTHS LATER

I did make it back to my real home in Colorado that night. Back to my own room with my stuffed zebra and my grandmother's postcards. And my Mama, Daddy, and Berg were right there waiting for me to finally wake up.

I still don't know if the whole thing was real, or if it was just a dream, but I am absolutely sure of what I learned. To love myself. Every annoying, frustrating, amazing, wonderful part.

Sweet Dillon never blamed me for his fall. I apologized for all the hateful things I said, and I made him so many cookies that he swears he gained five pounds. Charlie says he looks just perfect. He's the boy I caught Dillon kissing. They've been dating for three months, and really are good together. I'm totally giving them a white kitten if they ever get married.

I still have anxiety, but I'm trying not to bury it. I'm trying to feel all my emotions and not let them control me. And when I need help, I reach out to my family and to my friends. I even visited my old counselor, Ms. Foofaraw. She had no recollection of throwing my vape in the lake or even seeing me there- which was super weird- but she gave me other cool tools to help me feel less anxious, and she told me to visit her anytime.

Today's the first day of summer break so Berg and I are heading out for a sunset hike followed by an ice cream dinner. We try to have a brother-sister date at least twice a month, and I love every second of my time with him.

Berg peeks his head into my room. "You ready, Big L?"

I see he's wearing his special soccer jersey and that makes me grin. "You bet, Little B."

"Oh, I almost forgot." He hands me a postcard. "This came for you today."

The postcard is a beautiful photograph of a baby elephant with "Bangkok" written in black script above it. I flip it over and read the writing on the back.

Dear Kid,

The Venerable old gal gave me your address. Kam-Tong is settling in well, but he sure misses you. I do, too. Come visit soon!

Love, Rinzen

THE END

RESOURCES

If you have anxiety, or need to talk to someone, PLEASE tell a friend, a family member, a school counselor, or your doctor. They all care so much about you! And PLEASE reach out to the following for confidential help and resources in your area.

1.   Crisis Text Line – Text NAMI to 741-741

2.   National Alliance on Mental Illness (NAMI) Helpline :1-800-950-NAMI (6264) www.nami.org

3.   Teen Line: 1-310-855-HOPE (4673) or 1-800-TLC-TEEN (852-8336) www.teenlineonline.org

THANK YOU so much for reading I'M WITH ANXIOUS!

If you enjoyed Lottie's journey, will you PLEASE take a minute to **write a review on Amazon or Goodreads**? I want Lottie to help others learn to love themselves, too!

And if Lottie's story can help someone close to you, **PLEASE gift them this book**!

If you'd like updates on my upcoming books PLEASE contact me at www.sbrownbooks.com

www.ingramcontent.com/pod-product-compliance
Lightning Source LLC
Chambersburg PA
CBHW071907220626
47052CB00002B/241